ALL HIS BROKEN RULES

A FORBIDDEN PROFESSOR/STUDENT ROMANCE

THE BROKEN SERIES

MYA MORE

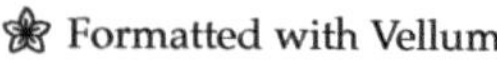 Formatted with Vellum

To the eldest daughter who followed every rule, met every expectation, and carried everyone else on her shoulders—I hope you find someone willing to break every rule for you.
And if he wants to tie you up and spank you, even better.

CONTENT WARNINGS

Sexual assault on page (not between main characters)
Attempted rape (not between main characters)
Child abuse (memory of event)
Death of a character by hate crime (descriptive memory on page)
Mentions of alcoholism and abuse
Mentions of immigration
Impact play with multiple toys
Light primal play
Mask play

You know your limits and triggers. Your mental health is important.

Any scenes with kink depicted in this book are for entertainment purposes and are not intended to be educational or accurate depictions of a kink lifestyle. Please do your research before engaging in similar acts to make sure you are your partner(s) are informed and safe.

DICKTIONARY 🌶

For anyone wondering where the spicy scenes take place—whether you're eager to dive right in or prefer to skip them altogether—you'll find them in the following chapters:

🌶 Chapter 1
🌶 Chapter 6
🌶 Chapter 8
🌶 Chapter 10
🌶 Chapter 16
🌶 Chapter 17
🌶 Chapter 18
🌶 Chapter 26
🌶 Chapter 30
🌶 Chapter 31
🌶 Chapter 32
🌶 Chapter 40

🌶 Bonus Chapter (download)

PLAYLIST 🎵

Luv Me A Little - ILLENIUM & Nina Nesbitt
Break the Rules - Charlie xcx
No Mercy - Austin Giorgio
Rain - Sleep Token
Can I Be Him - James Arthur
Once in a Lifetime - John Michael Howell
Pray - Sam Smith
Broken Rules - David Robidoux
Meant to Be - Kari Kimmel
Rules - DRKD
Into the Light - Honor by August
NIGHTS LIKE THESE - Benson Boone
Hot for Teacher - Van Halen
Provider - Sleep Token
Something In The Heavens - Lewis Capaldi
Train Wreck - James Arthur
Lose My Mind - Dean Lewis
Eternity - Alex Warren
Hunger - Of Monsters and Men
Gravity - Sara Bareilles
Imperfections - Céline Dion

Look What You Made Me Do - Taylor Swift
Emergence - Sleep Token
bad decisions - Bad Omens
Hard Place - H.E.R.
Made For Love - Archers
In the Air Tonight - Natalie Taylor
Touch Me - Avicii
when the party's over - Billie Eilish
We Go Down Together - Dove Cameron & Khalid
Love is Madness (feat. Halsey) - Thirty Seconds to Mars
Walk Me Home - P!nk
Say Something - A Great Big World & Christina Aguilera
Only When It's You - Bleeding Verse
Pillar of Strength (Cry Cry Cry) - Paul Greene

SPICY SPINE SISTERS
TBR

Because you totally need more to add to your
never-ending TBR and the Spicy Spine Sisters
have excellent taste in books.
Happy reading!

Sleet Kitten by SJ Tilly (mentioned in the book)
Brutal Obsession by S Massery (mentioned in the book)
The Heartbreaker by Sara Cate
Haunting Adeline by HD Carlton (mentioned in the book)
Learn Your Limits by Van R Som and Kay Thorne
Heart of Stone by Dakota Willink (mentioned in the book)
Right Man, Right Time by Meghan Quinn
Almost Ravaged by Abby Millsaps
Play the Game by SJ Slyvis
The Pucking Wrong Number by CR Jane

CHAPTER 1
EMMA
SOPHOMORE YEAR

I probably shouldn't let my brother's best friend take me to a sex club.

"Ethan's going to be so mad," I say out of the side of my mouth.

Alyx gives me the side-eye as we approach the entrance of Pulse. "Ethan's not going to find out."

"He would kick your butt."

"He'd do more than that if he found out I took his baby sister to a sex club."

"Cheese and rice, I'm not a baby. I'm nineteen, and he's only three years older. But, yeah, he'd be peeved about the schmex club part."

"You can call it a sex club, you know. I don't think your sisters can hear you from here."

"I know I *can*, but I choose not to. If I let one curse slip, then I'll get comfortable letting more slip, and before you know it, I'll be dropping f-bombs in front of Lizzy, Evie, and Erin." Ever since it upset one of my sisters, I've made a conscious decision to avoid cursing.

"That would be quite the scandal in the pony palace," Alyx teases.

I'm grateful that he's breaking the tension. "They've actually really gotten into these bird books lately."

"*Pajama Pigeon?*"

"Yeah, how did you know?"

"Becka's daughter is really into it."

"They are—" I start, but he cuts me off.

"Quit stalling. If this is too much for you, I can take you home." Alyx really is a good friend, as loyal as they come.

"I want to do this. I need to do this." Maybe if I keep repeating that, I'll eventually believe it.

"And you're sure this is *how* you want to do it?"

My fingers tug at the hem of my skirt as I roll the fabric against my skin and blow out a deep breath. "I'm sure."

I've had boyfriends—a few actually, most of them serious. It's easy to assume that I'd be a pro at sex, considering how many relationships I've had, but the idea of sex with them never felt right. Things would always start fine, but as soon as the guy would slip a hand under my clothes, I'd break out into a fit of giggles and slap them away. One guy made it to second base, but as soon as his finger connected with my breast, my elbow connected with his nose.

Believe me, I wanted more to happen, but my body just wouldn't cooperate. I know my way around a toy or two and can make myself finish with just my fingers, but as soon as a man touches me, my body rejects it.

My rotation through guys became something I was known for around high school. To save their fragile male egos, my exes got together and told all their friends about what we "did"—with the details embellished. None of those guys had even seen what was under my bra, but they didn't want their friends to know that.

College has been no different. I attend a local private school close to Columbus, and one of my exes ended up there too, so my reputation's followed me. I was determined to find someone my body wouldn't reject, but my freshman year proved unsuccessful on that front.

That changes tonight.

I've prepared for this, read everything I could find. Text-books, subreddits, romance books. I understand what this should be like, yet I'm still anxious.

We make our way into the club, and Alyx ushers me to his private room.

"Okay, sis, normally you'd have to go through a screening process and learn all about the club rules, but I'm trying to keep this under the radar since this is a one-time thing."

"He's not going to be here, right?" I panic, thinking about my stepbrother Ethan finding me and his best friend in a sex club.

"Who? Ethan? No, he doesn't even know I work here. Plus, he's busy taking care of this chick we met at a dance club a couple of months ago. She had to have surgery, and he's pretty much in love with her. He's got his hands full."

"Good," I exhale as I try to calm my breathing while I take in the space. "This isn't how I thought it would be. This just looks like a moody bedroom. And why is everything black?"

"You gotta problem with black?" he teases, crossing his arms with a smirk.

"Oh gosh, no, I wasn't being racist. I meant the walls, and the bed, and—"

"Relax, Em, I'm just fucking with you. Take a deep breath. It's not too late to back out. I haven't told my guy you're here yet."

He fixes me with his big brown eyes, concern etched in his brows. I will my heart to calm its rhythm, but it feels fruitless. I'm standing on a precipice, and while I know I could turn back, I force myself to look down, convinced that the jump isn't scary, that the journey to the bottom could be fun.

"And he knows about my… problem?" I lower my voice to a whisper on the last word, even though we're alone.

"He's aware."

I twist my fingers. "And he's okay with it?"

"He's dealt with a brat before. He can handle anything you throw at him."

"A brat?"

"It's a submissive who enjoys giving their dom a hard time."

"I don't want to give anyone a hard time. You're sure Ethan won't find out about any of this?"

"Emma, what's really going on here? There's something you're not telling me."

"I just don't want to disappoint him. Not that being in a schmex club is disappointing. I'm not saying you're a disappointment. He just doesn't expect this kind of behavior from me, like he does with you. He knows you like to keep your options open, you know? I'm not saying you sleep around, but you know what I mean, you've been with more people than I have. Biscuits. I'm messing this up and being a crappy friend."

"Breathe before you word vomit again." He pulls me into a hug and soothes a hand up and down my spine. "It's okay. I like sex and I'm not ashamed of that, but I understand not broadcasting everything to everyone, hence the reason I don't share my second job with most people."

I get that. Alyx and my sister Ella are the only two people I've ever told about my problem, and even they don't know *everything*.

He steps back, grabbing me by the shoulders. "I know you want to explore that side of yourself, and I think you should. And even if your brother never understands my reasoning, I brought you here so you can do that safely. Everyone has been thoroughly tested and had background checks performed. I'll be nearby, but not in the room with you."

"Okay," I say on a shaky exhale. "I think this will help. Do you think this will help?"

"All you can do is try. If you want to stop, give your safe word, and he'll stop."

"Safe word, got it. I read about that."

"And for fuck's sake, don't tell him about all your research. Just get out of your head and let him lead the scene."

I nod my agreement, and he squeezes my shoulder before letting go. "What happens next?"

"I'll text him, and he'll take you back to his room. It's a few doors down, and I have no plans tonight, so I can wait around for you after to make sure you feel okay about everything. You ready?"

"As I'll ever be. I mean, yes. I want to do this." Throwing my shoulders back, I try to strike a confident pose, hoping my emotions will catch up.

Alyx taps out a text on his phone. A few seconds later, there's a knock. A bead of sweat glides down my spine, and my breathing stutters as he opens the door.

He's tall, his body nearly filling the doorway, with broad shoulders and large biceps covered in tattoos that stop just above his elbows. His bare chest and abs are on full display, also covered in tattoos, and he has those V lines on his hips that disappear into his black pants. But the most alluring part is the black skull mask that covers his entire face. I can't even see his eyes.

"Follow me," a deep voice growls from under the mask. It sounds like there's a voice modulator built in.

Alyx gives me a thumbs-up and a crooked smile, and I follow the masked man into the hall. The muscles on his back ripple with each step he takes, his backside perfectly framed in his pants. I don't think I've ever checked out a man's butt like this before, but he has the most perfect behind I've ever seen, and refrain from grabbing it. He ushers me into a room down the hall, and once the door clicks, the noise from the club is silenced.

"Is it soundproof in here?" I ask nervously.

"It is." His tone is firm, giving nothing away as he stands with his arms crossed next to the door.

As I look around the room, there are all kinds of interesting devices, only some of which have come up in my research. "Is that a St. Andrew's cross?"

"Yes," the gruff voice answers.

"There's no bed in here. How are we going to…" I trail off as he approaches me, my eyes traveling up his form. My head tilts, attempting to see under the mask, but it's useless.

"I don't fuck subs, so I have no use for a bed."

"But I thought we were going to—"

"We're not fucking."

I let out a slow exhale as my eyes drop to the floor, not wanting him to see my disappointment.

"What's your safe word?"

"But I thought we weren't—"

"What's. Your. Safe. Word?" He takes a step closer to me with each word.

"Einstein," I blurt out.

He tilts his head, and the words spill out. "An ex used to call me that, and I hated it. If I willingly say that, you know there's a problem."

"Got it."

"I'm not sure how much Alyx told you about my situation—"

"I read over your survey. I'm familiar with your hard and soft limits. Your safety is my biggest concern. I will not cause you any harm, but make no mistake, I will test your boundaries and push their limits. If at any time you need me to stop, use your safe word. You have all the power here."

"I understand," I say determinedly. Straightening my spine, I open my mouth, but he cuts me off.

"Go stand in front of the cross with your back to me," he commands, making it obvious the scene has begun.

A shiver runs through me at his tone, and before I even

realize it, I'm following his direction. "Now what?" I ask shakily.

"Now you're going to shut your mouth and do as I tell you. No speaking unless I ask you a question. No moving unless I command it. Nod if you understand."

I nod as my panties dampen. No man has ever made my body react like this.

"Good. Since we only have one session, I'll focus on solving that problem you're having. Now tell me, pet, is there anything else I need to know, other than your aversion to touch?"

I preen at the nickname, and I'm not sure why. Maybe it's the overachiever in me, desperate to capture his attention? "It's not an aversion. I want to be touched, but for some reason, my body rejects it."

"If you don't like how I'm touching you, use your safe word."

"That's if I don't punch you first."

"You won't lay a finger on me."

"How do you know?"

"Because you'll be restrained." I inhale a sharp breath as something flutters in my stomach. "I'll prove that you want to be touched. That you need it. And then I'm going to make you come." He grabs my wrist, securing it so I'm facing the cross, and then repeats the process with my other hand and feet.

"You said we weren't going to do it."

"I said I don't fuck subs, but there are other ways to make you come. I also told you not to speak unless spoken to. If you disobey again, you'll be spanked. Do I make myself clear?" He pinches my chin between his thick, calloused fingers.

Desire courses through me at his naughty words, and I nod my head, unsure if I should respond verbally.

"I believe the words you're looking for are 'Yes, sir.'" His voice is menacing along the shell of my ear as I feel his hard body behind me.

"Yes, sir," I croak out.

"I knew you were a good girl. So good, you didn't notice my hands traveling up your skin."

My eyes close as his large hands cover my stomach over my shirt. Normally, I'd be slapping or punching by now, but instead my body relaxes, and I fight the urge to lean into his touch. How is he doing this? Is it because his identity is a mystery?

His pinkie moves down to the hem of my shirt and glides along the bare flesh of my abdomen as I suck in a breath.

"You like that." He sounds surprised, and I nod, unsure if that was an invitation to answer or move. He bunches the fabric, allowing his warm skin to hover over my flesh. The heat coming off his hand has me wound up in anticipation, and I arch toward his palm. "Don't move." His hand withdraws from my skin.

He steps back, and my disappointment is palpable. This is the first time I've ever looked forward to someone's touch instead of dreading it. Normally, if a guy tries to touch me, I'm too in my head, worried about my reaction. But being restrained, giving over control to this man, has me craving his touch.

There's movement behind me, and it sounds like he's opening a cabinet, but I dare not look. When he approaches me seconds later, I hear the thwack of what sounds like a whip, and I try to relax my shoulders. Is he going to hurt me?

"This is a riding crop," he says close to my neck. Moments later, I feel something hard gliding along the outside of my thigh and along my backside. It takes everything in me not to react, not to move. I want to clench my thighs together, but it's impossible with my bindings. I have this overwhelming need to please him, to obey and make him proud.

"You're wet. I bet you're soaking your little white cotton panties just thinking about what it would feel like if I touched you there. My fingers teasing your opening while my tongue flicks at your clit until you're begging me to stretch you with my cock."

A small whimper escapes me at his dirty words. No one has ever talked to me this way, and my arousal pools between my legs.

The tip of the riding crop moves slowly up my inner thigh. When it reaches my center, he rubs it back and forth, using the stiff handle to separate my lips through my panties, and the friction feels illicit. A wave of lust courses through me, causing my hips to rock against the implement.

"How bad does this good little girl want to come? Tell me."

"I… I need to… I need it. Please… Please, sir."

He mutters something unintelligible under his breath, and then the riding crop is gone, and I'm thrusting my hips against nothing but air. Is this my punishment? Is he going to keep teasing me, making me yearn for his touch before denying me the very thing I've rejected from every guy I've been with, yet somehow crave from him?

Is it the teasing? Normally guys rush right in, trying to grab every part of me they can, but he's drawing this out. Only focusing on me, not his pleasure. Is that why it's different? Is it because I don't know who he is? I can't see the way he reacts, can't read his emotions, and yet for some reason I've never wanted to please a person more.

Fingers glide up the outsides of my legs as he slips his hands under my skirt before wrapping them around my hips, pressing me back until my butt pushes against his front. Is he… hard? Oh, sweet mother of pearl, he *is* hard, and it's impressive.

The hard plastic of his mask grazes my ear as he speaks. "If I untie you, are you going to hit me?"

"No." My voice is husky with desire.

He bends down to loosen the cuffs on my ankles, allowing me to step out. My hands are still secured to the cross when I feel his fingers travel up the backs of my thighs before he pulls my skirt and panties down in one quick motion. Kneeling on the floor, he nudges my legs apart again and secures my ankles back to the cross. Everything happens so quickly, I barely have time to process it.

His hands wrap around my waist, his fingers easily touching as he encircles my back and stomach. Gosh, he has big hands. But I don't have time to dwell on that thought as he continues stroking his fingers under my shirt, until they're pushing under the cups of my bra.

I should be embarrassed at the moan that escapes me, but surprisingly I'm not. This is easily the most sensual thing that has ever happened to me, and I cannot contain my lust as he cups my breasts over my bra, squeezing them, pulling the cups down before he pauses.

"You're pierced?"

"Is that a question?" My voice is breathy and unsure.

"You surprise me, pet. Who did you let touch you here?" He delicately traces a nipple as he tortuously moves the barbell back and forth.

"I… uh… oh frick…" I moan as he continues teasing me, making it hard to concentrate.

"Answer me, pet."

"I went to a tattoo parlor hoping that I could trick my body into letting someone touch me there. Since it was a professional piercer, not someone trying to get in my pants, I was hoping that I'd have a different reaction. And it worked, he made it through unharmed." He continues playing with my nipples. When he dips one hand between my thighs, I gasp.

"So fucking ready for me. So fucking needy for me. Once I uncuff your wrists, raise your hands over your head and keep them there. No matter what I do, you don't move. Is that clear?"

"Yes, sir."

"Fuck, I love it when you call me that. Are you going to be a good little pet and do as you're told?"

"Yes, sir."

He moves quickly, uncuffing one wrist and then the other. I lift my hands above my head and inhale a shaky breath as his hands trail over as much of my skin as possible as he pulls my shirt up and off painfully slowly.

"So obedient for me, pet." He unhooks the front clasp of my bra, and then he's cupping me in his hands, kneading and pinching as my head falls back against his hard chest. "Already craving my touch, I see, but I didn't tell you to move."

My head lifts off his chest, and I immediately miss the comfort it provided. "Sorry, sir."

With my hands still in the air, he finishes removing my bra, leaving me completely bare as he refastens my wrists to the cross.

Once I'm secure, he extends his pointer finger, making a show of tracing each of my fingers with it, slowly swiping between each one, leaving no inch of my hand untouched by his. With the same single finger, he continues down my forearm, moving in lines up and down my arm, careful to cover every bit of flesh, before circling my elbow and then stroking my bicep. After he repeats the same motions on my other arm, his finger trails up to my shoulder and collarbone, mapping every divot and groove as my breathing picks up. His touch is gentle, a stark contrast to his earlier gruffness.

"Is this okay?"

"Yes, sir." I moan as his finger moves down to my chest. "Frick."

There are soft chuckles near my left ear, the modulator slightly distorting his voice.

His finger makes slow circles around the outside of my breast, and I inhale a sharp breath, forcing my chest up and out in a feeble attempt to get him to hurry the process along. I might die if he doesn't touch more of me soon, the anticipation making me sweat like a sinner in church.

"Patience, pet. You're doing so well, I'd hate to punish you now."

"What would my punishment be?" I ask eagerly as he removes his finger from my body.

"I warned you about speaking without permission." His voice gets softer. I fight the urge to look over my shoulder and curse myself for disobeying his command, worried he's done with me. I've spent years having physical reactions to men touching me, and this man was not only able to touch me but also make me crave him within minutes.

Soft footsteps approach, and he gently covers my eyes with a blindfold. "Not another word out of that perfect fucking mouth," he warns, tightening the blindfold as my heart beats rapidly in my chest.

A hand slaps the flesh of my breast, and I let out a gasp as the pain of the strike eases into pleasure when his fingers rub the skin after. His large palms easily cover both of my breasts as he pinches and kneads them. If I could rub my thighs together, I would. Instead, I worry about the flood of arousal that overwhelms me as he continues his sensual massage. My breath stutters as I feel a familiar tingle between my thighs. Holy crap, I'm going to have an orgasm. A man is going to give me the kind of pleasure I've only ever been able to give myself, and I don't even know his name or what he looks like.

"Are you going to come for me, pet?"

I nod quickly, unsure if his question is rhetorical. An embarrassingly loud moan escapes me as I drop my head, lolling it from side to side as I focus on his fingers. Each pluck of my nipple, each tug and twist of my piercings, sends a zing down my body straight to my core, and I can't concentrate on anything other than the electricity coursing through me.

"That's it, you're so close. I see how your body reacts to me. To my hands on you. The way I'm playing it like an instrument. Be a good girl and give me the melody I deserve. Come for me, pet."

And I do, I come harder than I ever have before, as if he's the maestro, conducting a symphony only my body can perform, my moans echoing off the cross in front of me in a chorus of ecstasy.

"Fucking divine." He releases my breasts, sliding down my torso in a sensual caress. Just when I think he's going to touch me there, he diverts his efforts outward, trailing down my outer thighs. "When I'm done with you, there won't be an inch of this perfect body that my fingers haven't touched. And then I'm going to replace my fingers with my tongue until I've tasted every part of you."

Oh. My. Gosh.

His fingers tickle the backs of my thighs before caressing my backside, but when he parts my cheeks, I flinch. "Don't move." His tone is soft and pleading, not quite a command, and I force myself to relax as he continues exploring my bottom. It actually feels quite nice, and I find myself pushing back against his finger as he circles my tight hole. "Fucking hell, pet, what are you doing to me?" This question is definitely rhetorical, but I can't help myself.

"Please. I need you inside me. Your fingers, your mouth, your—" My words are cut off when I feel something push inside me, in a place only I have touched, causing a loud moan to erupt from my mouth. Since I can't see, I can't be sure what's filling me, but my other senses are heightened, and I didn't hear him undo a belt or zipper. When I feel his hand grazing my lips, he adds what I'm confident is another finger into me, and I clench around it. I rock my hips as he continues thrusting his fingers in and out. That tingle starts again, and I'm so close to another orgasm when I feel him pull out abruptly. "Please, sir, please fill me. You're right, I need it. Need your touch. Please," I beg.

I hear him mutter something about rules, and I worry that I missed something in Alyx's briefing of the club rules earlier. It takes a second to register that his grumbles sound different, less distorted. He must've removed his mask. "This doesn't leave this room. Do you understand? No one can know." His head is near my core as he teases around the opening before moving his tongue up and down my thighs.

"Yes, sir." I nod in agreement, confused by the conflict I hear in his voice. Not sure who I would even tell if I wanted to.

"Good girl. Now I'm going to lick every inch of your magnificent body before I bury my face in this cunt, so if you need me to stop, use that safe word loudly," he warns before trailing his tongue over every inch of me at a pace much too slow for my liking, working me into a frenzy as I fight the urge to buck against my restraints. I can't stop the gasps and moans that escape my lips. I should be embarrassed or ashamed. A stranger is licking my body while I'm chained up in a sex club. This is so not me.

"Fucking dripping." His warm breaths bounce off my core before he feasts on me. Every lick and suck sends a bolt of pleasure coursing through me until I feel like an archer about to unleash a quiver of arrows, each one aimed at the same target—my complete and utter pleasure.

"Oh yes. Yes! Oh, jeez, that feels so good, yes, right there. Yes, sir. Oh heck, yes," I cry as my body convulses, and I come with the force of an earthquake.

"Fuck. Ughnnnn. Fuuuuck," he groans as his tongue stills, and he removes his fingers.

How did I get here? And what do I need to do for another round in pleasure town? Did he finish too? Is that what all his groaning was at the end there? I want to ask, but decide against it out of fear that my punishment might involve him refusing to see me again, and I definitely want more time with this man.

I want to tell him that when his hands were on me, it felt like lightning coursing through my veins, traveling a path straight toward my core. I want him to know that his touch made me feel more alive than I've ever felt. I want him to command every inch of my body with every part of his until I'm sated.

But I'm afraid I've traded one problem for another. What if he's the only person who can make me feel this way? The only one who could get close enough to me to do the things to my body that every other man has failed to do? How could I trust someone with my pleasure when I don't know who he is or what he looks like?

CHAPTER 2
JOHN

_W_hat the fuck am I doing? I don't fuck subs. That's rule number one.

Well, technically I didn't fuck her with my dick.

No, you just tongue-fucked her until she came all over your face while you came in your pants like a goddamn needy fuck, jackass.

I was supposed to touch her, maybe make her come. Just one session to show her that she could enjoy the touch of a man. But I lost control.

I _never_ lose control.

The minute the words "Please, sir" fell from her perfect lips, I knew I was fucked. And now I'm between her legs with a mess in my pants as she comes down from the high of her orgasm. I stare up at her wondering how I'm going to walk away from this. My eyes track a bead of sweat as it makes its way down the valley between her breasts, gliding along her smooth skin as it trails a path down her flat stomach. I arch up and swipe at it with my tongue before it reaches her navel. Goosebumps break out across her abdomen at my touch, and my cock jumps, delighted to have this effect on her. Then I put my mask back in place and crawl out from under her.

I need to get it together. I'm the dom. I'm in charge of the scene. She has given her control over to me, and I need to remember that.

Hovering close to her ear, I'm tempted to bury my hand in her hair and pull her mouth to mine, but since touch is a trigger for her, I restrain myself.

"Such a good pet. You came so beautifully for me." Her pants slow as her head turns toward mine. "Don't move. It'd be a shame to punish you now."

Grabbing what I need from the drawer to clean her, and changing into a fresh pair of boxers and pants for myself, I gravitate toward her, telling her what I'm about to do, where I'm about to touch before I proceed. Once she's clean, I release her from the restraints and slowly dress her.

"Is the scene over? Can I take this off?" She reaches for the blindfold. I grab her wrist and hold it in place, gently removing the blindfold for her. She blinks several times, her long eyelashes fluttering, casting a spell on me, testing my restraint.

Her eyes peruse my body, and I see the moment she notices my pants. They were black when we walked in, but I'm in jeans now. It's cute how her brows knit slightly, and her mouth drops open, before she closes it, clearly deciding against saying anything.

I cross my arms over my chest, and her pupils dilate as she stares at my biceps and pecs. I watch as she takes in all the ink there, and I'd love to know the thoughts swirling through her head as a hundred microexpressions cross her features. Fuck if it doesn't do something to my ego seeing the lust on this beautiful woman's face when she stares at me.

This can't happen again. She's way too young. I've got to be at least ten years older than her. She is way too inexperienced in the lifestyle, hell, in general. But fuck if I don't have the sudden urge to explore a corruption kink. Blame it on the religious upbringing.

This was not the plan. I was supposed to help tame a brat,

but she's not really a brat. She's clearly a sub with more than just an aversion to touch. She's got these big brown eyes that look like an innocent doe, but track every inch of my body. Light brown hair that can't decide if it's dirty blonde or brown, that I want to gather in my fist and tug when I fill her from behind. And those motherfucking piercings that hint that she's not as innocent as she seems.

"Follow me," I say, breaking the spell as she shakes her head slightly, raising her eyebrows as she tries to clear her thoughts.

I open the door and motion her into the hallway, following behind as she walks toward Alyx's room. I want to touch her, pull her back into my room, claim her with my hands, my mouth, and my cock. I am a weak, weak man. Instead, my hand grazes the small of her back, and she flinches slightly. Fuck.

"What was that?" I demand as she stops in her tracks, refusing to turn around and face me.

"I don't know," she squeaks out meekly as I circle around, stopping in front of her.

"You flinched."

"Did I?" She feigns innocence, but her fingers twitch.

I don't have time for this. If she's not going to tell me, that's fine. We're steps away from Alyx's room, steps away from her no longer being my problem. I arch my neck from side to side, cracking it to relieve my frustration. If she were actually my sub, she wouldn't be allowed to keep secrets from me.

All of a sudden, she drops to the floor, covering her head with her hands, making herself as small as she can as she cowers in my presence. "Einstein!" she cries as her breathing picks up and her petite body starts rocking back and forth.

Fuck. Fuck. Fuck.

"Whoa, whoa, whoa. It's okay," I soothe, crouching in front of her. "You're safe."

I make a show of grabbing my knees with my hands,

worried it was my touch that set her off. What the fuck happened? She was fine in my room, leaning into my touch, begging me to fill her. What changed?

"I'm going to touch you. Okay, pet?" I show her my palms and slowly lower my hands to her body. Her eyes are glassy, like she's looking through me, not at me. "You're going to be okay. I'm going to carry you to Alyx's room."

As delicately as possible, I scoop her into my arms and move quickly down the hall. Using the toe of my boot, I bang on the door, and Alyx throws it open with a look of irritation before he sees Emma in my arms.

"What the fuck?" Alyx asks as I push past him, gently setting her on the bed.

"We had a successful scene, and I was escorting her back to your room. She flinched when I touched her back, and when I pressed her about it, she used her safe word and dropped to the ground."

"Why are you wearing different pants?" His eyes widen. "Did you fuck her? You weren't supposed to fuck her. This is my best friend's little sister. He'll kill me if I let anything happen to her."

"Relax, I didn't fuck her," I assure him standing from the bed and crossing my arms. I easily have a few inches on him, and even though he can't see it through the mask, I glare down at him.

"Chill, Zade, you don't have to get all Daddy Dom on me."

"Zade?"

"It's a book about— you know what, never mind." He pushes past me to check on Emma. "Em, you okay? Talk to me, sis." He gently strokes her spine as she curls onto her side, facing away from him.

I'm hit with a confusing wave of jealousy watching him comfort her, and I shake my head to clear it. I need to get out of here. "You good with her?" I move toward the door.

"Yeah, man." Alyx doesn't look at me.

"Wait," a small voice rasps. I'm next to her in two strides, kneeling at the foot of the bed as her tiny frame faces me at eye level.

"What is it, pet?" I fight the urge to push the hair on her cheek behind her ear.

"I need to see you again," she pleads, locking those doe eyes on me, and even though my mask is tinted and she can't see in, I swear she's looking right into my soul.

"Don't know if that's the best idea…" Alyx starts, but she cuts him off.

"Please, I need to see you again. I need you."

It's clear she could use my guidance, and I was naive to think that one session would be enough. But it has to be enough—she is a risk I cannot afford to make. She's someone who will make me break all my rules. The kind of woman that men start wars over, like Helen of Troy. And suddenly I want to abandon everything to comfort her. Something about her triggers my hero complex, and I have an overwhelming desire to help her and protect her, but from what, I can't be sure. I should walk away. I have way too many fucking problems that I shouldn't drag her into.

"Please, sir. I need your help," she begs as a single tear glides down her slender nose, pausing on the tip, before dropping onto the black comforter.

My mind flashes to the last time a woman said those words to me. I couldn't deny her, and I know I won't deny Emma.

Her small hand reaches toward me, and I take it, bringing it up to my mask as if I'm able to kiss it. All I can do is offer her a small nod in response.

She deserves a lot more than I can offer her, but just like I always do, I'm going to help her anyway.

CHAPTER 3
EMMA

I lie on the bed in Alyx's private room for much longer than I should, but I'm afraid to move, and I can't pinpoint why. His hand is still making gentle, sporadic strokes on my back, making it clear he's probably scrolling on his phone.

Letting out a deep breath, I lean up on my elbow, knowing I need to move or I'll stay here all night.

"What did he do? To set you off," Alyx asks gently.

"I don't want to talk about what happened in his room." I'm not ready to tell him about anything when I'm still processing it myself.

"I'm not asking about that."

"He cracked his neck. In the hallway." I close my eyes to fight back the images in my brain.

Alyx gets it immediately. "Like the boogeyman in your dreams."

"It's not a boogeyman." I push to sitting before bumping my shoulder into him. "It's a man, I just don't know who it is."

"Has the therapy been helping?" He wraps an arm around my shoulder.

"I think so."

"Who does the therapist think it is?"

"She thinks it could be a memory I've repressed that my brain only seems to share with me at night."

He hums in response, seeming to accept the information. "When's your next appointment?"

"I need to schedule it. We definitely have some new developments to discuss."

"I'll say." A minute passes before he speaks again. "Do you ever think it's weird that *I* can touch you?"

"Not really. You're safe, like Ethan and my stepdad."

He laughs, throwing his head back. "So I can touch you because you know I don't want to fuck you?"

"I think?"

"You think? Emma, I definitely don't want to fuck you." He laughs harder, removing his arm from my shoulder and holding his hands out in surrender.

"No, I mean, I think that's why. I know you don't want to do that." I smile, comforted at how easily he can calm me down.

I pick at a loose thread in the comforter as a comfortable silence fills the space. I'm aware of the faint sounds of music and sex, and I concentrate on that, willing the thoughts in my head to be quiet.

"You're coming to my place tonight so I can keep an eye on you," he says, noticing a shift in my demeanor.

"That's not necessary."

"It is, Em. You scared the shit out of me. I need to know that you're going to be okay, especially if your nightmares are still happening."

"Ethan won't be there?" I ask, worried.

"Nope, he's been staying at his girl's place lately." He crosses the room and pulls his keys out of his pocket.

Alyx has been best friends with my older brother Ethan for as long as I can remember, and he's always treated me like family.

"Can Ella come too?" I ask, hopeful he'll let my younger sister crash the party.

"No underage girls in my apartment. I don't have a lot of rules, but that's non-negotiable. Ethan would probably freak out if he knew *you* were staying."

"Fine. I'll let Ella know to cover for me." Since I'm not in summer classes, I've been staying at home until I can move back into the dorms, and I don't want my mom to know that my nightmares are back.

––––––––––

The shadowy figure stalks closer to me, and I'm paralyzed with fear. My arms and legs aren't restrained, yet I can't move them. He towers over me, his presence larger than life, and I instantly feel small, insignificant.

I need to get out of here, but he's blocking the exit. How did he find me here? His tall, thick frame fills the door, illuminated by light from behind, casting his features in darkness.

His steps are slow and deliberate as he claps his hands, threading his fingers together and then flipping them out, palms toward me as he stretches them, cracking his knuckles before punching a palm with his fist as he approaches the side of the bed. I need to move, need to run, but I lay there motionless. He's going to kill me.

"Don't do anything stupid," he spits at me as he grabs my arms, pinning me to the bed, and then he climbs on top of me, straddling me and holding me in place. He moves his neck from side to side, stretching it like he's preparing for a fight. My adrenaline kicks in, but it's too late as I buck against his hold.

He leans down, using his chest to pin my torso to the bed, his hot, putrid breath enveloping my nostrils. His face is still in shadow as he speaks.

"Emma!" His voice doesn't quite sound right, and I thrash against him.

"Em!" the voice calls, more frantic, and my eyes open as I bolt up to sitting. Alyx wraps his big arms around me, and I sink against him. "Shit, Em, you scared me. You were screaming so loud. Shh, it's okay, I've got you." He rubs along my spine, soothing me as my heart rate slowly returns to normal.

A small light illuminates the room briefly, and he reaches over to grab my phone, answering it with a swipe and holding it up between us. My sister's face fills the screen.

"Ew, why is Alyx touching you?" She wrinkles her nose.

"Fuck you, Ella."

"Hello to you, too, Alyx," she shoots back with a smirk. "At least tell me he's clothed."

"For fuck's sake," he mutters, shaking his head in exasperation.

"Seriously, though, the man-child texted me that you were having another nightmare. You okay?" I see Alyx roll his eyes in the little picture of us on the bottom of the screen.

"I'm going to give you two a minute." He rests his cheek on my head as he hugs me.

"Need to get back to your flavor of the week?" my sister quips, and my eyes shoot to his, silently asking him if he has company over. He shakes his head vehemently, and I instantly relax. I don't care who he hooks up with, but I'm not in a place to be around any houseguests.

"How's Chad?" I swear steam billows from Ella's ears as he exits the room, closing the door behind him.

These two have been like this ever since Alyx told Ella that she couldn't hang out with him and Ethan when the guys were teenagers.

"Okay, now that Sir Comes-a-lot is gone, talk to me. He said you had another nightmare?"

I nod as I lean over to turn on the lamp next to the bed, propping the phone against it and cuddling into my blankets.

"Wanna talk about it?"

I shake my head as I shove my hand under the pillow, getting comfortable.

"Want me to come get you? Dad finally let me get my license last week. It's bullshit, I'm almost seventeen. I could steal his car and be there in an hour."

"No, it's fine. I'll be okay," I say, hoping she won't do something stupid but also wishing she would so she could cuddle me. "Can you just tell me a story until I fall back asleep?"

"I got you, Em," she says softly before launching into a rant about Dad and not living up to his expectations. I respond at the appropriate parts until my eyelids get heavy and I can't hold them open anymore.

When I emerge from Ethan's bedroom the next morning, Alyx is in the kitchen at the stove.

I only recently discovered his secret job. I'd spent weeks researching ways to solve my touching issue, reading everything I could to find a solution, and months talking to my therapist about it before I finally decided on my own version of immersion therapy—I haven't shared that part with my therapist yet, but I'm sure she'll be fine with it when she hears about my progress. But when Alyx reached into his wallet to hand me his bus pass and accidentally gave me his membership card to Pulse, I knew I could talk to him about it.

He wasn't thrilled with the idea of me hooking up with some random sex worker and suggested I meet someone he trusted at Pulse instead.

"I made breakfast sandwiches. It's just egg, cheese, and bacon on toast. I forget, do you drink coffee?" Alyx asks, pulling me from my thoughts.

"Yes, please." My voice is still adjusting to being awake, a little hoarse from the nightmare screaming.

"Is that how you normally sound in the morning? Like a bullfrog?" He grins as he hands me a plate and mug.

"Jerk," I mutter as he ruffles my hair.

"Yeah, but you love me." He takes a comically large bite, and yolk drips down his undershirt.

"You're a mess." I point to the stain on his shirt, and he whips it off, tossing it onto the counter.

"Ugh, can you put a shirt on?" I ask, averting my eyes.

"There's nothing wrong with the male form, Em."

"Yeah, but you're like my brother, and I don't wanna see him shirtless either."

"Fair point." He walks to his room. When he returns fully dressed, we stand at the counter, eating our breakfast in silence. "You wanna talk about last night?" He sips his coffee.

"Want to, no. Need to, probably." I pause for a moment. "Is it weird that I'm not comfortable with your shirtless body, but I can talk to you about my naughty exploits?"

He chuckles. "It's kinda quirky, but so are you, and I don't judge. I work at a sex club, there's nothing I haven't seen or heard." He hops onto the counter. "So, I'm all ears. Did Daddy Dom solve your problem?"

I shift on my feet, suddenly anxious at hearing about him. "Daddy Dom? Is Dom his actual name?" I'm a little too eager for his answer.

"Dom is his kink, not his name. He's known as Daddy Dom around the club, but very few people know who he really is since he's a pretty private guy."

"Why do I get the feeling you know a lot of people's secrets?" I stare at him pointedly, hoping he'll give this one up. I need to see him again, and for some reason, I'm afraid to ask.

"Why do I get the feeling you're hiding something?" He cocks an eyebrow.

I blow out a deep breath. "He was able to touch me. And, boy, did he touch me."

"You're cured?" he asks, his eyes full of hope.

"I thought so. He restrained me and touched me. Everywhere. And I mean, everywhere. And then he made me…" My cheeks heat thinking about his touch.

"You can say orgasm, Em. He made you come. Sounds like a successful session."

"What if the only reason it worked was because I was restrained? Or because I couldn't see his face? What if I'm not really cured?"

"You did let him carry you in the hallway after your freak-out."

"I don't know what came over me in the hallway. He did that motion with his neck, and it reminded me of the figure in my dreams. I know he's not that man, but it spooked me."

He doesn't say anything in response, and we eat in silence for several minutes. I'm afraid to say it. Alyx already did me a huge favor by letting me go to the club, and another by introducing me to his friend. It almost feels like a game of chicken to see who will break first. Staring at him, I give my best sad eyes, jutting out my lip a little while batting my eyelashes.

"Fuck, no. I know exactly what that look is, and the answer is no. You're not going back. That was a one-time thing, and we're pushing our luck if I bring you again."

"I need to see him again. He's the only person who's been able to get that far. I really think he can help me." My mind flashes back to last night, me on the bed pleading to see him again. He gave me a slight nod of agreement, but once we left, I had no way to contact him except for Alyx.

"This is a bad idea."

"Please," I beg, turning up the puppy dog eyes.

"You know, you're not the sweet little girl people think you are. But, fine, we'll figure something out."

I launch myself into him, hugging him tight.

"Kinda wish I was one of those people whose touch repulsed you cuz this is a damn tight hug," he grunts as I relax my grip.

"Thank you." A wave of relief washes over me. I don't know what's going to happen next, but I'm oddly comforted at the thought that spending time with a certain masked stranger is in my future.

CHAPTER 4
JOHN

There are rules by which I live my life. I need structure to quiet my brain. My household was pretty chaotic growing up, and having rules to follow helped me achieve what was expected of me. I had so little control over my life back then, and rules provided me a sense of comfort and order.

If I'm being honest, I don't have any control over my life at the moment either, so that's probably why these rules make me feel balanced. They let me know what I should and shouldn't do in this fucked-up situation I've found myself in. Though my current rules are much different than the ones my parents had for me.

My personal and professional lives stay separate.

I don't date students.

Consent is non-negotiable.

What happens at the club stays at the club.

Subs never come home with me, and we do not fuck.

I require complete submission.

Getting attached is out of the question.

I never show my face.

I didn't plan on living a double life, but certain situations forced my hand. My parents raised me to make good choices, but their version of good differs from mine. We went to church twice a week. I spent most of my life studying God's word and being expected to uphold it.

As a middle child who was desperate to please my parents and keep the peace in our house, I did everything right, according to their rules: I got good grades, I did mission work, I found a job at a Christian school. The deeper I got into my work and the more people I helped, the more the hypocrisy overwhelmed me. I was raised to love my neighbor by parents who couldn't do the same. I teach at a school where the mentality that reigns is "I love Jesus, but not you." I've never felt further away from God than when I was surrounded by *his* church people.

And that God failed me when I needed it most. And even though I eventually broke free from my family's religious oppression and their ridiculous rules, I'd already found my academic home at Faith Union. I've spent my time here searching for purpose, for a way to atone for the fuck-ups in my youth, to help others, even if I couldn't help myself. And along the way I made a new set of rules to keep me on the path I want for my life.

The only place that has given me true sanctuary is Pulse. The kink community there is open and accepting, and even though I prefer to isolate myself to protect my identity, I've never felt more welcomed or at home.

There are specific rules I'm expected to follow as a professor at Faith Union, and living out my BDSM fantasies at a sex club definitely isn't on that list. But it's the only outlet I have when I have little to no control over my life. While my work there is enjoyable, my encounters are transactional. I don't allow myself to get close to anyone.

Most of my clients are women, but I've helped a few couples too. It's a misnomer that all BDSM dynamics involve sexual interactions. People come to me for help. Some just want to turn their brain off and have someone else be responsible over their choices for a bit. Others want to feel cared for. And then there are couples that I've helped coach, instructing one partner how to top the other. While my interactions over the years have involved acts of intimacy, it's always one-sided. I might talk someone through their own self-pleasure or use toys on them. Normally I don't participate.

When I agreed to take on Emma as a sub, it was supposed to be just one session. But my savior complex kicked in almost immediately. There was something about her that grabbed my attention, as though her eyes were begging for the kind of help she couldn't vocalize. The last time I saw eyes like that... I can't go there.

I need to figure out a way to end this arrangement, it was supposed to be temporary, but damn if I don't need another hit of her sweet scent, to feel the taste of her on my lips again.

I've been attracted to subs before, but I've never been overcome with the urge to act on it until her. It's more than just lust with Emma; I've been under the limerence spell before and never felt this out of control. It has to be attraction and her innocence. And the fact that of all the men she's encountered, I've been the only one to successfully touch her. Make her come. And fuck if I don't want to do it again.

I'm going straight to hell for this.

Pulling out my phone, I note the time. She's late.

ME

If she's not here in ten minutes, I'm leaving.

ALYX

Chill, dude. I'm about to walk her down. It's my fault. Don't take it out on her. She's fragile right now. Had another nightmare last night. She's had one every night since she met you.

This is a terrible idea. I'm not a therapist. I'm not equipped to deal with emotional trauma. I just get off on spanking people.

Okay, there's more to it than that, and despite what happened last week, I don't usually get off with or around my subs. I wait until I'm home or alone and rub one out.

I open my door right as they approach, and I get a waft of her perfume. It's flowery and subtle and consumes my senses.

"You gonna be okay?" Alyx asks, releasing her shoulder as she steps into the room. She nods, and we speak over each other.

"Need to hear you say it, sis."

"Verbal consent, pet."

"Oh my gosh, yes. I'm fine. And the two of you are infuriating. I'm not a child, and I'm not that easily broken. If I were, I wouldn't be here trying my darndest to get over this. Instead, I'd be curled up on my bed, pounding energy drinks and ice cream while holding my eyelids open so the nightmares couldn't consume me. Can we just get on with this?" She throws up her arms in exasperation.

I take one step toward her, careful not to be too menacing and trigger another episode. "Got that out of your system?"

She nods.

"Good. I don't like taming brats, so that better be the last outburst you have tonight. If you want my help, you will fully submit to my rules. Is that clear, pet?"

"Yes, sir," she says without hesitation, and a rush of blood travels south as my cock thickens in my pants. Jesus Christ, what is it about this girl?

"I'll leave you to it. Try not to bring her back the same way you did last time, eh?"

Before I have a chance to respond, Alyx's gone, and I shut the door in frustration. Emma gasps, cowering slightly in my presence. There's a war inside me as I debate how to handle this. The humanitarian in me wants to rush over, scoop her up, and assure her that everything will be fine, that I'd never hurt her. But I've seen too many fucked-up parts of this world to believe that bullshit. The last time I gave in to that urge to do good, it got me into a mess that I'm still trying to clean up.

Instead, I listen to the devil on my shoulder that's shouting, "Good, you should be fucking scared of me. I'm not here to get attached. I'm here to make you submit."

Getting involved in this lifestyle has been the only thing that's helped me calm the beast inside. I take domination very seriously. It's not about hitting people until one or both of you get off; I never use it to take out my aggression. That's what the gym is for. Being a dom has its own code, its own set of rules dictated by the person submitting to you. Finding my submissive's limits fuel the fantasies I won't allow myself to partake in.

She stands stock-still, waiting for my instruction. Maybe she can be trained.

"You have permission to speak, pet."

She peers up at me with those big eyes, opening and closing her mouth. "I don't have anything to say."

"Bullshit."

All I get is a shrug in return.

"This isn't going to work if you're going to continue to brat."

"I don't want to talk about it, and I feel like you're going to make me share things I'm not comfortable admitting."

"I'm absolutely going to push you out of your comfort zone, but that's why you have a safe word. You can use that when I push too far."

"I don't want to talk about the nightmares."

"I'm not here to psychoanalyze you, but I need to know what you're dealing with so I don't trigger you again. I'm going to need you to answer me, even if it makes you uncom-fortable."

She lets out a sigh. "Okay."

I walk to the corner of the room and pull the lounger to the center, rearranging the wedges so she can lie flat on it. "Strip to your panties and lie face down."

Ever so goddamn slowly, she pulls off her top, revealing a black lace bra. She reaches behind her with one hand while the other holds the front in place, making eye contact with me the entire time like she knows what she's doing to me.

She arches a brow when she releases the bra, and it takes all my willpower not to bite my fist or reach out and touch her. As she carefully shimmies out of her pants, her tits jiggle with the movement, and my cock decides that now is the time to make himself known. I've gotten aroused during sessions before, but it never manifests this quickly, and it's never resulted in me coming in my pants until her.

After she's positioned herself on the lounger, her forehead resting on her forearms, I stalk around her, making slow circles like a lion about to devour its prey. "What does the man in your dreams do to you?" Maybe if I know, I can work her up to similar positions once she feels safe with me.

"How do you know it's a man?"

"Is it not? I presume this is why you have issues with men touching you, no?"

"I think it's a man, but I never see his face. He has a deep voice, but I never hear much of what he says."

"And what did I do to remind you of him?"

She's silent for a long time. "You cracked your neck. He does that… in the dream."

The way she hesitates makes me think this is more than just a dream scenario, but I don't want to press for more. "Thank you, pet. You're such a good girl for me. I'm going to reward you with my touch," I say, letting her know so she isn't startled, and then I gently caress the back of her neck.

A small whimper escapes her lips as her skin erupts into goosebumps.

"Are you cold?"

"No… uh, that feels… good," she gasps as my hands trail lower.

"Have you ever had a massage before?"

"Once, but it was a female masseuse. I wasn't sure I could handle a man."

"Are you feeling brave enough to handle it now?" I walk to the cabinets to grab some massage oil.

"I'd like to try, sir."

I pause my movements the second the honorific escapes her mouth. Many a sub has called me sir. That and "daddy" are my preferred titles. But it's never stopped me in my goddamn tracks like it does every time she says it. Taking a second to calm my heart and my hard-on, I blow out a slow breath as I stalk toward her. Once I lather my hands in oil, I slowly smooth them along her shoulders and arms. I'm thorough with my movements as I work out a few small knots in her shoulder.

"Oh, frick, that feels good," she moans before she instantly tenses, muttering, "Sorry, sir."

"You can speak freely." Suddenly, I'm desperate to hear every thought in her pretty head. What the fuck is wrong with me?

"Sorry, I thought I wasn't supposed to speak unless given permission, like last time."

"Would you like that? For me to have that kind of control over you? Are you willing to submit your speech to me again?"

"It was hard at first. I tend to ramble. But after a while, it was nice not having to share every thought or tangent in my brain."

My mind is at odds with giving her exactly that, and getting her to open up more about her nightmares when she continues.

"At times, in my dream, I'm unable to speak because of the fear or the way he's pinning me to the bed, holding my arms, or straddling me while he pushes down on my windpipe. I want to say something, but I can't. So it's nice to be given the choice not to speak, to know I'm safe not to, and to only have to do it when commanded. My brain was oddly at peace."

What the fuck do I say to that? The way she just summed up the reason why she'd make a perfect submissive, just beautifully explained the reason why I crave this type of dynamic, has more than just my cock swelling. She needs to give up her control for peace, and I need to harness her power and push it to the limits for mine.

This girl is the yin to my yang, perfectly matched to crave the very thing only I can give her, and there's not a damn thing I can do to stop it. Our demise feels like a foregone conclusion, because this can only end badly.

I should walk away, but she wiggles her ass ever so slightly, and I clench my fist to avoid spanking it. Instead, I decide to keep her talking as a distraction.

"I noticed on your intake form that you're open to exploring primal play. Can I ask why?"

She tenses under me before releasing a deep exhale. "For the same reason I checked off an interest in breath play, to take back my power. Whether he's chasing me, or pinning me down, he has control over me, and I need that control back. I don't want to live in fear forever."

"I want to try something, but it's going to require your total trust in me, and if you feel unsafe, you can use your safe word and I'll stop immediately. Can you do that for me?"

"O–okay." She turns her head to peek at me over her shoulder. I reach up and hold her chin between my fingers. "I trust you, sir."

It takes everything in me not to tear off my mask, flip her over, and worship her body from head to toe with my tongue. I squeeze my eyes shut as I try to calm the rush of adrenaline coursing through me at her words, for once grateful for this mask.

After a few cleansing breaths, I resume the massage, gradually increasing the pressure as I work my way down her body. When she's relaxed, I gingerly climb up, straddling her thighs as I run my hands along her spine.

"Wh–what are you doing?" She tenses slightly.

"Use your safe word if you need to tap out. Just know you can trust me, pet."

A soft moan spills from her lips as I work out some knots just above her ass. Jesus Christ, this ass. I want to spank it and leave my handprint, bite it and leave my mark, fuck it and cover it in my cum.

When I'm satisfied that she's at ease, I slowly crawl up her body, applying more pressure as I hover over her ass, careful not to put my full weight on her as I continue working upward. I need her to feel me on her, knowing I could hold her down, yet understand that she can wriggle free at any time.

Despite my efforts, she stiffens under me. "You're safe, pet."

Her breathing picks up, her back rising and falling rapidly beneath my fingers. I'm gentle with my movements as I work my way up her shoulder to the column of her neck, delicately tracing the soft skin there. I want to bite that flesh, mark it with my mouth, claim her, but I can't.

She flinches and I pull back. "Too much?"

"Sorry, it tickles."

I breathe a sigh of relief, worries of triggering her again slowly dissipating as I increase the pressure on the sides of her neck, dragging my fingers up and down. I lean over her, propping myself on my forearm next to her head, as I move in close to her ear, desperate to distract her. "Your body is exquisite, pet. I want to devour you. Would you like that?" I grip the back of her neck, squeezing it as I massage the tense muscles.

"Yes," she rasps, her thighs clenching under me.

"What else would you like?"

"I–I don't know."

Knowing I'm pushing the bounds of her comfortability, I press harder.

"I want to hear that pretty little mouth tell me all the dirty things you want me to do."

"T–touch me," she stutters. "I just want you to touch me."

"Where?"

"Touch me where he does. Make me think about you instead."

The man in her dreams. She's not asking for an orgasm, or even pleasure. Instead, she wants a distraction. "You should stop," yells the angel on my shoulder, but fuck that guy. I want this, I want her. For once in my life, I want to take something for myself.

I tip my mask up, breathing her in— soft and floral, like blooms after a spring shower. Delicate. Sweet. Full of promise. My nose trails along her neck as I inhale another deep breath.

She shudders under me. "What are you… doing?"

"Shhh," I soothe as I lean back and lower my mask.

After a long exhale, she relaxes under me as I touch the places she mentioned, holding down her arms.

"Breathe, pet. You can do this. You're safe with me." Once she calms, I lower myself, putting more of my weight on her, no longer hovering over her ass.

"I can do this, I can do this," she chants in a low whisper.

I pause my movements, expecting her to use her safe word. When she doesn't, I glide my hands up and grip the back of her neck. She mentioned him crushing her windpipe, and even though I'm on her back, I decide she isn't ready for that level of immersion. Instead, I wind one hand around the front, resting it just under her jaw, while the other squeezes tighter on the back of her neck.

"I'm so fucking turned on by how strong you are. It takes a fuckton of fortitude to do what you're doing right now."

"I don't feel strong," she says softly. "I'm a mess. I can't even get a decent night's sleep. And for some stupid reason, I can't even successfully let a man touch me like that."

"Do you feel my hands on you?" I squeeze her neck a little tighter, but still nowhere near cutting off her air. "You let me touch you. Another faceless man. You willingly submit to me. Let me touch you however I want. And I think that's pretty fucking strong, taking your control back."

"Can I see your face?"

I lean back, releasing my grip on her neck, then hop off the lounger.

"That's not a good idea," I grit out in frustration. My control is razor-thin, very little holding me back from ripping this mask off and making her submit the way I really want. But I force it down. This has already gone too far. If I cross that line with her, I could lose everything I've worked for these past four years. "Put your clothes on."

Her head pops up in surprise, and the look of disappointment on her face guts me. "When can I see you again?" she asks as she slips her clothes on.

"I gave Alyx explicit instructions for when he should contact me. If the criteria I've given him are met, I'll be in touch. There are some previous engagements I've committed to for the next few weeks, but if an issue arises, Alyx knows how to reach me. Do I make myself clear, pet?"

"Yes, sir." She deflates a little.

Me too, pet. But all good things come to an end, and I'd rather cut her free now than hurt her later.

CHAPTER 5
EMMA

W alking through the crowded hallway, I stay off to the side, careful not to bump into anyone. So far, my college experience hasn't been what I expected it to be. Everything came easily to me in high school, but I've had to make new habits and routines in college when life dialed up the difficulty to expert level.

But this is a new year, and I have a bag full of blank notebooks, sharpened pencils, and a fully charged laptop. There's nothing this school year can throw at me that I won't be able to handle. And now that I'm in my sophomore year, I get to take classes in my chosen major.

Once I locate the lecture hall, I pull open the door just as a guy pushes it open and shoulder-checks me, causing me to stumble and lose my balance. He continues walking, carrying on a conversation with another guy in a football jersey as a tall figure looms over me from behind.

"Are you okay?" a deep voice asks. As his eyes meet mine, his eyebrows lift, and I look away, overwhelmed by his attention. "Can I help you up?" He extends a hand, waiting for me to accept, and I place mine in his as he slides his other hand under my elbow, pulling me to my feet. A zing of something travels down my arm where he touched, but it's gone as quickly as his hands are as he opens the door for me, ushering me inside.

He has dark brown hair and just the right amount of facial hair to look devastatingly attractive. I can't decide if his eyes are brown or hazel. He has to be in his thirties, clearly making him the professor. His crisp suit covers his backside.

Jeeps, Emma! Do not check out your teacher's butt.

"This is Shakespeare, right?" I'm suddenly nervous as I follow him down the steps of the auditorium-style classroom.

"It is." He refuses to look at me as he reaches the podium and unpacks his bag, setting up a laptop. "But it's an upper-level class usually reserved for juniors or seniors." I'm confused by his abrupt change in demeanor. How does he know I'm not a junior or senior?

"My advisor recommended it, and I got approval to add it from the department chair." I bite my lips, confused by my sudden need to give him such a retort. *Not getting off to the best start, Emma.*

"I'll have to talk to them about that," he mutters as he fiddles with some plugs on his laptop.

"I'm sorry, I think we got off on the wrong foot. I'm excited to take this course. Professor Ali, right?" I swallow down the nerves bubbling to the surface and find a seat in the second row.

"As long as you know that other than helping you up just now, I'm not going to hold your hand all semester. You have to do the work."

Well, what crawled up your butt?

"What was that?" He looks up from his laptop.

Oh no, did I say that out loud? His gaze is penetrating, and his presence intimidating as he removes his suit coat and rolls up the sleeves of his white Oxford. Images of those strong hands flood my brain as I imagine him holding me down and having his way with me. I rub my thighs together as he clears his throat, refocusing my attention.

"Umm, what?"

He smirks for a split second, the look almost playful before it vanishes, replaced by a scowl. "I believe you said something about my butt?"

"Oh, heavens no, that can't be right. Must have bumped my head and my butt when I fell. And now my butt is sore and this chair isn't helping. I don't know why I'm talking about my butt. You're my teacher. I mean, you know you're my teacher. I'm stating the obvious. I'll stop talking now." I sink into my seat. That fall definitely left a bruise, I can feel it forming, the hard chair providing little cushion.

He seems to accept my answer, and I bite my tongue so his stupid handsome face won't fluster me any further.

Students filter into the lecture hall as I pull the laptop out of my bag. Syllabi are dispersed, and I look it over.

"Welcome to Shakespeare. This course will be rigorous as my expectations are high for a class at this level. I will challenge you, push you to expand your understanding, and question what you think you know. The demanding nature of this class will require you to adhere to the schedule, manage your time wisely, and follow the rules outlined in the syllabus. I expect you to familiarize yourself with it on your own time, but suffice it to say there are guidelines and rubrics for how I expect you to craft your essays, engage in classroom discussion, and turn in your assignments. I do not accept late work, no exceptions…"

Well, this is a vast departure from the kind gentlemen who just helped me up. I swallow down my nerves worried I'm in over my head as Professor No-fun drones on.

This is my year. I can do hard things. I am smart. I am more than people expect. I can handle this. I've got this.

I repeat the mantras in my head when a throat clearing pulls me out of my meditation. When I look up, Professor A-hole's eyes are fixed on me, a scowl on his face. It feels like all eyes are on me. "I'm sorry, I didn't hear the question."

"I was saying that you should be prepared to be called on at any time, and I expect you to at least attempt to answer my question or engage in a Socratic discussion with the class as that makes up a large portion of your participation grade, Miss Black."

I stare at him confused. "How do you know my name?"

He blinks for a second like I caught him off guard before he gestures to the sticker on my laptop. "I'm guessing your name is Emma, based on that, and there's only one Emma on my roster."

Blood rushes to my cheeks, and I squirm under his intense scrutiny. Maybe I *should* drop this class.

"I'll repeat the question. Can you tell me how many works Shakespeare wrote in his lifetime?"

This is where I shine. I'm not dropping anything. I'll show him. "Shakespeare is credited with writing thirty-eight plays, one hundred and fifty-four sonnets, two long narrative poems, and a few other poems. Though it has been speculated that Francis Bacon, Christopher Marlowe, or Edward de Vere may have had a hand in some of those works, it hasn't been definitively proven." I straighten my spine, satisfied with my answer, but then he moves on, calling on another student.

That's it? No acknowledgement? Was he testing me because he thinks I'm not ready for an upper-level class? I open my mouth to retort, then think better of it. *Don't pick a fight with your professor on the first day of class, Emma.*

Professor Power-trip asks me three more questions, and I can tell he's trying to test my knowledge and prove I don't deserve to be in his class. I nail the first two, but the last one trips me up, and he makes a note before dismissing me again.

The longer the class goes on, and the more he engages with other students, the more overwhelming my need to be seen and praised becomes. Why am I like this? I've always been a good student—learning came easy to me since it was some-thing I could control when the chaos of my life was too much. I don't have a lot of memories of my biological dad since he and my mom divorced when I was a baby. But my stepdad came into the picture not too long after, and I gained an older brother in his son Ethan. Then my parents had four more daughters. I love my siblings, but I spent a lot of time in the library because it was quiet, and I could focus.

Sometimes I think I try extra hard, overextending myself in hopes that I'll finally earn the good things in my life. Like if I don't work hard enough, I'll lose all the progress I've made. I feel broken and like my mask is slipping.

I clutch at my heart, trying to ground myself with touch, repeating what my therapist told me when these thoughts creep in. *I'm not broken, my body is healing. I'm worthy of love. I deserve good things.*

Shoot, what is he saying? Professor A-hole is standing behind the podium again, and I tell my brain to focus as I concentrate on his words.

"This is a fast-paced course with a heavy workload. It would be in your best interest to drop this class if you don't think you can handle it so you don't waste your time, or mine." He looks right at me on that last part, and I fist my skirt in my hand. "We'll be reading a good bit of the Bard's works, and there will be different essays assigned to each of them. While I don't adhere to the university's strict attendance poli-cies—because you're adults who are fully capable of managing your own time—a good portion of the midterm and exam content will come from our class discussions, so it's in your best interest to be here, or befriend someone who takes copious notes. My email and office hours are on the syllabus. Any questions?"

My head swivels side to side, looking around the room, but no one raises a hand. I want to ask him if he needs help removing the stick from his butt, but I refrain. He's probably just some boring, stuffy English professor who's too miserable with his mediocre life so he takes it out on his students. I bet he wouldn't know how to let loose and have fun if it smacked him in his cute, round butt.

Seriously, Emma, stop thinking about that A-hole's backside.

Two days later, I'm in my advisor's office, ready to explore my options. "Are you sure I can't drop the class?"

"Well, the deadline hasn't passed, but it *is* a required class for your major. It's up to you."

Frick.

"Can I take it with another professor?" Surely someone else teaches it.

"Professor Ali is the only one who teaches Shakespeare at Faith Union. He's also the only one that teaches the Shakespearean Acting course that you've signed up for in the spring."

"But he's an English professor, not theatre."

"This isn't a big state school, Ms. Black. We're lucky to offer these classes at all. He has office hours and is known to offer private tutoring. I'm sure he'd be willing to help if you needed it."

I slump into the chair, frustrated at my lack of options. He gave me a freaking C on my first paper. Who assigns an essay on the first day of class? It was a throwaway assignment, just an introductory essay that was only a couple of pages. I thought he just wanted a writing sample, not a dissertation. Heck, we've only had two classes. I know this is a mother-flippin' upper-level writing class, and it's probably normal to have papers due this early into the school year, but still! I've never gotten a C on my writing, and I'm convinced he did it to teach me a lesson. Or to get me to drop his class.

Since I need both of these classes for my major, I can either do them now, or put it off until they're offered again. I'll still have to deal with him at one point or another, and I'd rather stick it out now, so I don't have to see his smug, handsome face again.

Once I get back to my dorm, I drop my backpack and flop onto my bed, lying on my stomach as I hit FaceTime for Ella.

"El!" I cry once her face fills the screen.

"Em!" she screeches.

"N-O-P!" we say in unison as we recite our usual alphabetic greeting.

"I still think it's dumb that our parents named us all E names," she grumbles.

"You're extra surly today. What's up?"

"Nothing, Dad's just on my case to look at colleges. You know, the same old shit. How'd your first week of classes go?"

"Ugh." I look away from the camera as I gather my thoughts.

Her face moves closer to the screen. "Wait, I was just making small talk because school is so easy for you. Is it not easy? What's happening? See, this is why I don't want to go to college. If you're having a hard time, it'll be impossible for me. My grades suck."

"This is the first class in my major, and I was really excited about it, but the professor is kind of an A-hole."

"Oh my God, you have a crush on him. Is he hot?"

I give her my sternest look. "This is serious, Ella. I don't have conflicts with teachers, they usually love me."

"Oh no, poor little bookworm can't charm her professor." I stick out my tongue. "How's the new major going?"

"Shh, keep your voice down. Are you in your room? Is Dad home?"

She scoffs "He's not here. He's never here, but he sure likes to make sure I'm here all the time. Don't worry, no one can hear you, I have earbuds in." She tilts her head to the side to show me, and I nod in acknowledgement, breathing a sigh of relief.

I don't want to keep this from my stepdad, but I know he'd have opinions about my change in major to theatre. He'd probably encourage me to go major in social work since it'd be the cheaper route. I know he's just looking out for me, but I have bigger plans.

My sister Lizzy is nonverbal and on the spectrum. She's recently shown an interest in drama, and my brother Ethan did a lot of research on drama therapy for ASD individuals. There's a lot of evidence showing it can help with emotional regulation, and since it's an area of the spectrum Lizzy struggles with, I wanted to see if it was something that could help her. It's the reason why I changed my major to theatre, despite my stepdad's grumblings.

At one point I thought about becoming a teacher like my mom, and I've always loved literature. My stepdad is vocal about all of his daughters going to college since he never did. He got Ethan's mom pregnant in high school and barely finished himself, so he wanted more for his offspring. Ethan went to culinary school, so I'm the first of the kids to attend college. The plan is to get my master's in special education so I can help kids like Lizzy. The massive amounts of student loan debt I rack up will be worth it.

"I'll tell him eventually, it's just… you know how he is."

"Oh, I *know* how he is. Heaven forbid his children make the same mistakes he did. We *have* to go to college. We can't have sex in high school. Well, hate to break it to you, Pops, but it's too late on the second one and Lord knows there isn't a college that will accept my grades."

"Wait. You and Chad?"

She smiles and nods.

"When?"

"Last week in his car. You know the abandoned community pool in the neighborhood?"

"Yeah?"

"Well, the parking lot is secluded, and since the pool and rec center have been closed for years, there's no cameras or security. We hopped into the back seat and… you know. It was cool, but it was over in like ten seconds. I heard it gets better the more you do it, so we're gonna try again as soon as the warden lets me out."

Great. My seventeen-year-old sister has already done the deed, and I lose my cool if a guy even touches me.

"Earth to Emma!" my sister calls, breaking my train of thought.

"Sorry, I was just thinking about some ideas for my next paper for Shakespeare."

"You're such a bad liar. So, have you seen Daddy Batman again?"

"Oh my gosh, do not call him that." I shake my head in exasperation.

"When are you two going to bang?"

"I don't think it's gonna happen. I haven't seen him in weeks, and now that classes have started, I'll be in the city even less. Plus, he's so hard to read."

"It could be the mask?"

"It's more than that. Our first visit, he started off cold, but he really got into it by the end, but then he was back to being standoffish. And in our last session there was no smexy stuff at all."

"Maybe he's just really in character?"

"I don't think so. When I begged him to help me after that first scene, I could tell he had a heart, that he wanted to help me."

"How could you tell that? Wasn't he wearing a mask?"

"It was in his shoulders. The way his chest expanded when he'd sigh. I probably sound dumb, but I could feel the way he looked at me. He helped me through this major breakthrough, and I could tell he was moved by me and wanted more."

Ella blinks at me for several seconds, and my nerves get the better of me. "Or maybe all doms are like this. Maybe it's just a professional relationship and I'm seeing what I want to see. Projecting my own desires onto him because I long for more of a connection with the only person that's been able to touch me like that."

"Maybe," she says unconvincingly.

After we hang up, I get to work on my essay, but my thoughts keep drifting back to Daddy Dom. Even though we've only had two sessions, he's helped me more than anyone else. I wonder what advice he would give me for dealing with Professor A-hole?

Despite our conflict in class, I'm determined to prove that I can rise to his challenge. He doesn't think I'm ready to take his course? Well, I'll show him.

CHAPTER 6
JOHN

I can't believe she's my fucking student. What are the odds? I knew she was young, I just didn't know she was in college. *My* college. Everything in me is screaming to walk away.

I've tried to ignore the need to touch her. To light up her skin with my belt. I've been a cold, moody bastard to her. Hell, I'd even given her first paper a lower grade than she deserved to try to get her to drop my class.

But images of that fucker knocking her down on the first day still flood my brain, and I give in to the need to check on her.

I'm not her dom, and she cannot be my sub. I don't date students. There are definitely rules against this. Aren't there? There must be, but fuck if I know—the thought of getting involved with a student has never crossed my mind. Until now.

If I continue engaging with her as Daddy Dom, it will blur the lines my rules are so carefully built upon.

ME

Bring her to my room tonight. Eight o'clock.

ALYX

Who? You're gonna have to be more specific.

Emma

But she hasn't had any more nightmares. Or she hasn't told me about them, if she has. No more freakouts, she hasn't balked from someone's touch, and I haven't heard her talk about another man. Were there other criteria you forgot to tell me?

She did react to a man's touch. Someone knocked her down on the first day of class, and I helped her up. She doesn't know it was me, though.

Shit, is she okay?

I think so, but I'd like to check in with her. Bring her to my room tonight.

What if she doesn't want to come?

She will.

When there's a knock on my door at exactly eight, I breathe a sigh of relief. Why does this girl have me so twisted up in knots? And how the fuck can I release them? It's been three weeks since the massage, and I thought I'd be able to walk away. Clearly, I'm a bigger masochist than I thought.

"Bring her back when you're done, I know the drill." Alyx closes the door behind him as Emma stares after him in confusion.

Clearing my throat, I redirect her focus. "I want to reiterate that I have your consent."

"Yes, sir."

"That you're okay with this arrangement, where you don't know who I am under here, but I know who you are."

She blinks in confusion. "Has that not been the case this whole time?"

Now that I know who she is, it's important to me that I reconfirm her consent, if anything for my own selfish peace of mind. "And you're comfortable with that arrangement? I have your consent to proceed?"

"Yes, I'm okay with it, and you have my consent."

"If this is going to work, you have to abide by my rules."

"Aren't rules supposed to be negotiable in a BDSM dynamic?"

She's clearly done her research, and it turns me on more than it should.

"When it comes to a dom/sub dynamic, everything is negotiable, but when you're in my room, if we're going to do this, I have certain rules that are non-negotiable."

"Okaaay."

"Our dynamic only exists within the confines of these four walls. You cannot ask me about my life outside of the club. Is that clear?"

She nods and then speaks as if she already knows I'm about to correct her. "I understand."

"There will be no feelings involved. You may experience intense emotions while in a scene and feel the need to confess them. You need to remember that the things we do in this room are designed to test your limits, emotionally and physically. It'll make you feel things. I've held subs while they cried. I've watched them scream and curse and break down. This type of power exchange isn't for the weak."

Her shoulders visibly tense. "Got it."

"You have a problem, I'm helping to solve that problem. That's all there can be between us."

"No catching feelings."

"I'll reach out to you when I feel another session is necessary."

"Yes, sir," she says with bite, not her usual sweet submissive tone.

"And I know it's a double standard, but you have to be completely honest with me. I need a clear understanding of your emotional state, your health, and any concerns you may have so I can ensure your safety and trust."

"Yes—"

"Strip," I growl, interrupting her before she can finish the "sir."

She hesitates briefly before complying, and my cock swells with pride at her willingness to obey. When she takes everything off except her panties, I take a step toward her, backing her up against the door. "I said strip. I want you bare before me, pet."

"But last time I left my panties on. I just figured..." she trails off, her earlier fight gone as she removes her panties. "Sorry, sir."

"Is that a rule you want to negotiate?"

She thinks for a second. "No, sir."

"Go stand in front of the cross," I command, and she quickly complies. I follow the sway of her ass and clock the days old dark bruise on her left cheek. I blow out a deliberate breath for show and growl. I know how she got the bruise, but I need to pretend like I don't if I'm going to sell this. I stomp toward her, stopping inches from her body.

"Who did this to you, pet?" I gently trace the edges of the bruise, and she winces.

"It's nothing." She shrugs.

"Don't lie to me. Who gave you this bruise?" I grip the flesh above her cheek and pull her against me.

"It was a random guy. I wasn't looking where I was going, and I fell when I opened the door while he was exiting."

Why is she making excuses for that frat fuck? I saw the whole thing, watched her make herself small the entire walk to the classroom, and saw that fucker knock her over as she tried to get out of the way. She was looking where she was going; she was hypervigilant.

Overcome with the desire to teach her a lesson and dole out my punishment, I grip her by the neck, turning her face toward mine. "I prefer you wear my bruises, pet. Would you like that?"

"I... Uh, that sounds..." I wait for her to form words, but she continues to stammer. When I see her thighs clench together, I relax, knowing she's exactly where I want her.

"Use your safe word if you don't want that." I run my free hand down her right ass cheek. Cocking it back, I hover near her skin, ready to strike, or pull away.

"Please, sir," she begs in that breathy fucking whisper, and I fight the urge to rub my cock against that bruise. I release my hand, letting the sting of the slap reverberate against her cheek, before rubbing soothing circles around the spot.

"What else happened?" I ask as close to her ear as the mask will let me get, frustrated it won't allow me closer, but thankful for its existence, especially now that she might recognize my voice.

"I was excited about this class, but my super moody jerk of a professor couldn't decide what personality he wanted to try on. First, he helped me up after the bro knocked me down, then picked on me for the rest of class. He's such an A-hole."

Biting my lip to stifle my chuckle, I slap her ass cheek again.

"Oh! What was that for?"

"To teach you a lesson. Don't let a man pick on you or push you down. Think of it like another rule I expect you to follow, except this applies in all areas of your life."

"But he's my teacher. I can't just tell him to eff off if he's mean to me. What am I supposed to do?"

"Are you going to follow my rules?"

"Yes, sir. But what should I do about Professor A-hole?"

"Want me to teach him a lesson for you?"

"Could you really do that?" She seems to consider my offer before breaking into a fit of laughter. "He looks like he works out, but I think you could take him. Plus, you have this whole intimidating Dom thing going for you."

"Am I a joke to you?" I smack her cheek harder as she lets out a squeak of surprise.

"No, sir."

"Shut your mouth and spread your legs."

"What are you going to—"

Smack.

The sound of my hand slapping her wet cunt reverberates through my entire body as she gasps and grabs the cross to steady herself.

"It's taking every ounce of restraint I have not to crawl between your legs and lap at your perfect virgin cunt. I want to bury myself so deep in you that you soak the hair on my face. I want to be covered in so much of your arousal that my tongue alone couldn't clean it."

Her breathing picks up, and I stare at her tits as they heave and jiggle with each stuttered breath and she slides her legs apart further.

I want to drop to my knees, remove my mask, and devour her, but I can't. Instead, I cup her ass in my hands, squeezing each cheek firmly before smacking them both in unison.

She yelps, and I slide a hand between her legs and cup her pussy. "When you're in my room, this is mine. Do you hear me?"

"Yes, sir."

I deliver several quick hard slaps to her pussy before sliding a finger in and stroking her G-spot. Her hands tighten their grip on the cross and I remove my finger, dragging it up her front until I connect with her clit. I start with slow circles, reading her body as I increase the pressure and speed.

"I've touched every inch of this perfect fucking body."

She nods as a small moan escapes her mouth.

"Who does this body belong to?"

"You, sir."

"Who does it come alive for?"

"Only you, sir."

I shouldn't like that answer as much as I do.

"I want you to come all over my fingers like you'd come all over my cock. Fucking fall apart for me, pet. Drench me. Show me how much you want this. How much you need my touch. Come for me." I continue working her clit with one hand and use my other to fill her cunt with as many fingers as she can take.

"Yes, sir, I need it. Oh God, I need it so much," she cries as her pussy spasms around my fingers.

I don't dare remove my mask, but I can faintly smell the scent of her arousal as my mouth waters.

Once she comes down from her orgasm, I remove my fingers and slip them under my mask and into my mouth, savoring the taste of her as a low growl emanates from my throat.

Just like an addict, I swear this is my last hit. I've got to put a stop to this. Nothing good will come of this if I continue down this path, and she is too good, too pure. She deserves everything I can't give her.

After a generous amount of after care and returning her to Alyx's room, my phone lights up with a text as I'm getting in my car.

MARY

Hey John. I'm sorry to bug you during the semester.

I chuckle to myself. She starts most texts this way.

I promise you're not bugging me.

Okay. Sam is out of town again. Can you stay over?

Mary had a rough childhood, living in poverty in an area of the world known for violence. She scares easily and doesn't like being alone. She moved in with me a few years ago, and I let her stay at my place in Columbus with Sam and their son. During the school year, however, I rent a room from a fellow professor near campus so I don't have to commute from the city. Our living arrangement works for all of us, and I'm happy to help them out.

I'll be there.

This is the reminder I needed. Mary and her family need me. There are people in my life who depend on me to not get mixed up with students. I'm working toward a goal that is bigger than just me. I'm someone's white knight, even if it's not in the romantic sense. And I need to focus on that and not the young woman permeating my thoughts and dreams.

CHAPTER 7
EMMA

Seeing my therapist was high on my priority list this summer, but then classes started and my course load increased, and it got pushed to the back burner. I feel like I'm barely keeping my head above water and it's only a few weeks into the semester.

Last year I had a roommate, and she was nice, but I was always in the library or class so our paths rarely crossed. This year, I ended up with a solo dorm room. I'm excited to have a place of respite even if it is a little isolating. I really should get out more and make some friends, but I'll have time for that later, once I figure out how to write a paper that Professor A-hole won't tear to shreds.

Opening my laptop, I sign into the patient portal and click into my Telehealth link.

"So, Emma, how is the new school year going?" my therapist Brenda asks.

"It's good. There's this professor that's been really challenging, but I'll figure him out," I answer, shifting in my seat hoping she doesn't make me spend time talking about him.

"Have you had anymore nightmares?"

"I have. They started up again over the summer. It's the same recurring one."

"I see. Is there anything you can think of that may have triggered it?" I can tell she's taking notes as she looks off screen.

"No. Not that I can think of. I just wish I knew what was causing it."

"That's understandable, wanting clarity so you can make sense of your own experience."

"And since we talked about how I was able to figure out that I'm not responsive to just any kind of touch, you wanted me to explore the context of what makes me react."

"And did you do that?"

"I may have let a masked dom tie me up and blindfold me so he could touch every part of my body. Safely, of course. There were safe words, so I was in control."

"That's…" She hesitates, and for a second, I wonder if her video has frozen. "That's not the approach I would've recommended, but you know what's best for you. I do want to make sure you're not trying to shock your system into healing to prove a point. Reenacting past trauma can be detrimental if you're not being emotionally safe."

"But I can't remember anything traumatic happening to me. And I felt incredibly safe. Like, I was anxious about how it would feel and how I would react, but I did a lot of research first to prepare myself. There was this whole process beforehand where I filled out a survey with my limits, and he read it before the scene even started. Then we established a safe word, and he jumped right into the role."

"Trauma can be implicit. Even if you don't have memories in words or pictures, your body remembers. It can be risky to push yourself so far out of your comfort zone. The fact that you were holding space for curiosity and caution is a good step toward healing. Having a safe word is important since it gives you control in a scenario where you've historically felt powerless. Did it help?"

"It got me out of my head. He knew how to build up my anticipation so all I could think about was when he would touch me and where he would touch me instead of *danger, he's touching me.*"

"Well, in this scenario, you were choosing it. You sought him out. You set the scene. You shared your limits. And you dictated the rules. As long as you're going into this fully consenting to it, I don't see a problem."

I hesitate briefly, not wanting to disappoint her with the next part. She seems so thrilled with my progress.

"Based on the look on your face, I'm guessing there's more?"

Swallowing down my nerves, I blow out a breath. "After the scene was over, he cracked his neck like the man in my nightmares, and I panicked and used my safe word. It was really disappointing. I felt like I'd come so far just to ruin it with my stupid broken body."

She sets her pen down and looks straight in the camera. "First of all, you're not broken, you're healing. And even if it didn't end the way you'd hoped, I think there are a couple of important takeaways here. You let someone touch you. You explored it with consent. And when you felt triggered, you listened to your body, and you stopped it. Your nervous system was trying to protect you, and you honored that by using your safe word. That's what it's there for. You said stop, but you were still in control."

"I was kinda hoping that one visit would be all it took. But I've seen him three times now and the nightmares are still happening."

"Healing isn't linear, Emma, and one experience with a masked man isn't a magic fix."

"There are no magic fixes," we say in unison.

"That's right. But you made some progress, and you should celebrate that."

I end the call a few minutes later and blow out a deep breath. A sense of peace washes over me and I open a blank document, determined to write an essay that Professor A-hole won't eviscerate.

CHAPTER 8
JOHN

The start of the semester—when beginnings are new, hopes are high, and possibilities are endless—is my favorite time of year. This year should be no different, but a pit of dread forms in my stomach at the thought of where this year could take me if I'm not careful.

A Christian college may seem like an odd choice for someone who also moonlights as a dom at a sex club, but my strict religious upbringing was a huge factor in my decision to work at Faith Union. It took a while to overcome the need to please my strict parents, but by then their chokehold on my life was too far-reaching. I'm fairly certain my need to top—to be in control of a sub—stems from me wanting to break free of the church's control over me. My own secret act of rebellion.

Even the fact that I teach Shakespeare is due to my parents deeming it one of the few appropriate types of literature I could read aside from the Bible.

Students file into the lecture hall, and I push everything down, determined not to give in to my desires. I have more discipline than that.

I will control myself.

We're a month into the semester at this point, and most students have developed a routine, sitting in specific spots throughout the room every class without fail.

I feel her presence before I see her. My eyes flick up, and I watch her make her way down the steps and across the second row.

She's so fucking beautiful, so perfect, drawing me in like a siren calling to a sailor. I'm enthralled by her beauty, enraptured by the sound of her voice. I find myself calling on her before anyone else, craving that sweet lilt. It's probably shitty of me to tear apart her essays, but there's a part of me that hopes it'll be the reason she'll come to my office and give me more of her attention.

A relationship between us is forbidden and wrong for more reasons than she's aware. I'm thirteen years her senior and her professor. There are rules that forbid me from acting on any of these impulses. And I can't screw over Mary's future, not when she's depending on my help.

Pulling up my notes for class, I force down my desire, taking several deep breaths to even out my racing heart. This is the same thing I do at Pulse when I put my mask on. *I am in control.*

"Today we're diving into *Henry V*. Can anyone tell me what you think the main themes of the play are?"

A student in the back raises his hand. "What makes a good leader." I nod my agreement when Emma's hand shoots up. I fight my smile as I nod at her.

"It goes deeper than that, exploring the complexities of leadership. Henry's public persona versus his private self."

"Could you expand on that a little more, Miss Black?"

"I think we should question what makes a good leader. Does he need fear or respect to be deemed good? Does he need to be ruthless in achieving victory and maintaining order? And how is that compatible with goodness, morality, and compassion? It examines how someone appears versus their true nature. The qualities that make Henry a great king are not the same qualities that would define a good person." There's a hint of a smirk on her face like she knows her words hold a deeper meaning, and fuck if it doesn't make me hard.

"It must be hard having all those responsibilities. Worrying about your country, its people, their well-being and safety in the threat of war, and then having to put aside your own desires, your own needs, for the good of your nation," she continues.

"I can't wait to read more about your findings in your next essay, Miss Black." My tone is flat, giving nothing away. While I'm no king, and certainly not leading anything other than a classroom full of half-interested students, I know what it's like to subvert my own desires for the greater good. To be part of something larger than myself. And it makes me wonder what she'd think of me if she knew who I really was.

Once class is over, I pack up my laptop as Emma approaches. Her soft floral scent washes over me, causing my cock to thicken in my pants.

"Can I speak with you, Professor Ali?"

"Office hours are Tuesdays and Thursdays from two to four, Miss Black," I reply, not making eye contact.

"It's about my last paper." She continues, not acknowledging my dismissal of her, and the fact that she's obeying Daddy Dom's rule makes me want nothing more than to bend her over my knee and spank her until she comes.

"What about it?" I continue packing up my bag.

"I'm having a hard time wrapping my head around the grade. I worked extremely hard on that paper. I've never gotten a C before, let alone two, and I want to learn from my mistakes so I can improve my writing."

I look up and hold eye contact with her, doing my best to stop my perusal at her face. When I cock an eyebrow, she crosses her arms under her perfect rack, pushing them up so her cleavage is more prominent.

"Honestly, it was lacking depth. Your thesis was compelling, but you failed to provide sufficient proof to back it up. Most of your evidence was circumstantial, and what little that was spot on was overshadowed by your lack of analysis. You spent entirely too much time on quotes that didn't prove your point while glossing over your valid evidence. It was shallow drivel at best, and something that may have gotten you praise in high school but won't cut it here."

She appears stunned, blinking several times as her mouth opens and closes. "Thank you for that." She waves her hand in a circle at me. "Even if it was a pedantic take on a decent essay," she mutters the last part, and I get a little turned on at her willingness to stand up to me, while also fighting the urge to toss her over my knee until she submits.

"What was that, Miss Black?" I taunt.

"I'll work harder to make it a decent essay." She smiles as she marches up the steps of the auditorium, my eyes tracking her perfect ass as she goes.

Once I make it back to my room later, I text Alyx, silently cursing myself for being so quick to break a rule and talk to her outside of the club. Is it technically breaking a rule if I told her that we can only see each other at the club? This isn't part of our dom/sub dynamic. It's a gray area, and I've learned how to bend my morals to navigate those over the years. I'm still in control, and while I feel my resolve slipping, I'm confident I could rein it back in when it matters.

> I need Emma's number.

ALYX
> Always so bossy.

Do you want me to continue helping your friend or not?

Don't be a dick, of course I do.

Seconds later, her contact is saved in my phone. I don't give my cell out to students, only my office number is in the syllabus, but it forwards calls to my phone when needed.

Have you been a good girl for me, pet?

I cringe knowing how creepy that must sound coming from an unknown number.

Who is this?

Who do you think?

Daddy Dom?

Know anyone else that calls you pet?

How should I save your contact?

Fishing for my name?

Maybe...

How about Batman Dom?

???

You know, because of the mask, and the voice.

I laugh. This feels natural, familiar, like I've known her for years. I get comfortable, lying back on the bed.

I'm taking your silence as permission.

I'll allow it.

Goody! To answer your first question, I have been a good girl. You'd be proud of how I stood up to my professor today.

I smile at her confidence. This is what I was hoping to instill in her.

Want to see how proud I am?

Yes

I snap a pic of my hand gripping my erection through my slacks. Once I look it over, making sure there are no identifying details, I send it to her. What the fuck am I doing?

Holy erection, Batman!

Laughter spills out of me at her ridiculousness as I somehow manage to get even harder. My laughter quickly dies when I see the picture she replies with. Instead of calling me out for breaking a rule I created, she's seeking her own pleasure from me, sending me a picture of her skirt hiked up showing off her lacy white panties and the hand she's slipped into them.

I need to be the adult here. I should stop this and follow my rules.

Fuck it.

Breaking one won't hurt, and really, it's more like bending since we can't technically see each other anyway.

I free my aching cock from my pants and give it a few hard strokes as I stare at her picture when my screen lights up with a call. Scrambling off the bed, I grab the mask with the built in modulator buried in a bag at the bottom of my closet and slip it on as I hit the answer button. "Yes, pet?"

Silence permeates the line, and I pull it away from my ear

to be sure the call connected when I hear her stuttered breathing. Holy fuck.

"That's my good girl. Touching yourself, taking what you want. I'm so fucking proud of you," I grit out as I continue fisting my cock.

"I'm your good girl. I'm being so good. Waiting for your permission."

The way she naturally submits to me is the biggest fucking turn-on. "I want you to take two fingers and slowly rub circles around your clit."

"Yes, sir."

"So fucking good for me. But only for me, pet."

"Only you." A soft whimper hits my ear.

"Now slip those fingers in your soaking cunt and use the palm of your hand to apply pressure to your clit."

"Oh, freaking A. Oh God, I'm so close, sir."

"Don't come until I command it, pet." I continue working my cock, pumping furiously as I imagine her pretty lips swallowing me down while I fist her hair.

"Yes… sir," she moans like it's hard to speak.

"Ughhnn, fuuuuck. Now. Come for me, Emma," I groan as hot ropes of cum spurt out of my dick, coating my hand and stomach.

Her answering moans are music to my ears, and I can picture her writhing around on her bed as her fingers fall still.

"You called me Emma," she pants as I reach for something to clean myself with.

I falter for a moment, trying to remember if I've used her name as Daddy Dom. I'm sure I have. "That is your name, no?" I say with confidence I don't feel.

"Yeah. I like it when you call me that. I mean, I like 'pet' too, but you hardly use my name. It feels more meaningful when you do."

What the fuck do I say to that? What did I just do? It's obvious she's getting attached, and considering I demanded

Alyx give me her number just to check on her after our run-in today, it's safe to say I'm getting entirely too comfortable with her.

This is why I have rules. I'm not supposed to get attached, but I can already feel myself slipping.

CHAPTER 9
EMMA

There's nothing more beautiful than Faith Union College in October. The air is crisp enough to wear a sweater and enjoy a pumpkin latte while I walk to class. Leaves fall from trees in vibrant shades of reds, oranges, and yellows, blanketing the green landscaping on the quad.

I'm determined not to let the A-hole get under my skin. He's been less grumpy in class the past couple of weeks, but I know better than to let my guard down around him.

It's been well over a month since I've been to the club and seen Daddy Dom in person. Getting him on the phone has proven difficult as well. He's gone to great lengths to conceal his identity, and I'm beginning to wonder why that is.

Is he ugly under the mask? Or a burn victim with scarring on his face that he's self-conscious about? That doesn't explain why he's disguising his voice, though. Maybe he's famous and he doesn't want the world to know about his secret bedroom activities? It would explain him masking his face and voice. But I can't think of any A-list celebrities with tattoos like his. Could he be an athlete? A hockey player? He certainly has the build of one.

Our text conversations have been somewhat regular,

though. He's even given me a few rules that he thinks will help me get along with my professor.

Don't take it personally. Easier said than done when everything out of Professor A-hole's mouth feels like an attack on either my character, my intelligence, or my skills.

Pick your battles. This one came after I told him I confronted the A-hole about my paper.

Set clear boundaries and stick to them. This one seems fairly simple, and since I don't plan on being around this man any more than I have to, it should be easy to implement.

When I enter the classroom, I take my usual seat in the second row. I like being close to the front in most classes, but with as much as Professor Ali walks around, there's not a seat that's safe from him.

"We've talked a lot about his plays and themes, but I'd be remiss if we didn't cover the rules and conventions that Shakespeare would adhere to when writing his works. It's widely known that he used iambic pentameter when writing in verse. And he often used verse to show higher-status characters while prose was used to show humor or lower-status. But even he would break his own rules for dramatic effect to showcase a shift in a romantic relationship between characters."

He pauses after the last sentence, and I glance up from my computer screen, my fingers hovering over the keys. There's a look on his face that I can't quite place, a mixture of disgust, anger, and hope, like he's coming to terms with a revelation. His eyes dart up to mine before I quickly drop my head, glancing over my notes.

He clears his throat and continues. "There were also rules about what style and color clothing individuals could wear based on their social standing. For example, purple was reserved for members of the royal family and those close in nobility. Another rule, or more of a status quo perhaps, was the fact that all the actors in the shows were male, including those playing female parts."

I nod my head and carefully pull my phone out of my pocket holding it close to my laptop screen to conceal it while I type out a message to Alyx.

Save me. I'm bored in class.

What do you expect me to do? I'm working a double today. You're lucky you caught me after lunch rush.

Entertain me.

Send me memes.

I'm not sending nudes.

I said MEMES!

I need a distraction from this droll speech filled with facts I learned in high school.

I'm not your puppet, Emma.

[gif of a marionette on strings dancing]

Classy

Pretty please. Anything to distract me from Professor A-hole.

With as much as you complain about the man, I'm starting to think you have a crush on him.

Do not.

Do too.

I do not.

I think one more time will really convince me.

You're infuriating.

You got it bad.

Stop it.

Got it bad. Got it bad.

For Pete's sake.

[I'm hot for teacher gif]

I cover my mouth with the back of my hand trying to hide the silent giggle that slips out at Alyx's last message.

"Care to share your thoughts with the class, Miss Black?" His booming voice startles me, causing my phone to slip out of my hand like a bar of soap, landing right at his feet.

Frickity frick frick.

He picks it up looking at the tail end of my conversation with Alyx. "What's more interesting than our discussion of *Othello* and its themes of jealousy, racism, betrayal, and reven…" His voice trails off, and my face heats, knowing what he's reading. When his thumb moves to scroll further up in the thread, I lean over and attempt to grab the phone out of his hand. He lifts it out of my reach and clasps my wrist, stopping my movements.

My eyes fixate on his hand. How is he able to touch me? Why am I not freaking out? I can't stand this man; he's the last person I want touching me. There's no way he would ever make a move on me. That must be it.

He must feel my tension and quickly releases my wrist. Leaning over my desk, he places my cell face down, covering it with his large palm. I look down at the phone, and my eyes trace the thick veins popping out of his hand and follow them up his forearm. His sleeve is rolled up to his elbow, revealing a tiny swirl of black ink on the inside of his arm. Does the uptight professor have a tattoo? Maybe there's more to him than I realized.

His voice is a low whisper. "See me after class."

———————

I remain in my seat as the classroom empties, slowly packing up my things while I watch Professor A-hole out of the corner of my eye, trying to gauge his mood. He's always so hard to read, a million microexpressions crossing his face before he quickly schools his features, shoving whatever he's feeling down deep. I wonder how he deals with all that pent-up emotion? Maybe he gets secret tattoos to torture himself?

Ever so slowly, I approach the front of the room, unconcerned with how timid I must look. This is one of those times that I'm going to pick my battles. I was caught red-handed, and there's not much I can say to defend myself. I'm just not sure how much of Alyx's teasing he read. Does he know those texts were about him?

"I'm sorry. I shouldn't have been on my phone—"

"Am I a joke to you? Do you think my class is a joke?" He leans against the table, cutting me off as I drop my gaze to the floor.

"No, sir." I cringe at my choice of words, hoping he just assumes I'm being polite.

"Sir?" There's a lift in his tone, and I fight the urge to look at him. "Look at me." His tone is firm yet pleading, and I obey his command.

"Good… That's good. That's *better*. It's rude not to look at someone speaking to you."

Was he just about to say *good girl*? Why does that make all the blood in my body rush to my face and also between my legs? Wait, did he just scold me like a child for not making eye contact? This man is infuriating. Before I can open my mouth in response, he slaps a palm on the table next to him.

"I don't know what you want from me—I mean, from this class. I don't know what you're hoping to get out of this class when you write uninspired papers and refuse to heed my feedback. And now you're texting during my lecture. I warned you that the midterm and final come from class discussion. The more you know, the more you pay attention, the more capable you are. Knowledge is power, Miss Black. Don't come crawling to my office begging to redo your paper when you decide you aren't happy with the mediocre grade *you* earned."

The nerve of this freaking man. I want to punch his stupid perfect face. A million emotions channel through me as I gather the courage to speak without saying something I'll regret.

But before I get a chance to respond, he grabs his bag off the podium and walks past me, leaving me alone in the classroom.

———————

John

Stop teasing my student while she's in class.

ALYX

Shit, man. Sorry. You should really talk to her about texting in class.

Trust me, I did.

That sounds ominous.

You put me in a difficult situation. Daddy Dom couldn't handle it so Professor Ali had to.

When are you going to tell her that they're the same person?

I don't know if I am.

I wish you would. It was fine when you agreed to help her for the night, but then she ended up in your class, and now I feel like I'm lying to her.

I can't be involved with a student. It's against the rules.

That ship has sailed.

Besides that, I can't be with her. She's too young. And I have too many obligations weighing me down.

That's cryptic AF.

You better not hurt her.

Wouldn't dream of it.

Then figure out a way to tell her or walk away before she gets too attached.

Fuck

Yeah, fuck

CHAPTER 10
JOHN

We're well into the school year, nearly approaching the Thanksgiving holidays, and I'm no closer to letting this woman go. She permeates my thoughts and dreams. I wake up hard every fucking morning, jacking myself in punishing strokes to rid my brain of all the images its conjured of her delectable body throughout the night.

It's a necessary evil if I want to control myself from touching her in class. I've had to stop meandering through the lecture hall because I'd catch whiffs of her sweet, flowery scent, and my cock would swell in response. I'm now relegated to hovering around the lectern, hiding behind my podium to conceal my errant erections.

This fucking girl.

EMMA

I hope it's okay that I'm texting you.

More than okay, pet.

Good

What's going on?

My professor. He was a jerk in class today. It always feels like he's picking on me.

It feels wrong deceiving her like this. I'm supposed to be keeping my professional and personal lives separate. Would she still talk to me if she knew who I was?

Sometimes weak men need to assert their dominance to feel powerful. He's probably intimidated by you.

It feels like he's constantly annoyed by me.

So no offense, but I know you like to dominate, how is that different?

I chuckle to myself, impressed by her perceptiveness.

For me, being dominant is about being in control. Of myself, my urges, my sub. I only feel powerful when I've harnessed your power, not weakened it.

So what kind of dom are you?

There are a few kinds that fit my kink. It's a misnomer that all dominants fall into one type. Tastes change, kinks change, depending on the person or situation. I definitely live up to my name of Daddy Dom. I like protecting and praising my sub, but I also enjoy spanking and scolding them when they get out of line. But I'm not into age play like some daddies are.

Is it weird that I don't like thinking about you with other subs?

That shouldn't make my heart flutter like it does. I clutch the phone harder in my hand, cursing myself for this reaction. She's my student. And my only sub, and she really shouldn't be the latter if I was following school rules. Clearly, I'm willing to break rules for her, even if they're ones I didn't make.

No, you just signed a fucking employment contract.

But I'm not technically dating my student, so I'm not breaking my rule, and we haven't had sex, so depending on their definition of intercourse, I haven't broken the school's rule either.

Keep telling yourself that, asshole.

I blow out a breath and start typing.

> I don't like thinking about you with other doms.

So what are the other kinds of doms you identify as?

> Well, I think you unlocked the pleasure dom in me. I don't normally engage with subs sexually, but I can't stop thinking about all the ways I want to make you come.

So that thing you did with your tongue was just for me?

> Yes, pet. Only you. There are subs that will climax in a scene with me, but it normally doesn't require my hand or mouth.

I feel... honored.

> I also am a bit of a white knight dom.

Wait, that's a thing? I haven't read about that!

> All it means is I enjoy taking care of my sub, protecting them, helping solve their problems.

I don't tell her that my white knight extends into other areas of my life. And it's the real reason we can't be together right now.

> Morning, pet.

Morning, sir.

> You know how hard that makes me.

Do I? Show me.

> Behave.

Yes, sir.

> Fuck.

> I want you to do something for me.

Anything.

> I want you to go to class without panties today.

The dots bounce on my screen for several minutes, and I curse under my breath, worried I've pushed her too far.

Why don't I show you instead?

> It's for me.

How is that for you?

> I want you to walk in that room in a skirt with no panties.

> I want you to show that asshole what he can't have.

> Tease him with that perfect pink cunt and then tell me all about his reaction after.

I dunno, this feels risky. What if I get in trouble?

You won't.

How do you know?

Trust me.

?

How is showing my A-hole teacher my privates going to accomplish anything?

Her response has blood rushing to my cock.

Are you questioning your dom?

I'm sorry.

As your dom. I need your total trust. I want your total submission. You may not understand my methods, but you will obey or you'll be punished.

Yes, sir.

I smile at how quickly she sends that response. She is the perfect submissive for me. She may question me on things, but it's often her inexperience showing. I find that once I explain the why, she complies quickly.

He can't do anything about it.

You can claim it was an accident.

You didn't know he could see up your skirt.

You were doing laundry and ran out of clean underwear.

You can flip it on him if he pushes and accuse him of being a pervert.

Why was he looking up your skirt?

> You have multiple excuses at your disposal.

Yes, sir.

> Keep your phone on you and answer me when I text you.

I will.

I'm a fucking masochist.

———————

She walks into class wearing a white sweater with a black skirt and boots that end just below her knees, taking a seat several rows up from where she normally does. I track her every movement, my heart beats rapidly in my chest.

Normally, Professor Ali would call her out for her change in seats, but I want to play this differently, watching her submit to me without knowing she's submitting to her dom.

My phone sits on the shelf of the podium, on silent, and hidden from sight. I glance down at it, swiping open my text thread with her.

> Are you in class?

I watch as she looks at her phone, quickly typing out a reply.

I am.

> Good. Spread your legs.

Fuck, I wish I could type out everything I want her to do and really guide the scene, but I refrain.

"Can anyone tell me about the key themes in *A Midsummer Night's Dream*?" For once, Emma doesn't raise her hand, so I focus on someone in the back. I was hoping she'd answer the question, making sure my focus is on her pussy while she talked, but my timid pet isn't that bold. I'll get her there.

The kid blathers on, and for once I couldn't care less about my back-and-forth with the student. When he finally finishes, I turn my focus back on Emma. "Anything to add, Miss Black?"

She shakes her head, knees slightly parted. I can't see anything, but she quickly snaps her legs shut, crossing one over the other when I focus on her.

"Surely, you must have some witty retort to add to Mr. Anderson's insights."

"Nope." Her eyes cast down.

"Pop quiz." The class groans. This was the plan once I gave her orders this morning. Get the class to focus on something so I could play with her inconspicuously. "I want you to write five hundred words exploring the idea of love's blindness in *A Midsummer Night's Dream*. Consider the effects of the love potion and the role of magic. How do external forces change the characters' perception of love? You can use all the resources at your disposal, including electronic devices. Consider it open book."

There are grumbles around the room about having to write a paper on the fly, and how it's not so much a quiz as an impromptu essay. And the thought of grading this shit later is worth it for the control I'll have over Emma. I'll just give them a participation grade and call it a day.

Pet

??

Are your legs open?

Not anymore.

Open them.

Show that asshole what he can't have.

Can't talk, writing paper.

Fuck, I didn't think this through all the way. Her desire to please her teacher is overriding her desire to please me. I look around the room, making sure no one's watching me and then text her again.

Pull your skirt up your thighs and stretch your legs out while you write.

K

Keeping my head down while lifting my eyes, I watch as she shifts nervously in her seat, awkwardly hiking up her skirt as her torso leans back in the chair, one hand still typing on her laptop. I want to praise her for following my command, but I can't.

Even though I can't see under her skirt from where I'm standing, my cock hardens at her act of submission and the fact that she's unknowingly pleasing both sides of me: The teacher who assigned her work, and the dom who gave her a command.

Several minutes pass as the clicking of keyboards fill the space. Once my urges are under control, I leave the podium, moving up the left side of the room to answer questions. When I walk back toward the front, I slide through the empty row of seats in front of her chair. She's so engrossed in writing that she doesn't see me coming.

Her brows are pinched together as she types. I'm too close to her to get a good look under her desk without bending over and making it obvious. But it's not about seeing her bare right now. It's about her submission.

Clearing my throat to get her attention, I grip the edge of

her desk, leaning on it. She snaps her legs closed and sits up taller as a shudder runs through her.

"Cold?" I asked in a hushed tone, careful not to draw too much attention.

Her mouth hangs open, but nothing comes out.

"Ten more minutes!" I warn the class, pushing off her desk, and she startles at my volume. Returning to my podium, I discreetly send her another text.

> It's killing me not being there.

> I would devour every inch of your cunt in front of him.

> Make him watch as I turn you into a needy mess for me.

Okay

Keeping my head still, I flick just my eyes back up to watch her clench her thighs together. I'm so fucking hard it's torture. Why the fuck did I think this was a good idea?

The devil on my shoulder answers for me. *Because you want what you can't have and you're punishing yourself for touching the forbidden fruit.*

I adjust the bulge tightening my slacks and glance around the room. "Time's up," I call, shifting the focus back to me. "Email me what you wrote, and you can head out."

There are a few murmurs of appreciation at my announcement of class ending early as the students file out.

Emma remains in her seat, fingers still flying furiously over her keyboard as the last student leaves.

"Class is dismissed, Miss Black."

Her head pops up, a startled expression on her face as she swivels her head finally noticing the empty classroom.

"Sorry, I guess I was really into it… uh, my work… I mean, the paper."

I should wish her a good day and leave the room. But I stand there willing my dick to behave. Watching my innocent little lamb shed her wool is the hottest fucking thing I've ever seen.

CHAPTER 11
EMMA

A week later, Professor A-hole's stupid smug face is peering up at me across the lecture hall as he tries to stump me with yet another impossible question. I swear he's doing it on purpose, and I wonder if his distaste for me is obvious to anyone else in our class. I can't wait for the day that he's no longer my teacher.

"Miss Black, do you think Hamlet's madness was genuine or a calculated performance he put on to hide his true intentions?"

"I don't think there is a definitive answer on the topic. There's merit in both arguments."

"Which camp do you find yourself in then, if you had to pick?" he asks, clearly not willing to let this go.

I grip my hands together under my desk trying to discreetly conceal my frustration at his insistence. He's always interested in my opinion on a topic, but when I write a whole paper stating my case, with quotes citing my sources, he gives me a fricking C.

"On the one hand, he tells Horatio and Marcellus that he will pretend to be mad, and later he appears to feign madness around Claudius and Polonius, while acting rationally around

Horatio. And people are suspicious of him, including Rosencrantz, Guildenstern, and Claudius, calling him crafty or thinking he's acting strange, but not crazy. Those examples argue that his madness is something in his control, that he's choosing when to appear that way depending on the person or motivation. But it's hard to refute the other times during the play when Hamlet is not in control, appearing genuinely mad. He has violent outbursts and acts impulsively, killing Polonius."

"Spoilers!" a guy jokingly shouts in the back of the class as people break out into laughter. Professor A-hole shoots them a withering look and shifts his focus back to me, walking out from behind his podium as he crosses his arms and nods for me to proceed.

I continue, desperate to prove my point so he can call on anyone else and I can shrink from his spotlight. "He treats Ophelia horribly, and she seriously thinks he's mad at times."

Kind of like your constant treatment of me, Professor.

"Also, Horatio voices concerns about the fact that Hamlet is seeing his dead father's ghost and how that could be driving him to madness. In fact, even before he finds out about his father's death, Hamlet is suicidal and has thoughts that hint at some mental health issues, which one could argue he isn't faking. So, it's really hard to say whether his madness was real or fake when sometimes it appears he can control it and other times it appears to be controlling him."

There's a smug look on his handsome face as he sits on the edge of the table in the front of the room and leans back on his arms. "But if you had to pick?"

"Then I guess I would say that he is truly emotionally unstable." I cross my arms in satisfaction, secretly hoping that he will pick up on my subtext.

"Okay, Einstein," a voice calls out, and a snicker breaks out around me.

"That's enough," Professor Ali yells loudly, his tone unforgiving, as the class falls eerily silent.

I drop my head, my chin pressing against my chest as I feel my cheeks heat in embarrassment.

"Chill, bro, it was just a joke," the guy counters.

"I'm not your bro, and I don't tolerate bullying in my classroom. You're dismissed."

"Whatever, I'm outta here," he calls out.

I feel everyone staring as the bully noisily leaves the room. Slinking down in my chair, I try to make myself as small as possible, just wanting to move on from this awkward encounter. This isn't the first time I've been called Einstein. I've heard it all. Know-it-all. Suck-up. Teacher's pet. Miss Smarty Pants. Frankly, the insults aren't even creative at this point. But I get Einstein the most, and it's my least favorite, which is why I made it my safe word at Pulse that night.

A throat clearing from someone next to me pulls me out of my thoughts, and I look up to see Professor A-hole leaning over a chair in the row directly in front of me.

"You okay?" His voice is low, and the concern etched on his face reminds me of the day we met when he helped me up in the hall.

Giving him a quick nod, I focus my attention on my computer screen, trying to end this uncomfortable disruption. His attention is overwhelming, and I'm confused by his abrupt shift in demeanor. This man has picked on me in every class I've attended so far, but someone teases me and he tosses them out of class? I guess *he's* the only one who can tease me. That's got to be it. The thought of him doing that for any other reason doesn't make sense. This man doesn't like me. And I'm not a fan of his either.

John

When class ends, Emma packs her bag to make a quick escape. I don't know what I'm doing, but I can't seem to help myself around this girl.

"Miss Black, can you stick around for a few minutes so I can talk to you about—" I pause. What the fuck do I need to talk to her about?

She looks at me, her big doe eyes blinking, eyelashes fluttering as she waits for me to continue. "About what, Professor?"

Think, man. I glance around quickly, noticing we are attracting the attention of several other students. "About your last paper… and what I suspect may be the assistance of AI used in writing it."

Her nostrils flare as she stares me down. "I did not use AI to write my last paper, or any of my papers, *Professor*," she spits the last word through clenched teeth.

Fuck, did I have to accuse her of cheating just to get a minute alone with her? What the fuck am I doing? "Have a seat." I gesture to the front row of the lecture hall.

She reluctantly sinks into the chair as I wait for the rest of the students to file out of the room. Her head swivels around watching everyone leave. Once we're alone, she turns to me, ire radiating off her.

"I have not and will never use AI to help me write. I prefer to think for myself and come to my own conclusions, not have a robot do that for me. And the fact that you would ever think that one of my essays is anything other than my own words is insulting and infuriating," she says with a quiet intensity that has blood coursing south in my body.

"I know you didn't, I just wanted to talk to you alone about what that asshole said in class today, and it was the first thing that came out of my mouth."

She stares at me, mouth agape as her eyes narrow. "Some prick calls me a name, and your first thought is to publicly accuse me of cheating so you can check on me? And how is what you just did any different than what that jerk said to me? He called me a stupid name that I've been labeled my whole life, and you just questioned my integrity in front of my classmates. You're both bullies as far as I'm concerned. And why do you even care?"

Shit. I have royally fucked this up.

"I'm sorry, I should've considered my words more carefully and not accused you of something I know you didn't do. I just know you hate being called Einstein."

"How would you know that?" she asks suspiciously.

FUCK.

"You just said you've been called that your whole life."

"Yeah, but I just told you that. You didn't know that when you kicked him out of class."

A bead of sweat trickles down my spine under my suit jacket as I wrack my brain for a way to get out of this.

"I could tell by the look on your face. When he said it." I pause, unsure of how much to share. When her doe eyes lock with mine, I continue. "You wrinkled your nose and flinched when he said it. I could tell it bothered you." I place my arms on the desk in front of her and lean toward her.

"Why do you care what bothers me?" Her soft floral scent fills my nostrils, making it hard to concentrate. My dick is having a Pavlovian response to the smell and decides this is the time he wants to stand at attention. Apparently, that's how much this woman has fucked with my psyche.

I stare at her beautiful face for several moments, taking in all her delicate features, when she arches an eyebrow at me, waiting for my response. "I care about all of my students." My words hold a deeper meaning that I pray she doesn't read into.

"You have a weird way of showing it," she mumbles. "Cruel to be kind."

"Hamlet." I fight the urge to touch her, to tilt her chin forcing her to look at me. "I think you have a lot of potential.

As a student. If I'm hard on you, it's because I see greatness in you."

I should leave it at that, walk away.

She looks up at me, her face filled with a mix of emotions: wonder, hope, confusion. She schools her features, settling into a look of determination. "I am made of sterner stuff. I've been called worse, endured harder trials, only to come out of the other side stronger. I can handle myself, and I don't need you to intercede on my behalf. Nor do I need your false public accusations. I have plans for my education, for my life, and I don't need you pushing my face into the mud every time I've climbed my way out of the pit just because you think I could handle more."

Oh, but you do, pet. You just don't realize that the devil on my shoulder pushing you is Daddy Dom.

CHAPTER 12
EMMA

My sophomore year definitely isn't as easy as my freshman year was, and with each passing day, I question my decisions. As the end of the semester approaches, I can't wait for the break from classes. And from Professor A-hole.

Daddy Dom's rules have come in handy and have made dealing with Professor A tolerable.

Nothing worth doing is easy.

I repeat the mantra in my head.

This will all be worth it. I'll be able to do so much good in the world. I'll be able to help people like Lizzy.

I've somehow managed to earn an A in my Shakespeare class, and as long as he doesn't eviscerate my final paper, I should be able to maintain my four-point-zero GPA. Grades have always been important to me, but lately they haven't felt like the mark of success they once did.

Now if only I could solve my other problem.

I haven't seen Daddy Dom in person since the first week of classes, but now that I'll be in the city for winter break, I'm dying to visit the club.

He's been so hot and cold, and it's infuriating. I think he

likes me. He'll call or text me so I know I mean *something* to him, but when I bring up seeing him again or going to the club, he either shuts it down or ignores it.

One minute he's opening up to me through text, then he's ghosting me for weeks. Every time I feel like I've had a breakthrough with him, he goes silent. I wish he'd make up his mind about what he wants. I'd love to enforce some rules of my own, but I'm afraid it would push him away even more, and I'm desperate for every little morsel he gives me.

And I wish I could see him in person again. He hasn't been clear about why we can't see each other right now, but I want to believe it's that he's busy and he wants me to concentrate on school. Our texts and phone calls haven't been enough to satisfy the overwhelming need coursing through me anytime I think about him. I need his hands on me, his mouth on my skin. No one else has ever brought this out in me, and I think I'm finally ready to take the next step.

The December air assaults my senses as I leave my parents' house and head to my car, loaded up with my bags. I'd planned to spend winter break at home, but there's a lot of tension there, and after a day it was stressing me out. That's how I end up at Alyx's.

The entrance and hallway leading up to his apartment are cramped, and we awkwardly maneuver all my luggage to his door.

"Thanks for letting me crash here for a couple weeks."

"Your eighteen suitcases would say otherwise," he groans as he lugs two more bags in from the hallway.

"It's not that many." I watch him struggle with the last three bags, barely getting through the door before tripping over a rug and nearly falling over.

"Holy shit. What do you have in these? Bricks?"

"Just a few books."

"That feels like a whole freaking library."

"So all those muscles are just for show?"

"Sis, stop playin'." He flexes a bicep with a cocky grin, and I roll my eyes.

"I'm a mood reader. I have to bring a bunch, because I never know what I'll feel like reading."

He shakes his head, using his foot to push the bags away from where they were blocking the door. "Remind me to buy you a Kindle."

"I've got one! But sometimes I just like to hold a book, ya know? To feel the weight of it in my hands. The satisfaction of turning the pages and seeing your progress. To run my nose up the center and take a big ole sniff."

"I don't wanna hear about you shoving your face in cracks to sniff things."

My head falls back against the couch in laughter as he plops down beside me, pulling my leg into his lap as he rubs the heel of my foot with his thumbs.

"Things are weird at home," I admit, wanting to break the silence.

"What's going on there? Oh wait, I think I know."

"What do you know?"

"You're going to need to talk to Ethan about that. Speaking of, you might need to tell him you're staying here. I don't need him accusing me of sleeping with you again."

I laugh, thinking back to earlier in the semester when I came to his apartment to escape classes one day and walked in on my stepbrother humping his girlfriend in the living room. I saw so many things I can never unsee. "Why do I need to tell him? It's not like he's ever here."

"Actually, he was here after Thanksgiving for a few weeks. It's the longest he's spent the night here since meeting Bridget."

"Is everything okay with them? I really like her," I ask worriedly.

"I think so? He said Bridget needed some space, but I think they worked out their issues because he came back a week ago and packed a big bag of shit. He's also got that dopey grin at work again."

"I wonder what happened." I pull out my phone and Face-Time my sister.

"El!" I cry when her face fills the screen.

"Em!" she echoes.

I turn the phone, pointing it at Alyx as she continues. "N-O-P. Ugh, E. Nope, not the stupid face I wanted to see."

"Good to see you too, princess," Alyx snaps.

"Why are you with the playboy? I know things are weird over here, but you don't have to stay there. Come back here," she whines.

"Cuz you're so much more pleasant to be around than me." Alyx rolls his eyes.

"Don't you have a kitchen to burn down?"

"It was one fucking pan that caught fire, not the whole kitchen," he claps back.

"Oh my God, I was joking, but this is even better. You're a walking disaster."

"Says the princess in her tower. So high and mighty on your high horse," he taunts.

"So this is fun," I say awkwardly, caught in the middle of their bickering.

"Em, come back home. Lizzy and I miss you. So do the other two."

"Jeez, learn your other sister's names, princess. Even I know them," Alyx quips.

"I know their names!"

"Okay, you two." I shoot each of them a look. "Ella, I can't stay there right now. The energy is off."

"Tell me about it. Lizzy's having more meltdowns than normal, and Dad is super grumpy, which means I'm on lockdown. Shit went *down* at Thanksgiving."

I'm filled with guilt at the thought of not being there for

Lizzy, but my mom is an excellent caretaker. "What happened? You never told me the one day I was there."

"Ethan brought his girlfriend over, and everything was fine. I was in the basement, and then I heard shouting. Lizzy started freaking out, and when I went to find Ethan, he was yelling at Dad on the porch."

"Well now I'm glad I skipped it to work on my paper. What were they yelling about?"

"Hell if I knew, no one would say anything. Wait, man-child lives with him, I bet he knows something, point me back at him." I tilt the phone toward Alyx.

"Nope, I'm staying out of this. Talk to your brother if you want details. It's not my story to tell." He releases my foot as he heads to his room.

"Useless," she mutters as I prop the phone on my knees so I can talk to her. "So why are you really at Alyx's? Wanted to be closer to Dommy Batman?"

I laugh at her ridiculousness. "Maybe. But I didn't really have anywhere else to go since the dorms are closed for break."

"Are you going to see him again?"

"I hope so. Oh, I meant to ask you, how are things with Chad?"

"I think man-child ratted me out because Ethan mysteriously showed up last month when Chad and I were alone at the house. We were finally going to do it again, and Ethan cockblocked me."

I laugh and then she quickly moves on, catching me up on her senior year of high school and plans for the future. "Don't tell Dad, but I haven't applied anywhere, and I'm not going to."

"Your secret's safe with me," I assure her. "Besides, I'm starting to second-guess my decision."

"Now I know I made the right choice. Have you thought about transferring schools?"

"Not really."

"I always wondered why you picked a private Christian school. It's not like we grew up in church."

"Faith Union does have a good reputation, and the theatre department is great. I think I just wanted to stay closer to home. But I'll probably apply for a graduate program at a state school. I'll either do a master's in special education or social work."

"Are all the guys there horny and repressed? Maybe I should come out for a visit."

I can't help but laugh at her teasing. When we hang up an hour later, I feel refreshed, thankful to connect with one of my favorite people, and equally bummed that I bailed on her to stay in the city.

———————

Later that night, I'm curled up in bed doom scrolling when I get a text.

> Have you been a good girl today?
>
> Staying hydrated?

>> Yes, sir.

> Where are you right now?

>> Alyx's. The dorms are closed, and there's too much drama at my house.

> What's going on?

>> I'm not really sure, I can't get a straight answer out of anyone. Tension is high, so I came over here.

> Just wanted to make sure you were safe.

I am. I wish I could see you.

The dots bounce for several minutes, and my insecurities grow as my impatience wanes.

Me too.

I wonder what he must've typed and deleted only to send that. Even though I'm desperate to keep him talking, clinging to every small scrap of himself that he shares, I can't bring myself to ask for what I really want.

Are you at home?

Yeah. I have some friends staying over for the holidays. What are your plans?

I'll probably go back home at some point. I do want to see my mom and sisters.

What about your dad?

Now it's my turn to pause as I ponder what to share.

My dad passed away when I was younger, but I'm excited to see my stepdad.

I'm sorry, pet. I didn't know.

It's okay. He was pretty awful. My mom doesn't talk about him much, but I know he was abusive towards her. I don't really remember much about him.

Did he ever hurt you?

I don't think so. Or I don't remember it if he did. I was really young when my mom left him.

Is he the man in your dreams?

I thought you said you weren't a therapist.

I'm not, but it would make sense.

That's my therapist's theory as well.

I wish I was there so I could hold you in my arms while you sleep, keep you safe from your nightmares.

His text is surprisingly honest, and I'm shocked by his candor. He's not normally one to share how he feels, especially since he made not sharing feelings a rule.

Breaking rules, sir? I want you here too.

Can we meet at the club?

The dots bounce for several minutes and then disappear, and I'm left feeling empty and alone. Why did I push him like that? He's the only person I've made a connection with this year, and I don't want to lose that. Sure, I have Ella and Alyx, but I spend so much of my time studying or reading—or trying to make sure I pass Professor A-hole's stupid class— that I've pretty much given up on trying to make new friends. But it's almost a new year and a new semester. Who knows what it will bring?

CHAPTER 13
EMMA

I swallow my nerves as I walk into my Shakespearean acting class in January. When I spot Professor A-hole already in the front of the room, I quickly drop my gaze to avoid making eye contact with him and I find a seat near the back. This classroom is much smaller than the lecture hall we were in last semester. Normally, I'd choose a seat closer to the front, but I'm determined to fly under his radar.

Setting my bag in the seat, I pull out my notebooks and pens.

"Is that seat taken?" a voice asks. When I look over, a guy is gesturing to the desk beside me.

"There are several seats open up front," booms Professor A-hole, his loud voice startling me.

I look between my professor and the guy just trying to find a place to sit.

"Are you saving it for someone?" the guy asks.

"It's not taken." I finally manage, as I grab my bag.

"Can I squeeze by you?"

I step back to let him pass, but when his hand settles on my shoulder, I flinch. The touch feels foreign, and I cover it by dropping quickly into my chair.

"If we're done playing musical chairs, Miss Black, can we begin?"

What the heck is his problem?

I nod quickly and spend the next few minutes hyper-fixated on a syllabus that someone hands me so I can avoid Professor A-hole's scrutiny.

"Sorry about that. I'm Jeremy." He has a boyish smile on his face.

"Emma. And it's okay. Professor Ali's not my biggest fan." I roll my eyes.

He chuckles softly. "I can see that."

The rest of class is uneventful, and I'm almost disappointed that Professor A-hole has given me the cold shoulder. Normally by now he'd have called on me several times. What is wrong with me? Why am I desperate for this man's attention?

"Your first assignment is a soliloquy. I can't wait to see what you come up with." Professor A-hole folds his arms over his chest before focusing his attention on me. "Class dismissed."

I quickly pack my things and pull on my hat, scarf, and gloves.

When I walk outside the theatre building, all bundled up from the bitter cold, I shove my hands in my pockets hoping to warm them. "It's so freaking cold," I mutter to myself through clenched teeth.

"Now is the winter of our discontent," a deep voice intones from behind me, startling me. When I turn, Professor A-hole is staring at me.

"Professor," I say, quickly turning away.

"What monologue are you thinking of performing?" he asks with a tone that almost sounds like interest.

"I don't know yet."

"The world is your oyster, Miss Black. I know you'll make

the right choice." He walks past me toward the English building.

Frozen in place, I watch him walk away, my gaze lingering over his broad shoulders, before dropping to his perfectly round butt. Ugh, what is it about this infuriating man? It's not like he'd ever show any interest in me like that.

I watch as he pulls his phone out of his pocket, taps on it quickly, then puts it against his ear, when my pocket vibrates.

Pulling off my glove with my teeth, I fish out my phone. There's a text from Daddy Dom.

BATMAN DOM

How'd your first day of classes go?

I smile to myself, happy to shift my focus to a man that actually seems to want my attention.

It was good. Professor A-hole left me alone for the most part.

I can't wait for this class to be done so I never have to deal with him again.

When I look up, Professor A-hole is gone so I decide to go to the caf to grab dinner, but I stop when my phone buzzes again.

New rule. As long as we're engaging in this dynamic, you're loyal to me. No other men. You only play with me.

I stare down at the text for several seconds, thrilled by his need to claim me and confused by it. He created the rules—no feelings, just solving my problems. This feels like more. Like monogamy.

Where is this coming from?

Do I have your total submission on this?

A cloud of water vapor escapes my mouth when I huff out my frustration. This hot-and-cold is tiresome, and yet I crave his approval. Yearn for him in a way I never have before.

Yes, sir.

"What monologue are you going to do?" a voice asks from behind me.

I startle. "Mother of pearl!" I fumble with my phone as I clutch my scarf.

"Sorry, didn't mean to scare you." He comes up next to me, a boyish smile on his face. He's got a beanie on, his wavy blond hair poking out around it, making it look like a halo.

"Jeremy, right?"

He beams as he looks down at me, his blue eyes twinkling. "You headed to the caf?"

I nod, breaking eye contact, suddenly nervous from his attention.

"Mind if I join you?"

"Sure." We make our way down one of the few sidewalks that's been shoveled and salted. Patches of ice appear every so often, and I step carefully to keep my footing. Each time we approach a slick spot, Jeremy shoots an arm out to offer me assistance, but I ignore it, not ready to share my touching hangup with a stranger.

"So… monologue? Any thoughts on what you're picking?"

I mull it over before answering. "I'll probably just do one from *Romeo and Juliet.*"

"*O Romeo, Romeo! Wherefore art thou, Romeo?*" His voice is way too high as he mimes dramatically looking for someone.

"That was terrible. You definitely shouldn't do that one," I tease.

"So, the balcony scene, then?"

"Actually, I was going to do one of her last ones, right before she takes the drugs. It's a powerful scene where she's wrestling with her decision. Plus, I did it in an English class in high school and already have it memorized. What about you?"

He holds out an arm, and I interrupt him before he starts. "Please don't tell me you're going to do the *Hamlet* speech."

"Why not?" There's a hint of disappointment in his voice, and I worry I've offended him.

"I'm sure you're great at it, but every guy in our class is gonna do that one, and then we'll be sitting through like ten dudes talking to skulls."

He barks out a laugh. "You're probably right. What do you suggest then?"

"Ooh, there's a good one in *Richard III*. It's in Act One, I think? It starts, '*Was ever women in this humor wooed*,'" and it's Richard talking about how he's just wooed Anne after killing her father. It's deliciously dark and evil, and it would be really fun to play."

"That sounds good, I'll have to check it out."

A throat clears behind me, and I turn my head, not paying attention to where I'm going. "You totally sh—" I start, but the words die on my tongue when I slip on a patch of ice and my arms flail out, spinning in circles as I try to keep from falling. It feels like everything happens in slow motion. My legs fly out and I fall backwards as I scramble to grab something to keep myself upright.

I end up yanking the bottom of Jeremy's coat, pulling him down with me as I go. His body twists and his legs go right, while he goes left and when we land, we're in the shape of a T with his chest draped over my stomach.

Hysterical laughter bubbles out of me and I can't stop it, no matter how hard I try as I squeeze my eyes shut. Jeremy chuckles against me too as we lose it on the sidewalk.

I hear a growl, and my eyes fly open. I'm met with a pair of murderous brown eyes. Professor Ali is standing over us, his penetrating gaze locked on mine as his fists clench at his sides.

What the heck is his problem?

He's probably just mad that we're blocking his path, preventing him from getting to whatever boring, grumpy professors do in their off hours.

When he extends his hand, I look at it in confusion, blinking several times. I feel Jeremy roll off my stomach, but I continue staring at Professor A-hole.

"I'm not sure why I keep finding you like this, but here." He thrusts his hand closer.

The minute I slip my gloved hand into his, something warm fills me from the inside out. He pulls me up, but just as I'm righted, he takes a step forward, slipping on the same patch of ice that caused our demise and his hands grab my waist for balance before he pitches backward, pulling me on top of him.

It's oddly silent when I look down at him from where I've landed on his chest. I slide off to his left, when something hard presses against my center. My eyes shoot to his in surprise.

Oh my God, does Professor A-hole have a boner?

"My phone," he says through gritted teeth. I breathe a sigh of relief as I flop onto my back on the sidewalk next to him.

"Shit, Emma, are you okay?" Jeremy hovers over me.

I can only nod my head as my mind races trying to dissect the intensity of my encounter with Professor A-hole.

The anger on his face when he first approached.

The way it felt when he helped me up.

The look on his face when I landed in his arms.

I might have more than just a crush on my professor. And it's starting to feel like I'm cheating on Daddy Dom. But that's crazy, we're not even together.

Are we?

Taking Jeremy's hand, I carefully stand and leave the scene

as quickly as I can, not looking back out of fear that if I did, I wouldn't be able to walk away from that infuriating man.

CHAPTER 14
EMMA

Wrapping my jacket tighter around my body, I silently curse myself for not bringing my hat and gloves as the cold March air whips my hair into my face. I squint to keep the chill out of my eyes as I cross the campus, headed for my dorm. There's no such thing as spring in Ohio. The weather plays a constant game of ping-pong between arctic tundra and sweltering humidity, and you never know which one you're getting on any given day, or if you're going to get multiple seasons in a day. While it isn't currently snowing, it feels like it could at any minute, and piles of long-plowed snow line the walkways on campus, making gloomy, crunchy gray hills of frosty misery.

When I reach my dorm room, I hear my text notification chime and pull my phone out of my pocket.

BATMAN DOM

Did you make it back to your dorm?

I swear he has my walk timed, knowing exactly how long it takes me to get from class to my room.

Yes, sir.

Fuck, pet. You know what that does to me, and I'm not in a place where I can indulge you.

Sorry

I set my phone down and flop onto my bed when I hear it chime again.

That doesn't mean I can't text you, though.

Sounds like someone misses me.

I do.

Me too.

What are your plans for your spring break?

Not sure yet. I want to see my sister Lizzy. I don't get to see her as much during the school year.

So you're going home?

Probably not. She's attending a drama camp for autistic kids so she won't even be home. I want to volunteer at it next year because it's the kind of stuff I want to do after I graduate.

You'll be great at that. You have such a kind heart, it sounds right up your alley.

And it's important to give back. I volunteer whenever I can.

You do?

Yup. Usually it's through my work. I've served a lot of soup.

And what do you do for work again?

Nice try.

Seriously, though. This camp is great, and they do important work.

What do you love about it?

I love the way they treat these kids. How patient they are, never treating them like a burden. I see that so much, especially with Lizzy. People treat her like she's not a person, like she can't understand the cruel things being said about her. It's horrible.

I have experience with that too, with someone in my life.

Someone with ASD?

No, but something similar. My brother was different from his peers. And he was treated like shit because of it.

I'm sorry. I've seen people treat Lizzy like she's not even in the room just because she's nonverbal. Like she's not part of a conversation simply because she can't use words to join in. But she communicates in other ways. And she has emotions like the rest of us. It's hard when people can't look past someone's looks or abilities.

Why do you think I wear a mask?

Sorry, that was a joke. Just trying to make you smile. Wasn't sure if that came through in text.

Bummer. So you're not rocking a Phantom of the Opera situation under there?

I am not.

When do I get to see what you look like?

Several hours go by before I give up waiting for a response. This back-and-forth has been going on for about nine months, and I'm nearly at my wit's end. I'm ready to see the man underneath the mask. He's probably worried that I won't find him attractive, but that's the last thought in my mind. I've spent a lot of time getting to know him through text, and I couldn't be more attracted to him.

I can't wait to go back to his room at the club for another session. He made all these rules for us to follow, but sometimes I wonder why we even have them when we're constantly breaking them. Our dynamic was only supposed to exist in the club, but he sought me out through text. I started opening up about my personal life and he never stopped me when I broke his rule and asked about his. He's definitely done more than just solve my touching problem—heck, he hasn't even touched or seen me since August. And it's obvious we're both catching feelings.

His lessons at the club last summer helped me more than he knows, and I ache to feel his touch on my skin again. And even though it should, the thought of his hands on me doesn't scare me.

———————

I end up staying on campus for spring break. The resident advisor on my floor, Lindsey, says it's okay for me to stay because she is too, even though the school normally closes the dorms all week. But they lock the buildings when they close them to students, and our keys only work on interior doors.

"This is my number." Lindsey hands me a slip of paper as she stands in my doorframe. "If you leave the building this week, you'll need to text me to get in."

"Thanks." I pull out my phone and add her number to my

contacts. "I'm not really planning on many excursions, but I'll text you."

"I'll see you around." She backs out of the room and then adds, "Oh, and don't prop open the exterior doors. It'll trigger a silent alarm if it's left open for too long."

I nod and hop up onto my loft bed ready to cuddle up with my book for the night.

When I wake up a couple hours later, my book's propped open on my chest. I must've dropped it when I fell asleep. Looking around my solo dorm room, there's not much to eat. Food delivery options are limited out here, and I'm not in the mood for pizza or Chinese.

Reluctantly, I pull on some clothes and head out to the store to get some groceries. There's not a lot in my bank account, so I remind myself to text my mom to make a deposit later.

When I get back to the dorm, arms loaded up with several bags, I swipe my keycard. Nothing.

Son of a bee sting. I totally forgot I have to text Lindsey to get into the building this week.

Fumbling with the bags, I pat my pockets for my phone and come up empty. I set my groceries next to the door and run up the pathway back to my car. Once I find my phone, I'm walking back on the sidewalk, not looking where I'm going as I text Lindsey.

It feels like I run into a brick wall, but when I look up, a familiar set of green eyes peers down at me. I take several steps back.

"You really should watch where you're going, Em," Trent takes a step closer to me.

"I told you not to call me that." I attempt to step around him, but he throws his arms out, preventing me.

"Aw, I thought we were going to play nice. Fine, if you're going to be a bitch about it, I don't really give a fuck what you say."

"Classy." Hiding my phone behind my back, I call Daddy

Dom's number. I really hope he picks up, or this is going to be a weird voicemail to explain.

Trent takes a step closer, and I back up again.

"Don't come any closer, Trent." My voice comes out a little louder, and I hope he thinks I'm just trying to draw attention from anyone nearby—not that I'm hoping my phone picks it up. Not that anyone would hear me right now. Campus is a ghost town.

"Poor little Emma, all alone. Didn't your daddy ever teach you not to walk alone at night?"

I can't believe I ever dated this turd of a human in high school. Girding my loins, I stiffen my spine and cross my arms over my chest, keeping the screen of my phone facing me so he can't see it. "You don't scare me. You're a bully, just like you were in high school." When I look down, I see the call has connected and I pray that he's listening on the line. "Still mad I wouldn't sleep with you, so you have to slink around campus at night and prey on me when I'm alone?"

"Listen, you stupid bi—"

I cut him off with a finger, pretending I'm getting a call as I hold the phone to my ear. "Hey, Daddy, I'm just walking back to my room."

"Where the fuck are you, pet?" Daddy Dom's voice growls into the line.

"I just left the parking lot, and I'm on the way back to my dorm now. I sent you my location." I try to keep my face neutral as I continue my lie, hoping it will scare Trent off. If he thinks my dad's tracking my movements, maybe he'll be less likely to try something.

"Are you alone?" Daddy Dom asks.

"I'm not alone." I make eye contact with Trent. "You'll never guess who I ran into. Do you remember that guy Trent that I dated in high school?"

Trent's eyes shift nervously side to side.

"Laugh and pretend I just made a joke about the sorry fuck."

I laugh, looking at Trent again. "It *is* the guy who took me to senior prom, and I agree his tux was too small for him."

"Put me on speakerphone."

"Sure, hold on." I hit the button. "He wants to talk to you."

"Hey there, Trent. I hope you're watching out for my little girl on campus." He affects the most chipper voice I've ever heard him use, sounding nothing like the man I know.

Trent shoves his hands in his pockets. "Uh, hi, Mr. Black. You don't have to worry. I'll keep an eye on her."

"Excellent. Are you headed back to your dorm, sweetie? You know how your mom worries about you."

"I'm headed that way now." I step around Trent, shooting him a stern look.

"Good. I'll stay on the phone until you get inside."

I walk at a brisk pace back to the building, picking up my groceries right as Lindsey opens the door for me. I take my phone off speakerphone as we walk down the hallway, parting to go to our rooms. Once I get inside, I hold the phone to my ear.

"Okay, I'm in my room. I'm sorry, I didn't know who else to call."

"You don't ever have to apologize to me for that. That was quick thinking on your part."

"Thanks. I've seen those videos that you can play when you're alone in a rideshare, where a guy has one side of a conversation so it sounds like you're on the phone. It kinda gave me the idea."

"What the fuck was that? Who was that guy? Do I need to keep watch outside your door?"

I giggle at the thought of this masked man standing watch outside the dorm at a private Christian college.

"What's so funny?"

"Would you wear the mask when you act as my bodyguard?"

"Probably."

My heart sinks a little at his words, wondering if I'll ever get to know the man underneath. I clear my throat and circle back to his earlier question. "I did date that guy in high school, I wasn't lying about that. We went to prom together." I lie back on my bed.

"Did he touch you?"

"Tonight or back then?"

"Don't answer that, I might want to hurt the fucker if I knew."

"He got in my face tonight, kept stepping toward me, but he didn't touch me. Something about his vibe was off, though, I can't explain it. He was never aggressive like that in high school, but he was part of this group of guys that spread rumors that they got in my pants."

All I hear in response is a low growl.

"Can you come outside?" he asks after a minute, and I shoot up to sitting.

"Are you here?"

"Yes."

"Gimme a minute." I hang up the call.

I can't move fast enough as I slip on my shoes, quickly throw my groceries in their designated places, fridge, shelf, snack drawer, and head down the hallway to give Lindsey a heads-up that I'm stepping outside for a little bit.

"Just text me when you need back in." She waves me off, and I walk down the hallway. It's been *months* since I've seen this man, and I can't wait to get my hands on him.

When I open the door, he's leaning against the side of the building, and he pushes off the wall, stalking toward me. If I didn't know him, his swagger, combined with the menacing mask, would be terrifying, but my face lights up with a grin as he approaches.

"I need to touch you, pet. Can I?"

I barely get out the "yes" before he's pulling me against him, leaning down and sliding his arms under my thighs and picking me up as I wrap my legs around his waist and burrow against him.

"How did you get here so fast?" I ask against his shoulder as his strong arms grip me tightly.

"I was in the area." His heart is beating rapidly in his chest, and I smile against his shirt, elated that I have this effect on him.

His answer finally registers, and I pull back, pinching my brows as I look at him dubiously. "But you live in the city, like an hour away from here."

"You gave the bat signal." He shrugs, pulling me back into him. "And I needed to hold you. That's all I can offer right now."

Something cracks in my chest at the desperation in his touch. If this is all I get from him right now, it's enough, especially if he's willing to break his rules for me.

CHAPTER 15
EMMA

It's close to the end of the spring semester, and I'm weeks away from being done dealing with Professor A-hole. His Shakespearean acting class has been enlightening, and after several months, it's obvious why this class is paired with the writing one. While reading the Bard's works is gratifying, they were meant to be performed, and I often find that the cadence of reading it aloud helps me work out the meaning when I'm having difficulty with a particular passage.

Our final assignment for the semester requires us to act out pivotal scenes with a partner. When I enter the classroom, my acting partner Jeremy is noticeably absent. I slink down into a desk, hoping to remain invisible for the rest of class. There's not much I can do if Jeremy isn't here, so I pull out my script and look over my lines.

"Miss Black, why aren't you rehearsing?" Professor A-hole stops right in front of me. Everyone's eyes are on me as I shrink in my seat.

"My scene partner isn't here." I try to keep the snark out of my tone, but there's just something about this man that gets under my skin. I want to slap him in the face, but he's also so attractive that I want to kiss him at the same time, and I'm not sure how I feel about all of that.

"Get up." Several more heads turn our way at his command.

"What—"

"I'm going to fill in for your scene partner." He gestures toward the small stage in the corner of the classroom. Unlike last semester's lecture hall, this space feels far more intimate. Most of the class has scattered around the room and into the hallway to rehearse.

"But I only have my copy of the script," I protest, desperate for a reason why this shouldn't happen.

"Don't need it. I know that scene by heart. Played Benedick in college," he volleys back, stepping onto the stage.

"That must have been decades ago," I mutter. Holy frick! Why did I just say that out loud? I never talk back to teachers. I grimace, looking up at him to gauge his reaction. There's a hint of a smirk on his face, but he schools his features quickly, his standard scowl back in place.

"Can we go out in the hall? Or maybe your office or another classroom?" Suddenly I'm full of nervous energy at the thought of my peers watching me perform this scene with my hot professor.

"Actually," he starts in a voice that is way too loud to just be addressing me, "This is a great learning opportunity for the class."

Kill me now.

"But you don't know our blocking, and I only have one script," I repeat, desperate to get out of this.

"Honestly, you should be off book by now, Miss Black," he retorts, and my cheeks burn with embarrassment.

"I am… mostly."

"And I'll follow your lead on the blocking." He crosses his arms tilting his chin up at me.

Gripping my script tightly in my hands, the paper crumples as I slowly inhale through my nose, nodding at him once I take my mark and begin.

"*Lady Beatrice, have you wept all this while?*"

I turn my back to him. "*Yea, and I will weep a while longer.*"

He takes a step closer, close enough that I can feel the warmth of him. "*I will not desire that.*" His voice is rough, edged with something that sounds dangerously like desire. It's nothing like the way Jeremy acts the scene with me, and it throws me off guard.

"*You have no reason. I do it freely.*" I'm so used to playing this bit with humor, and I awkwardly wait for laughs that don't come.

"*Surely I do believe your fair cousin is wronged.*"

"*Ah, how much might the man deserve of me that would right her!*" Our dynamic is off. I feel like a petulant child acting next to him.

"*Is there any way to show such friendship?*" He steps closer, my back to his front. The urge to lean into him is strong and confusing. There's only one person whose touch I crave, and it isn't his.

"*A very even way, but no such friend.*"

"*May a man do it?*" He grabs my hand.

Blood rushes to my face as I try to hide the shock I feel at his touch. There's something exciting yet also comforting about the caress of his hand against mine. It took weeks of rehearsals and dozens of different excuses before I could get this far with Jeremy. Is it because I find him attractive? Or is it because I don't see him as a threat since there's no way he would ever date me?

Before I can overanalyze it, I pull my hand from his, putting myself back in Beatrice's shoes. "*It's a man's office, but not yours.*"

"*I do love nothing in the world so well as you. Is not that strange?*" He clears his throat as I look down at my script. "Alright, let's stop there for a minute."

I breathe a sigh of relief. Why didn't we pick a scene from the beginning of the play when Benedick and Beatrice hated each other? Or why couldn't my scene partner have just shown up for class?

He crosses upstage of me. "I need more emotion from you, Miss Black. Make me believe you want this man, that you love him. And that only he can help you with your…problem."

"These two are infuriating. Even when they're confessing their love for each other, they still bicker back and forth," a guy in the back of the room laughs, and my cheeks pinken.

Professor A-hole nods at the guy. "You're not wrong." He turns, looking me directly in the eye. "What do you want in this scene? What is Beatrice's motivation?"

I squirm under his scrutiny while he paces in front of me. "She wants Benedick to kill Claudio for ruining her cousin Hero's name, for leaving her at the altar. For breaking her heart."

"But she doesn't really want him to kill Claudio, does she?"

"No, she's just angry and protective of Hero. She wants vengeance. And maybe she's testing Benedick's love for her?"

"Is that a question?"

"No, sir." His head whips to mine, and I can't decipher the look on his face. He swallows thickly and I track the way his Adam's apple bobs. "Before I can believe a word you speak, you need to fully understand this character and live that on stage. Continue, Miss Black."

"*As strange as the thing I know not. It were as possible for me to say I loved nothing so well as you, but believe me not, and yet I lie not; I confess nothing, nor I deny nothing. I am sorry for my cousin.*"

He takes a step toward me, crowding my space. "*By my sword, Beatrice, thou lovest me!*"

"*Do not swear and eat it.*" My words come out sharper than I intend.

His features soften as he looks down at me. "*I will swear by it that you love me, and I will make him eat it that says I love not you."*

"Will you not eat your word?"

"With no sauce that can be devised to it." He cups my cheek. *"I protest I love thee."*

The air leaves my lungs at his touch. *"Why then, God forgive me."* My words are a whisper.

"Louder. You won't be mic'd," he chastises before continuing. *"What offense, sweet Beatrice?"*

"You have stayed me in a happy hour. I was about to protest I loved you."

He smiles down at me, swiping his thumb across my cheek. My heart skips a beat, and my face heats. *"And do it with all thy heart."*

"I love you with so much of my heart that none is left to protest."

"Come, bid me do anything for thee." He's looking at me so intensely. His eyes flick to my lips. It almost looks like he wants to kiss me.

He's just acting. We're just acting.

"Kill Claudio," I say weakly.

Instantly he drops his hand, crossing his arms over his chest. "I don't believe you, Miss Black. Make me believe you. Make me feel it here." He stabs his chest. "Make me question if you're just acting."

"Kill Claudio," I repeat louder. Frustrated. Embarrassed.

"No!" he shouts. I rear back, startled by his outburst. "You're not giving me enough; that's the worst thing you can do as an actor. I can always pull you back if you go too far, too over-the-top, but I can't make you give more to the scene."

"I don't know what you want me to do. I'm not an actor. Sure, I've been in plays before, but this isn't what I want to do with my life. I just have to take this class for my major," I snap.

"That's it, get angry at me. Use that anger. Channel it. Beatrice is mad. You're mad and you want vengeance. You're so mad you make an extreme request of Benedick. Think back to a time in your life when you wanted vengeance. When you were so mad you wanted to fight back. Try it again."

I close my eyes and try to picture a time when I was that mad, that emotional. "*Kill Claudio,*" I say with more force, as sweat trickles down the back of my neck.

"Again!"

"This is ridiculous, I'm not actually going to act the scene this way."

"I don't care how hard you're going to act it later; I want to see you take direction. If I tell you to go harder, you do it. Again."

"*Kill Claudio,*" I shout.

"More! I know you've got it in you."

Something inside me snaps, and I drop my script as I lock eyes with him. "Kill him. *Kill Claudio,*" I shout, my emotions boiling over as I drop to my knees. I'm not just talking about a fictional man who wronged my cousin. An image flashes in my mind, but I can't make sense of it as I squeeze my eyes closed, willing it away. It felt real. Whatever I just tapped into, felt so real, I'm having a hard time composing myself as I pant for breath.

His dark figure looms over me, threatening, menacing. Like he's going to pounce at any minute. He hurt me. No, he hurt my mom.

I don't think it's just a dream, I think it's a memory. And pulling from memories for this exercise has unlocked something in my brain. I was running from him, something wasn't right. She needed my help. My heart was racing, and I was overcome with fear, so I ran. I needed to distract him, so he didn't hurt her. I made it halfway down the stairs when he grabbed me, jerking my arm. But I fought back, I scratched him, and he let go. That's when I fell and landed on my arm, my wrist absorbing the impact from the fall. My mom told me I broke it at camp.

She lied to me, to protect me from him, from remembering this.

The room is silent, except for my hiccupping breaths as I try to unpack the thoughts and images in my head.

Oh my gosh. It *was* my dad this whole time. I can't believe it.

"Thank you, Miss Black. Excellent work today, everyone. Class is dismissed."

I collapse onto my butt, crossing my legs and folding my body over them, making myself as small as I can as I come down from the rush of emotions. Students shuffle about, and I wait. For my heart rate to slow. For the classroom to clear out. For my mind to make sense of what just happened.

My father was abusive toward my mom. Once I was older, she'd shared stories of how he'd hurt her when I was a baby and how she'd escaped that life. But I don't really have any memories of him. So why was everything so clear in my head just now as if I was recalling a memory and not a dream?

A hand clasps my shoulder, and I flinch, instantly pulled out of my bubble as I scramble away from my professor.

"I need to go."

"Miss Black, that was…"

My cheeks flush and my heart races as mortification swallows me. I don't need to know how he finishes that sentence. I stumble off the stage to grab my bag so I can escape when his next word stops me.

"Incredible."

I'm frozen in place resisting the urge to look at him. I can't face him, afraid of the pity I'd find in his eyes, so I run out of the classroom, not stopping until I make it back to my dorm.

I send my mom a quick text as I throw a few things in an overnight bag then drive to her house. As soon as I walk in, she pulls me into her arms.

"Oh, sweetie. I'm so sorry."

She smells like cookies, and I let go of everything I'd been holding in on the way here. Years worth of fears in the form of nightmares that were shielding my brain from the truth I was too young to understand.

When I pull back there's a comically large wet spot on her shoulder and chest from my tears and snot. "I'm sorry," I say, pointing to it.

"It's okay. Once I had kids, bodily fluids stopped grossing me out." She laughs, and I relax as she leads me into the living room. I sink onto the couch. Why is it that there's no couch more comfortable than the one in your childhood home?

"What happened, sweetie?"

"I know what's been causing the nightmares."

She nods solemnly, not looking at all surprised.

"It was dad. My birth dad, not Hank."

Her eyes fill with tears. "I was really hoping you wouldn't remember anything about him."

"Why didn't you tell me what happened?" I can't hide the hurt in my tone, and I cross my arms, willing myself to breathe.

"You were so little when it started. The abuse." She shifts uncomfortably. "I was hoping you were too young to have any memory of what you saw. And it was never directed at you, only me. You were around a year old when we left, and I didn't see any point in bringing it up and upsetting or scaring you if you didn't remember it anyway."

"But I was older in this memory, probably five or six. Not a baby."

"Your dad was an alcoholic. The more he drank, the worse it got. He pushed me a few times, and I had some bruises. Nothing I could report him for without it being a he-said-she-said situation. I was still technically married to him when I met Hank."

I stare at her in shock. "But you and Hank got married. I was like three at the wedding. There are pictures of me and Ethan."

"It was for show. I was still technically married to your

dad. He refused to grant me a divorce. We got legally married at the courthouse a few months after your dad, Matt, died in the car accident."

Shaking my head, I try to make her words make sense in my brain. "I don't understand."

"I wanted to move on with my life, and Hank wanted to make me happy. The right man will do that for you. He was so different from your dad. Fun and adventurous and willing to go along with what I wanted. And it sounds dumb, but I wanted to play house. I wanted to get married and have his babies and have the family and the love I craved but never got from Matt."

"But what does this have to do with the nightmare and the stairs?"

She looks away. "Around your fifth birthday, your dad reached out and wanted to see you. He told me he'd gotten sober, even showed me his AA chip. Something didn't feel right about it, but he spent months convincing me that he'd changed. He wanted to spend time with you and have a relationship with you. So I agreed to let you go over for visits as long as either Hank or I were present, and you were comfortable with it. Everything went better than expected. He seemed to have healed, and you were begging to see him."

"What changed?"

"He told me that he'd give me the divorce if we could work out a custody agreement. The visits were like a trial run to see how it'd go. After a month, we agreed to let him have unsupervised visits. Shortly after, you came home with a bruise on your shoulder. I asked you about it, but you seemed fine and didn't know how it got there. It was weird, but kids get bruises, so I dismissed it. Then you came home with bruises on your arms and legs. And he said you fell down playing tag with some of the neighbor kids."

A flash of the figure in my dreams pops into my head, but this time the shadows are gone, and I see my father's face.

"It's him. I can see him now. He's not in shadow anymore."

Tears spill down my mom's cheeks, and she buries her face in her hands. "He… he hurt you, and I didn't know. I thought he'd changed. The last time I picked you up from his house, you had bruises on the side of your neck, and I lost it. You were standing behind him at the top of the stairs. I was halfway up the steps when I confronted him about the bruises. He started shouting, and as he got closer, I could smell the alcohol on his breath and he reared back like he was going to hit me. Suddenly, you ran toward me, and he grabbed your arm, throwing you down the few steps between us. It all happened so fast. You hit your head on the wall, and I screamed for help. Hank came running in from the car, and we got you to the hospital. When you awoke with a concussion and a broken arm, you didn't remember anything that had happened with your dad. So we told you that you broke your arm at summer camp. I should have told you the truth when you got older, but I didn't think the nightmares were about him. I should've known, I should've figured it out. I'm so sorry, sweetie."

I pull her against me as she weeps against my chest. "It's okay. It's not your fault."

A shuddering sob overtakes her as I rub her back. "Really, Mom, it's okay. I have a great therapist, I'm okay, I'm going to be okay. We'll figure this out. Plus, there's kind of someone that's been helping me."

She pulls back, searching for the truth in my eyes. Her shoulders visibly relax. "Is it a guy? I want to hear all about him."

I tell her about Daddy Dom, sharing only vague details, referring to him as Don since I don't know his name and don't want to explain what a dom is to my mom.

CHAPTER 16
JOHN

When class starts and Emma's second row seat is empty, I know I've pushed her too far. I struggled with whether or not I should reach out to her as Daddy Dom after class last week. But her professor witnessed her meltdown, not her dom. If she wanted to talk to me about it, she would've texted. If she had any more nightmares, I would've heard.

More than anything, I want to hold her in my arms and assure her that everything is going to be okay. But I can't make that promise.

I go through the motions, barely interacting with anyone as they run through their scenes, trying to make it through the rest of class so I can check on her.

I'm not one to cancel classes, but I send out an email and add an announcement to our online message board letting the rest of my students know that we're not meeting this afternoon.

There's a good chance she's just avoiding me, but just in case she's not, I need to make sure she's okay. What the fuck has gotten into me? I don't normally get involved in my subs' personal lives outside of the club. But I also haven't had many subs since meeting her. I've done enough to keep my room at Pulse, but anyone I've engaged with over the past year has been platonic and required very minimal physical interaction from me.

And no one has held my attention. Yet Emma consumes my thoughts and there's not a damn thing I can do about it as John, and barely anything I can do as Daddy Dom.

I hurry back to my place near campus, thankful that the professor I share the space with is in class for the rest of the day. Once I'm in my room with the door locked, I fish my mask out of a bag in my closet and hit FaceTime on my phone, making sure my background is neutral giving little away.

The call rings, and I fight the urge to lay into her if she picks up, reminding myself that Daddy Dom doesn't know she's skipping class.

"Hey! I wasn't expecting to hear from you today." She's out of breath—and she's not in her dorm room or her bedroom at her parents' house.

"Where are you?" I snap.

"Well, hello to you too," she mocks as I clench my teeth.

"I don't recognize the background is what I meant," I say a little softer. "Hey, pet."

"I'm at my other home away from home, Alyx's apartment. He's at the restaurant right now, so I'm by myself."

"Aren't you supposed to be in class?"

"Jeez, do you have my schedule memorized or something? Why are you so obsessed with me?" she teases.

I grin behind my mask. "You have no idea," I murmur. "Just answer the question."

"Well, I was supposed to be in Professor A-hole's class, but I decided to skip since he was such a jerk last week. I can't wait till this semester is over and I'm done seeing him every week."

It seems I've done too good a job at pushing her away as Professor Ali that I doubt she'll ever link my private persona to my public one. And fuck if I'm not reminded of her speech and paper on *Henry V* and that very topic during her first semester in my class. Maybe it's better if she hates him—it'll make breaking this off easier.

"You shouldn't be skipping class."

"Is that a rule I'm supposed to follow, sir?" Her voice is husky, and my cock jerks in my pants.

Running a palm along my length to ease the ache, I blow out a deep breath. "Fuck, you know how sexy your obedience is to me."

"Is it?" she says coyly.

"Strip," I bark, and she obeys easily.

"What about my earbuds?" She points to her ears.

"You can keep those in. Now, get on the bed and spread your legs. Let me see how you touch yourself."

She angles the phone in place and lies back.

"No, pet. I want to see your cunt. See the way your fingers glisten as you plunge them in and out. Watch as you play with your clit until you're covered in your cum."

She moves the pillows so she can prop herself up, lying diagonally on the bed. When she parts her legs, baring her pussy to me, I suck in a breath.

"I wish you were here." She reaches between her legs and teases her lips.

"Me too." Fuck, if only I could hear the noises she makes as she pushes a finger in and out, spreading her wetness.

"Oh gosh, this feels so good."

"That's it. Pinch your clit with one hand and fuck your fingers with the other. Can you do that for me?"

"Oh God, yes," she moans.

I undo my belt and pull out my cock, aching to be free of its confines as it stretches up my stomach, peeking out of the top of my boxer briefs. I debate what to show her. She's never seen my cock, but I figure this is the safest way to play with her, because if we were in person right now, there'd be nothing stopping me from filling her up with my cum.

"Can I see you?" Her voice is breathy, pleading.

There's no way I can deny her when she asks like that. I prop the phone against some pillows and lie back.

"Where are your tattoos? I want to see them." She's writhing on the bed, her eyes hooded as she stares at the screen.

I quickly remove my shirt, giving in to her demands. There's not much I wouldn't do at this point, if only she'd ask me.

"That's better," she rasps. "I'm so close. Can I come, sir?"

Oh, sweet fucking Christ. "Don't you dare fucking come, pet. Not until I tell you. Do you understand?"

"Yes, sir."

Tilting my mask, I spit into my palm. I tug furiously at my cock, wishing it was her warm cunt enveloping me, overwhelming my senses. The way she's barely keeping it together, turning her head into the pillow to quiet her moans, has me teetering on the edge.

"Oh God, I can't… I'm going to—"

"Come for me. Come all over those fingers like the good submissive fucking pet you are. Oh fuck, fuuuuck. Unghhh," I grunt as warm jets of cum spill out of my cock, covering my abs and chest in warmth.

"Oh God! Oh my God!" she whisper-yells, and I immediately know something is wrong.

"What is it? What's wrong?" I sit up and grab the phone with my clean hand.

"Ethan?" she calls out, confused. She scrambles off the bed, going out of frame before I see her again, briefly, covered in a robe.

My heart rate slows, remembering Ethan is her brother.

"Emma? What the fuck? Is Alyx in there with you?" an angry voice bellows.

"What? Ew, no!"

"Open the door, Emma!"

"Fine! But it's super embarrassing."

I set the phone down just in case, cleaning myself off while she talks to her brother.

"Do you have someone in there with you? You better not be fucking my best friend."

"Oh my gosh, gross! He's at work. Shouldn't you know that?"

It's quiet for a minute before I hear Ethan's voice again.

"What are you doing in there? Is someone with you?"

I hear her sigh and I grin, wondering how she's going to spin this. "This is so embarrassing. I'm in human biology this semester, and I was studying for a test on reproductive health. I think you can see where I'm going with this. Okay. Thanks for stopping by."

"Emma," Ethan scolds.

"Fine! I got turned on and decided to take care of it, if you know what I mean." She's so quiet that I probably wouldn't have heard her if her earbud wasn't still in.

"You're telling me your textbook made you so horny you masturbated?"

"Cheese and rice, Ethan!" she cries, and I silently chuckle.

"Well, I'll let you get back to studying." I hear a door close and then moments later she's back on screen, sitting on the bed.

"How much of that did you hear?"

I grab my phone off the bed, now fully cleaned and dressed. "All of it." I gesture to her earbud.

"Frick, I forgot I still had that in."

"Human biology? Did you just lie to your brother?"

"I had to come up with something, and it was the first thing that popped into my head. Now he's going to think I'm some weirdo diddling myself to anatomy books." She drops her head in her hands, sighing before she flops onto the bed.

"Emma," I say sternly, and her head pops up, locking onto the screen as she pushes up on her elbows. "Here's another rule for you. Don't worry about what other people think. It doesn't matter. Your brother can think what he wants about you; it doesn't change who you are. And if I had to guess, he probably didn't buy your story but didn't want to press you for more details after that excuse you gave."

"You're probably right," she sighs, a small smile on her face.

I feel like the biggest fucking hypocrite telling her that when it's one of the reasons I've kept her at arm's length. We can't be seen together. Hell, we can't be together, not now anyway. Even though I've bent some of my rules for her, I need to remind my savior complex why this is the worst timing. Mary needs me and I need to be there for her.

"When can I see you in person again? I'm almost done with the semester, and then I can be closer to the city. I can come to the club," she offers eagerly, pulling me from my thoughts.

"I don't know."

The look of disappointment on her face guts me, but I know I need to end this soon. This call was a reminder that we could be caught at any moment, and as much as I want to throw away every obligation in my life for her, some things are bigger than my selfish desires.

CHAPTER 17
JOHN

This ends tonight. What we do here will have to be enough to last me through the next year. Even though I'm consumed with the overwhelming desire to help her, protect her, I need to walk away now.

She easily agreed to see me again, considering the last time we were physical like this was at the beginning of the semester. While I wait for Alyx to bring her down, I set up the lounger, arrange the cushions and inserts to resemble a flat surface, and grab the massage oil, then put my mask in place.

Alyx knocks and gives me a nod, then turns back in the direction of his room. I close the door behind him and look down at her small frame, letting my eyes roam over each delicious curve of her body. "Strip and lie down."

"Yes, sir." There's no hesitation in her voice when she obeys. And fuck, that willingness makes her even harder to resist. She climbs onto the table, gently placing her forehead on her folded arms.

"When was your last nightmare?" She has a problem; I'm helping solve the problem. If I keep it transactional, no feelings need to be involved.

"A week ago, sir." Her voice is weak, like she's afraid to admit this.

"Why wasn't I informed?"

"I didn't tell Alyx about it. I was alone in my dorm studying for finals."

"What happened in this one? What did he do to you?"

"He straddled me and held me down." She lets out a shuddering breath as her breathing picks up. She told me about her breakthrough with her mom recently, and I'd hoped her nightmares would lessen, but I know it could take time. Do I keep pushing or let this go and hold her?

"How did he hold you down?"

"My throat. He cut off my air and I couldn't breathe," she says through a sob, and my resolve cracks.

"Look at me, pet." I stroke her cheek. Her head shifts to the side, one of her eyes peeking out. Her lashes are thick as they flutter, and I shift slightly to block the light so she doesn't have to strain.

"You're safe with me."

"I am." It's not a question. Her agreement is everything I need to continue.

"Do you trust me to reenact that scene?"

"Yes, sir." There's no hesitation in her voice.

Something stirs in my chest. It's thrilling when a sub hands you total control, but there's something about Emma's submission that makes every part of me come alive for the first time in my life.

Like this is how it's supposed to be.

Like every other person I've been with was just practice for this.

Like this is real.

Only it can't be real, and it can't be her. Not now.

I climb onto the table, moving gently as I straddle her. Once I'm over the small of her back, I lean down, getting as close to her ear as my mask will allow. "Turn over."

She shakes her head. "I c–can't."

"Can't isn't your safe word. My full weight isn't on you, and there's just enough room for you to flip under me. Show me those perfect fucking nipples, pet. I've been dying for another peek."

She shifts under me until she's on her back, tits bared. My dick hovers over her pussy, my clothing the only thing between us. I grab her hands and place them on my thighs as my fingers slowly tickle up her arms, those fucking goosebumps following in my wake. Her breathing stutters as I get closer to her neck.

"You can stop this at any time."

She shakes her head as she releases a shaky breath.

"You have all the control here. You can grab me by the neck or the balls. I'm not going to stop you."

She squeezes her eyes shut, grabs my forearms, and guides my hands to her neck. "Show me how it's supposed to be done. I don't want to be afraid of it. I want it to feel good, like the hand necklaces in the books I've read. If I can show my brain that it's not always scary, maybe it won't terrify me in my nightmare."

Her lithe body grows still under me as I grip the sides of her delicate neck, careful to avoid her windpipe. I lean in as close as I can, praying she can't feel the way I'm stiffening in my pants. "The key is not to cut off your air supply completely. Breath play is an art and requires complete trust. I'm happy to grip your neck for now, but you're not ready for that kind of play yet."

"Yes, sir," she rasps, and my hips buck in response, rubbing my erection against her as she moans.

Get it the fuck together. Do not allow this girl to cause you to stray from the plan. The rules are there for a reason.

"Harder, please."

I don't know if she wants me to increase the pressure on her neck or thrust harder against her clit, but against my better judgement, I do both.

"Oh f–fuuuh, fudge." She finishes the last word on a slow moan.

"You can do better than that pet, say it for me. Just once. I want to hear that sweet voice moan 'fuck' in my ear. You have no idea what it would do to me to hear that dirty word come out of your clean little mouth. No one can hear you but me. Give it to me." It comes out as a command, but it feels like I'm begging. The urge to corrupt this innocent sub takes over, and I pick up my thrusts, pushing hard against her clit as she clenches beneath me.

"Oh God, I'm going to… oh f–fuhh— can't, I'm—" Her words are interrupted by a guttural cry as she shudders against me, her fingers digging into my arms as she squeezes them.

I ignore the voice in my head telling me to stop as my orgasm builds quickly, she was so close to swearing and the thought alone is enough to unravel me. "Fuck, Em. Fuuuuck, such a good fucking girl for me," I growl as I explode in my pants, sweat trickling down my face as my heavy breathing threatens to fog up my mask.

As we come down, she stares up at me, a look of wonder on her face, her big brown eyes boring into me.

Tucking a strand of hair behind her ear, I gaze at her, awestruck. "You didn't use your safe word."

"I didn't need it. I liked it. It was freeing."

"Are you okay?" I stroke the side of her neck.

"More than okay. Thank you, sir."

I climb off the table and move to the tall cupboard that houses my extra outfits and costumes. I clean myself quickly, keeping my back to her. What the fuck is happening to me? My control is too weak.

"Get dressed," I say with more bite than I intend. I should apologize—this isn't my normal level of aftercare, and I feel like an asshole for leaving her on the table while I tend to my needs instead of hers, but my scalp is hot, and I feel like my body is covered in ants. I want to scratch or scrub every inch of my skin until I bleed.

She makes quick work of putting her clothes on, and it takes everything in me not to pull her into my arms and shower her with praise at the progress she's made.

I open the door and extend my arm, motioning her into the hallway. She hesitates for a second, a look of confusion and hurt on her face before she sighs and walks into the hall.

When we get to Alyx's door, I grab her wrist before she knocks. My fingers linger on her skin as I pull her against me, her back to my front as I lean close to her ear. "Thank you, pet. You were so good for me, but our time is up. That was our last session."

I release her wrist and back away, turning down the hall so I don't have to see her reaction. I'm a fucking coward for abandoning her, but this needs to happen. Her soft pleas and sobs reach my ears, but I don't turn back regardless of the pain in my chest. Despite the spiral I'm in, maybe this is good. This is what I need to walk away.

CHAPTER 18
EMMA

M-

From the moment we met, I knew you were it for me. But we come from two different worlds that are determined to keep us apart. I promise you I will find a way for us to be together. Don't give up hope.

Stay safe and know I'm thinking of you always.
J

The letter appears under my door on the last day of school. I don't recognize the handwriting on the envelope. I rip open the door and look around, but the hallway is empty.

I read it half a dozen times, growing more confused with each pass. Was I the intended recipient? It's addressed to "M," which I guess could be a nickname for Em, but when I search my brain for who the "J" could be, I come up short. I don't know anyone with a J name who would write me a letter like this. And the only person on campus I have any sort of romantic connection to is Trent—and he's never expressed feelings for me this intense.

Could it be from Daddy Dom? And could his name start with a J? I think about texting Alyx, but that man's a vault, and I know he won't say anything even if I did guess.

It feels like something Daddy Dom would say, but given the fact that he broke up with me and hasn't returned any of my calls or texts, I doubt it's him. Plus, he lives an hour away in Columbus.

Regardless of who sent it and whether I was the intended recipient, it breaks my heart to read, so I stuff it in my bag along with all my feelings as I pack up my dorm room and remind myself to schedule another appointment with my therapist. I have too much to cover with her lately.

It's early June when I get a text from Ethan asking me to bring him groceries while he recovers from his vasectomy. I moved back into Mom and Dad's after finals, and I haven't left my room in days. And while I'm thrilled to finally be done with Professor A-hole, I'm reeling over the loss of Daddy Dom.

What is wrong with me? I never even saw the man's face, never heard his real voice, and I don't know his real name. So how can it hurt this bad when I don't know who he really is?

Because he saw the real me. Not the version of me I show to the world. The real me, broken and messy. And I thought he wanted me anyway, but his abrupt dismissal of me still has me reeling weeks later.

ETHAN

Make sure you get everything on the list.
We're making one of Nonna's recipes tonight.
You're welcome to join us.

> I don't want to drive an hour to you. Can't you just use a delivery service?

I could, but then I wouldn't get to see you.

> Mom or Ella?

Huh?

> Which snitch texted you?

I don't know what you're talking about.

> Cut the crap, Ethan.

Since when are you this bossy?

> ETHAN

Mom. She said you haven't left your room in days. And she's been bringing you food. Come over and cook with us. I'd come get you, but I just had surgery and can't drive.

> Ugh, fine. Just text me the list.

After I pick up everything on Ethan's list, drop it at his place, and unexpectedly cry in his girlfriend's arms, my plans change for the night. Bridget and Ethan have been cooking some of Nonna's recipes lately, and Ethan's lounging on a stool, an ice pack on his crotch, bossing me and Bridget around in the kitchen.

The two of them are ridiculously cute, and it's a stark reminder of how alone I am, hence the spontaneous tears. The only man that's ever been able to touch me walked away without a second glance. It hurts how easily he was able to do that, like our time together meant nothing to him when it meant everything to me.

"So what are your plans this summer?" Bridget asks as she snuggles into Ethan's side on the couch.

"Hellcat," he warns, "I'm going to need you to sit somewhere else. No snuggling against me until I'm fully healed."

"Ugh, you two are so cute, it's gross."

"He's just being a baby. Vasectomies are very common procedures." Bridget moves over to the loveseat next to me as Ethan swings his legs onto the couch, readjusting his frozen peas. She looks at me expectantly.

"I'm taking a couple summer classes, but nothing other than that."

"How are you with kids? My best friend Becka is looking for a sitter to help with her daughter. It could turn into more than the one night since they don't have a lot of options with their families, and Ethan and I aren't always available."

"I'd love to." This could be the perfect distraction to take my mind off my pathetic love life.

"Great. Can I give her your number?"

"Sure. Now, I believe I was promised face masks, and I really need to see Ethan in one. Ella is never gonna let him live it down. She still has pics of the makeovers we gave him on her phone as blackmail."

"Oh, he still has those on his phone too. You girls made him look very pretty." She laughs as Ethan smiles at her.

Once we eat and don our face masks, I turn on a movie and settle into the couch. I can feel my brother staring out of the corner of my eye, and once Bridget excuses herself to use the bathroom, I pause the movie and glare at him. "What is it?"

"What's what?"

"The reason you're staring at me. You're doing that thing you do where you stare at me as if you can hear my thoughts."

"I heard about what happened with your dad," he admits quietly.

"What? How?" My cheeks pinken at the thought of my mom sharing this with him.

"I was picking Lizzy up to take her to therapy, and overheard Mom telling Dad about it in the kitchen."

My nerves ease slightly at his words.

"Are you still having nightmares?"

I sigh. "They started up again recently. My therapist said it's just my body's way of watching for danger. She said I'm not going to erase my triggers overnight, but I need to trust that when they do occur that I'm not letting them define me. But it's hard not to feel discouraged. Once I knew who was haunting my dreams, I'd hoped they would stop. But it doesn't work that way." I don't tell him that a new masked figure has been making guest appearances in my recent dreams.

"I'm so sorry you're dealing with that but thank you for sharing it with me. Need me to look up some resources for you?"

I smile at his offer. He does this for Lizzy too. She shows an interest in something, and he learns everything he can about it. She has a problem, and he's looking for solutions on every corner of the internet. "I'm good. But could I stay here tonight?" I ask through a yawn.

He looms over me as sweat trickles down my back. I take off in a sprint, my heart beating wildly in my chest. I climb the stairs two at a time, then race down the hall into the nearest bedroom. There's not even time to shut the door behind me. I can hear his footsteps, practically feel his hot breath on my neck.

I make it into the closet, but before I can shut the door behind me, a hand snakes in, grabbing hold of my ankle, pulling me out. I try to kick with my free leg, but I can't see, can't make contact with anything. The carpet drags against my skin as I flip onto my stomach, grabbing at anything I can find to hold onto, but I lose the game of tug-of-war we're playing.

There's no point in trying to fight it. I lay there motionless as he straddles the backs of my thighs, pressing his hard body against mine. "You can't escape me. Stop trying."

Goosebumps prickle my arms as he slowly traces his fingers along them and my panties dampen at his touch.

Strong arms slide under my torso, flipping me onto my back. I peer up at him, anxious to finally see his features, but the room is too dark and his face is in shadow. His rough palm cups my cheek, and I let out a stuttered breath.

He leans down and his lips brush my skin as he speaks. "Let me take care of you. Open your legs." My obedience is on autopilot as I widen my thighs so he can settle between them. He pushes my skirt up before tracing the side of my panties, running a finger along the crease of my leg as a shudder rocks through me.

I'm all frantic need and anticipation as he slowly lowers his head, pushes my panties to the side, and licks me. It's relentless, all-consuming, and a rush of heat courses through me. He sets a steady pace, flicking and rolling his tongue against me, applying firm pressure on the spot I need it most as I buck against him.

When his head pops up, I whine, groping around in the darkness so I can push his mouth back where I want it. Where I need it.

"Use me. Show me exactly where you want it most. Let me hear how needy you are for me to make you come. Soak my face, drench my fingers, make me taste you for days."

I can hear the wicked grin in his voice, feel the smirk in his dirty words. And then he's moving back to my core, pressing his face against me as he tortures me with that filthy tongue. My fingers thread through his hair as I move him to the exact spot I need and rock against him, taking what I want.

"Oh yeah, right there." His mouth feels amazing, and my orgasm builds as I writhe underneath him. "Please, sir, please make me come."

His mouth feels incredible, like a dream. Better than any of my toys. How is this possible? How can it feel this good? How could he walk away from me?

"Emma." He's still buried between my thighs as he gently kisses me, dragging his tongue in long, slow licks that feel like a massage.

I'm still pulsing, my orgasm refusing to let up as I convulse against him.

"I can't… please… I can't stop—"

"Emma!" a loud voice booms.

I bolt upright, stunned from the abrupt noise. When my eyelids flutter open, I wince in pain. They're puffy and swollen from crying and it feels like I have a hangover, but I haven't been drinking. When fat tears fall down my cheeks seconds later, they burn against my tired skin.

"Was it another nightmare?" Ethan asks, pulling me into a hug. I nod against his chest, unsure of what else to tell him.

"Do you need anything? Some ice water?" Bridget's soft voice asks from the hall.

"Make her one in a tumbler with lots of ice, like you like." I want to give him a hard time for answering for me, but I don't have the energy to fight him.

It felt so real. I thought he was here. I thought he was back. More tears streak my cheeks when I remember how alone I actually am. And now my brother thinks I had another nightmare, and there's no way I can tell him I had a sex dream about my masked-dom-sorta-boyfriend who recently dumped me.

"Do you have any cucumbers?" I hiccup around the words.

"I'm a chef, I always have a fully stocked kitchen. Want me to throw some in your water?"

I shake my head. "For my eyes."

"I got you." He presses a kiss to the top of my head and walks gingerly over to the kitchen.

As soon as I see him wince, I stand, about to walk to the kitchen. "Sorry, I can do it myself. You just had surgery."

"I'm fine. Just feel like I've been kicked in the nuts. It's nothing I can't handle."

Bridget appears in front of me with a tumbler. "He's fine. A bit of a baby, if you ask me." She sets the water on the table, taking a seat on the couch as she pulls me down next to her. "Wanna talk about it?"

"Can you keep a secret from my brother?" I whisper, hoping the sound of Ethan cutting cucumbers masks my voice.

She hesitates for a second, looking at him in the kitchen, and it warms my heart knowing my big brother has someone in his corner.

"Trust me, he doesn't want to know what I'm about to tell you."

"Then yes, I'll keep it a secret," she says quietly.

Ethan walks over with a plate of cucumber slices and sets them on the table. He looks between Bridget and me for a few seconds, picking up on our conspiratorial glances at each other. "I'm gonna head back to bed. You coming, Hellcat?"

"I'll be there in a few, Pup."

Jeez, even their nicknames are cute.

He kisses her forehead and disappears down the hall.

I turn to Bridget once I hear the door close behind him. "I was having a sex dream, not a nightmare."

"Holy shit!" She laughs, and I can't help but join her. "He heard you screaming and came running out here only to wake you up from a naughty dream. Oh fuck, this is gold."

"He's too protective for his own good," I say as we continue our fit of laughter. "Told you he wouldn't want to know."

She swipes at her eyes, and I notice how pretty they are. The deepest shade of blue with slight wrinkles around them. I've never had a big sister before, but I really like her, and before I know it, I'm spilling everything.

"He broke up with me."

"Who broke up with you? The guy in the dream?"

"Yes? Maybe? I don't know." I blow out a breath. "I couldn't see his face."

"In the dream?"

I nod, trying to decide how much to share. "But also in real life."

"What do you mean?"

"We met through a friend. He's into a certain type of lifestyle and doesn't like to show his face, so he always wore a mask around me. It started last summer, and it continued throughout the school year. We didn't see each other a lot, but we texted and called when we couldn't meet up because of my class schedule. But I don't even know his name, or what he looks like."

"But you were being safe, right?"

"Yes, absolutely. My friend introduced us, so he's not some rando. And we messed around a little bit, but never went all the way. I wanted to, we just never had the opportunity. So we were safe on that front too."

"So, you dated an unnamed masked man for a year?" I don't hear any judgement in her tone. She's calm, like she's just recapping the facts.

"Yes."

"Yeah, definitely not telling your brother any of that. He freaked out for a week when you caught us at his place. He was convinced something was going on with you and Alyx."

"Gross, no. I love Alyx, but he's like a brother to me."

"And this lifestyle he was into, would that involve a certain club Alyx likes to frequent?"

I grab a cucumber and shove it in my mouth to avoid the question as I smile awkwardly.

"And this friend that introduced you is Alyx, isn't it?"

Shoot, why did I open my mouth? I should've just called Ella after they went back to bed.

Bridget reaches out and places a palm on my thigh.

"You look like you could use a friend. I don't have any

sisters, and I tend to ghost the one friend I have, so I'm probably not the best person to dole out advice, but I'm here if you want to talk."

I grab another cucumber, turning it over in my hand, my eyes fixated on it as I speak. "It just hurts so much. I don't know why he broke it off. And I don't want to bug Alyx and put him in the middle of it since he knows him too. We had something, a real connection. I have a hard time trusting men—"

"Oh, I've been there."

"So you get it. It's hard when every man I've shown an interest in has let me down. Except him. He's the first person that saw me as more than my issues. He saw me, when I was broken, and he thought I was strong. And I trusted him *completely*. So why would he walk away? I just feel like a stupid foolish child."

"Emma, you're a grown woman. A powerful, strong, kick-ass chick. You know what's best for you, and I'm not here to judge your choices. And I'm certainly not going to tell Ethan that his best friend took his sister to a sex club so she could hook up with a masked man. It's not my place to share. But you're not the only one with secrets. And you're not the only one who's felt broken." There's a glint in her eye that tells me there's something she's not telling me. And I can't explain why, but it comforts me knowing that whatever skeletons she has haven't prevented her from living her life and falling in love.

"So you don't think I'm a freak?"

"Fuck, no. You're doing the best you can in a shitty situation. And I know what it's like to feel like everyone's out to get you. I pushed everyone away for years until your brother saw me for who I really was, broken pieces and all. He helped me put myself back together after a… uh… shitty situation in high school. So, I get what you're feeling."

"But your person stayed. He didn't break up with you," I cry, a tear falling down my cheek as my voice cracks.

"Believe me when I tell you that Ethan and I have overcome some shit together. It wasn't easy, and I almost let my baggage keep us from finding our way back to each other. But maybe he just needs some time to figure things out like I did. Maybe this is a 'see you later' and not a goodbye."

I drop my head back against the couch and let out a loud exhale. When I look over, Bridget is grinning at me. "That's how I feel every day I walk into my office. A deep sigh, an eye roll, and I'm ready to deal with whatever shit men throw at me."

"I really like you."

"I really like you too." She smiles. "Hey, whatever happened with that asshole professor you had?"

"Ugh, Professor A-hole. He's the last person I want to think about right now. I'm just glad I never have to see his stupid handsome face ever again."

CHAPTER 19
JOHN

I decided to pick up a few summer classes. Anything to take my mind off the mess I put myself in or the coward I've become. I'm keeping my head down, sticking to my rules, and honoring the commitments I made before this bewitching woman entered my life.

Before Emma, following the rules was easy. Sure, I'd bend them from time to time, but it was always for the greater good. Like breaking the speed limit to rush someone to the hospital.

But the longer she's in my life, however, the more I find myself breaking my rules, taking bigger risks that could not only ruin my life, but the lives of others as well. If word got out that I was involved with a student, I could lose my job. And Mary depends on me, and not just for her housing situation. Her friendship is important to me, and her safety is paramount.

In so many ways, Emma reminds me of Mary. They've both overcome abuse at the hands of a man they should have been safe with. They both came to me for help, but under much different circumstances. And they both love fiercely and want to help others. I think if they met, they'd be friends.

Walking away from Emma was necessary, but it feels like

the worst mistake I've ever made. I can't come clean with her, not now, and she deserves my honesty. She deserves someone who can take her out, treat her right—in public and in private. And that's not me, not right now—maybe one day, but I can't ask her to wait.

Hell, I can't even walk into my private room at the club without thinking about her, and she'd only been there a handful of times. But fuck if Emma wasn't the perfect natural submissive for me. My good little pet. Even though I'm only coaching couples now at the club, I keep expecting her to walk in my door, yet she never does.

I'm keeping myself busy so I don't have time to think about her, but there aren't enough clients I could take on at Pulse, not enough classes I could teach to erase her from my mind completely.

I pull up the classroom portal to double-check my roster for any last-minute additions. Relief washes over me when I don't see Emma's name. Not that I was really expecting to. I was successful in my mission to drive her away from my professor persona, determined to make her hate me so she didn't figure out who I really was. But we only saw each other in person a handful of times last year, most of which were in a dark club, and when we spoke, I either wore my mask with the built-in modulator, or I masked my voice. I even carry myself differently on campus, playing the role of the buttoned-up, scholarly English professor.

I'm aware that I'm known for having difficult classes, of being tough yet fair. But nothing worth doing in life is easy, so I push my students to be the best version of themselves they can be. Just like I push my subs to know their limits.

Not everyone loves being challenged, so my reputation of being a hard-ass is earned, but despite my demeanor, my student evaluations have always been favorable.

I'm not sure what her summer plans are. It's killing me that I can't check in on her, but I decided to end this, and I made a rule that I'm not going to ask Alyx about her. I'm determined not to break that one like I have so many of the others.

This is going to be a long summer.

Emma

This summer is about trying new things, and I'm determined to move on from the events of last school year.

When I walk into the cozy bookshop, I'm in awe of the atmosphere and selection. There's not a single bit of wall that isn't covered in shelving filled with thousands of brightly colored spines and covers, and little tables dot the open space with books propped on stands and little signs denoting the tropes and blurbs. It's a book lover's dream.

Becka's been begging me to come to book club all summer, and I finally had time between summer classes to make an appearance. The shop is so cute, and I can't believe I've never been here before.

"Emma!" Becka squeals as she waves her hand wildly, motioning me over. When I reach her, she pulls me into a hug. "I'm so glad you came."

"Me too. Luckily my course load is light this summer, and I've already read this book, so it worked out." I offer her a small smile.

"Oh, you don't really have to read the book. I mean, we do actually talk about the books, but no one's gonna care if you haven't read or finished it."

I nod as she's speaking when a book behind her catches my eye. "Is that a shirtless hockey player?" I ask in astonishment.

She looks over her shoulder and laughs. "*Sleet Kitten*, that's a good one."

"You've read it?"

"I have. This is a whole wall of hockey romances." She waves her arms like she's a model on a game show.

I laugh incredulously. "Wait, this is a thing?"

"It's one of the largest subgenres of romance, certainly the largest of the sports romances. It's Amanda's favorite, hockey romance. She's the store owner, have you met her?"

I shake my head as Becka continues talking excitedly.

"She's great, you'll love her. And I love how she's organized the store. This section here has all the sports romances, but this wall is all hockey, and she has them organized from light at the top down to dark at the bottom."

"Wait, there's dark romance all about hockey?"

"Girl, those are some of my favorites. S. Massery writes some great dark stalker-y hockey romances. Start with *Brutal Obsession*." She points to a book with a hot guy on the cover. "You should also check out S.J. Sylvis and C.R. Jane. Oh, and Rina Kent has a series too."

"I had no idea this was a thing." I run my fingers along the spines as she talks. "Are there other dark books you would recommend? Like maybe some that involve BDSM?" I ask, nervously.

"I love BDSM romance. There's this series that I love by Dakota Willink. The first book is called *Heart of Stone*, and it's billionaire, sex club, with BDSM. And the FMC is a virgin."

"That sounds..." Oddly familiar. I'm unsure how to finish my thought worried that Becka will realize how on the nose that recommendation is, but luckily, she keeps going, mentioning more books as she flits between shelves motioning for me to follow.

"What else do you like to read? I'm sure I could recommend dozens of books in that subgenre." She smiles eagerly.

"Is it weird that we're talking about this? I mean, I work for you." I shift on my feet as I look around the store noticing a woman moving chairs into a circle.

"Emma, you watch my daughter so I can fuck my husband. This is totally fine." She flicks her wrist in a circle, and I laugh, recalling our first conversation when she shared way too much about her sexual rut she and how she needed time away to reconnect with her husband. "Reading romance helped save my marriage. It introduced us to new kinks, new positions, new ways to role-play. I will never shy away from singing its praises. But if it makes you uncomfortable, we don't have to talk about it."

"It's not that," I say nervously. "I'm just not as experienced in all this."

"Reading romance?" I shake my head vigorously. "Oh. *Oh!* Gotcha. Are we talking the *virgin* trope?"

I nervously look at her.

She smiles, placing a hand on my arm. "It's okay. I've got you. Your secret's safe with me. And I can totally give you some recs for that trope if you're interested."

"That would be… great. I really hope this doesn't make things weird between us."

"Girl, everyone has sex. Oof. Insert foot in mouth. Maybe not everyone, but you know what I mean. It's a normal part of life if you choose to do it. I'm definitely not judging you for your choices, and if you ever need someone to talk to about this stuff, I've always wanted a little sister. I'm the youngest, and let's just say my older sister isn't the best."

"Thanks."

She gestures to the circle of chairs, and we grab our spots as others fill in. "So how are summer classes going?"

"Good. Luckily all my professors are laid-back. Nothing like that A-hole I dealt with last year."

"Ooh, tell me more about that. I feel like you're just giving me breadcrumbs." There's a mischievous twinkle in her eyes.

"Like Hansel and Gretel?" I laugh at her turn of phrase.

"Exactly! I had to explain it to Bridget a couple times before she picked up what I was putting down. That one does not like puzzles."

"I could see that. She seems very straightforward."

"Oh, she is. But before she met your brother, she used to

regale me with tales of all her hookups. We'd meet for coffee, and she'd fill me in on all her wild nights."

"If any of them involve my brother, you can skip ahead."

She lets out a full-body laugh. "No worries, not going to share about that. Anyway, she'd give me highlights without filling in all the details. 'He was tall, average dick, and had two moves, three out of ten.'" She does a spot-on impression of my brother's girlfriend. "I was like, 'girl, I'm an old married woman who isn't getting enough action and is living vicariously through you, Imma need more than that!'"

"Seems on brand for her. Straight to the point."

"Straight to the dick!" Becka throws her head back in laughter, and I can't help but join her. "So tell me all about the A-hole. Wait, that sounds dirtier than I meant it."

"Ugh, I'm so glad I'm done with his classes. He's just so frustrating. Always pushing me. Calling on me more than anyone else in class and asking me really difficult questions, so I either look like a total know-it-all or an idiot if I don't know the answer. And one time someone teased me for getting his obscure question right, and he got all alpha and threw the guy out of class."

Becka raises an eyebrow.

I shake my head. "Nope. I know what that face is, and I can tell you with certainty that he did not like me. He was hot and cold and wildly inconsistent. One minute he was picking apart my papers with ridiculous precision, and the following semester he pushed me so hard emotionally in a scene that I nearly had a panic attack in class, recovering a traumatic memory I'd buried from my childhood. And shortly after that, the guy I'd been seeing broke up with me and I cried to Bridget about it and she introduced us and here we are."

"That rabbit trail was incredible. I was totally with you for the whole ride."

I laugh at the way she views my verbal diarrhea. There's something about her that feels safe yet wild, like a fun aunt who sneaks you drinks but then holds your hair back when you get sick later.

"What did this hot-and-cold professor look like? I bet he wasn't bad on the eyes." She wiggles her eyebrows rapidly.

I let out a deep breath, deciding that if I'm going to share all this with anyone, Becka feels like the best person to do so with. "Ugh, he's probably the most attractive man I've ever seen. Tall, at least six feet. Dark brown hair, and facial hair he can't decide if he wants to grow into a full beard or shave every day, so it looks like a permanent scruff I want to run my fingers through. His shoulders are broad, but the way his waist tapers, you just know he has those V lines. He's always in these perfect tailored suits that hug his behind. And the way he carries himself? He's older, and I imagine he knows exactly what he's doing in the bedroom which is really appealing because I have no experience there."

"Ooh, I love a tall, dark, and scruffy man so much I married one." She has a dreamy look on her face.

"Yeah, but then he opens his stupidly attractive mouth and ruins everything. That's why I call him Professor A-hole."

Becka laughs. "To his face?"

"Oh, biscuits, no!"

Amanda calls the book club to order, and we spend the next hour talking about a small-town baseball romance and baseball pants. The group is fun and feral, and I love their energy. It's a welcome distraction from the heartache I feel about Daddy Dom.

CHAPTER 20
EMMA
JUNIOR YEAR

After a summer full of babysitting, I'm excited to start the new school year, even though I'm going to miss spending time with Becka's little girl Hallie. She's the sweetest, but has a lot of energy, just like my younger sisters Erin and Evie.

I also got to spend a lot of time with my sister Lizzy and was able to play some improv games with her. It reinvigorated me, reassuring me that the path I'm on in my educational journey is the right one. And my father took the news of my change in majors surprisingly well; it doesn't hurt that I told him the day after he found out that my sister Ella was sexually active. He was less concerned about my future in that moment.

My class load this year is packed full of theatre classes, and I'm really starting to enjoy this little community on campus. They're welcoming and accepting in a way I've yet to experience at this school. The reason I chose theatre and not social work as my field of study was because the majority of the girls in social work aren't actually interested in going into that field. I found out after my freshman year that majoring in anything under the health science umbrella was code for looking for a husband. These women don't want a job after graduation; the building is next to the business school, and they're actually looking for their MRS degree.

And the business guys are no better, looking for their perfect version of a Stepford wife while they network and make connections as future CEOs. And anyone that doesn't fit their mold is labeled a black sheep, like us theatre kids.

I'm not even thinking about marriage at this point, and I have other goals for myself. I want to help people like Lizzy find a place they belong and can thrive.

Growing up with a special needs sister, I'm used to being treated like an outsider. Kids didn't want to play with us at the park. People would stare at us at the grocery store, especially when we forgot Lizzy's headphones and the noises overwhelmed her. But the worst was when we took Lizzy to a camp she'd been excited about. It was just a regular summer camp, and my mom made sure they could accommodate Lizzy's needs when she signed her up. They assured her they could. But they couldn't, or didn't, I'm not really sure.

When we visited her on family day, I got so mad at how she was being treated. After I overheard a counselor talking badly about her, I got in her face, yelling and shouting, and I let fly a curse word—and not just any curse, the worst freaking one. Lizzy had a huge meltdown because of it.

At first, I thought all the yelling and noise had upset her auditory processing issues. I asked her a series of yes or no questions, trying to figure out what was wrong. When I asked her if my cursing upset her, she nodded emphatically. Since then, I've gotten creative with the way I swear, avoiding words that bother her, even when she's not around.

After that, I wanted to find other places that would offer Lizzy similar experiences while also meeting her needs. We found Camp New Hope, and Lizzy's been going ever since. She found a community that supports her, and I'm finally starting to feel like I've found mine on campus.

I let a few new friends talk me into going to a frat party,

and we agreed to meet in the quad and walk over together. Rylee and Megan have been very sweet, and even though I'm not that enthused about the party, I'm excited to spend time with them.

"The guys in this frat are so hot." Rylee links her arm in mine during the short walk across campus.

"I heard they throw the best parties," Megan adds.

"I thought it was a dry campus, being that it's a Christian school and all?" I ask, confused.

"Frat Row isn't actually on campus, so that's how they get around the university rules. Back in the fifties, a bunch of fraternities bought up houses that backed up to the college. Eventually they paved footpaths to connect them to campus, but their addresses technically make them off-campus," Rylee explains.

"I've never been to a frat party," I admit.

"Girl, seriously? You're a junior. How have you never been to a frat party?" Megan asks.

"I dunno," I say, suddenly self-conscious. Actually, I do know. I spent most of my freshman year with my nose in a book, and my sophomore year trying to get a certain dom to pay more attention to me, and a certain professor to pay less.

"Well, we got you," Megan says. "If you feel uncomfortable, just scratch your nose and we'll leave. Okay?"

"Okay." I exhale. I've opened up to them about some of my issues with touch, and Megan suggested we come up with a code to communicate with each other in situations like these. It suddenly reminds me of having a safe word with Daddy Dom.

Nope. Not going to think about him and mess up my mascara. I've been doing so well. Frick.

Rylee must sense the change in me, and she stops walking. "Emma, what's wrong?"

I look up at the sky, blinking rapidly, hoping the cool fall air will stop the tears threatening to spill out of my eyes.

"Sorry, something just reminded me of someone and—" I cut myself off from saying more, realizing I haven't told them anything about Daddy Dom.

"Do you need a minute?" Megan places a hand on my shoulder, and I glance at it. "Sorry, is this okay?" She pulls back.

"It's fine. The touch thing is just with men. I think? Actually, I'm not sure. It could be anyone trying to get in my pants." I'm rambling, my nerves getting the better of me.

"You're hot, but you're not my type, so I'm not trying to get all up in that." Megan waves a hand in front of my crotch.

We burst into laughter.

"Thanks, I needed that," I swipe a finger under my eye.

"Anytime. Comedic relief is my specialty." Megan laughs.

Rylee turns to me, drawing my focus. "We don't have to go to this party if you don't want to."

"I want to," I assure her. "I want to have normal college experiences. Go to parties, have a drink, all that. I don't want this hang up preventing me from living my life."

"Maybe it's like Cinderella!" Megan squeals. "You have to try on a bunch of shoes until you find the one that fits. You just have to let a bunch of guys touch you till you find the one that doesn't make you want to throat-punch someone."

"Cinderella didn't try on a bunch of shoes, just the one. The prince had to go through a bunch of women before he found her. Totally not the same," Rylee says.

"Close enough," Megan chirps.

"Also, you do realize that in this scenario you're suggesting our friend let a bunch of randos touch her?" Rylee adds.

"Metaphorically, not literally." Megan groans.

"Do we need to go over the definition of those words again?"

Their banter always makes me laugh, and I'm thankful for the distraction. "I want to go, and I'm fine. I'll scratch my nose if I get uncomfortable, but I'm not trying on any shoes tonight."

We resume our walk to the frat house, but as soon as we are inside, I get a bad feeling. The vibes are off, but I shove it aside not wanting to ruin the night for my friends. I just made this big speech, and I want to show them that I can do this. I can handle hard situations.

I make my way to the kitchen to grab us drinks, and when I return to the living room, I can't find my friends among the crowd. They were just here. I continue moving through the house on my search. They wouldn't just abandon me, but there are more people here than I thought there'd be, and my anxiety is making it feel like the walls are closing in on me.

The door to the deck is propped open, and I step outside, my hands full with our drinks. I hear voices below, so I walk down the steps to the patio but it's empty.

"Is this the infamous Emma?" a voice behind me asks.

When I whip around, I'm face-to-face with the guy that knocked me down when I was opening the door to Professor A-hole's classroom last year.

"How do you know my name?" I ask nervously.

"Oh, you're famous around here." He circles me like a shark about to devour its prey.

Then he's behind me, close to my ear, his hot breath on my neck as he speaks. A chill runs down my spine.

"Wanna go upstairs? I'll make it really good for you. I don't even care if you bleed on my sheets." He snakes a hand around my waist, covering my stomach as he pulls me against him. Bile rises in my gut, and my heart rate increases when I feel his erection press against me. I need to get out of here. My elbow connects with his gut as I throw the drinks behind me and run.

"Come back here, you little bitch."

I take off around the corner of the house, running as fast as

I can to get away from him. There's shouting behind me, but I ignore it, squeezing my fingers into my palm, balling them into a fist as I pump my arms and legs harder, scaling the slight incline to make it around the house.

"Hey! Whoa, man, chill the fuck out, it's not what it—" His voice is cut off, and I run faster, taking a shortcut to the path back to student apartments.

I burst into my front door, slam it behind me, and lean against it. I'm out of breath and panting as I pull out my phone. The adrenaline coursing through me makes it difficult to type, and I force myself to take several deep breaths to still my shaking hands.

> MEGAN
>
> Where are you?
>
> RYLEE
>
> Where did you go?
>
> Are you okay?
>
> MEGAN
>
> OMG someone just said they saw you take off running. What happened?
>
> Can you guys come to my apartment? I had to get out of there.

Ten minutes later, Megan and Rylee are on my couch and I'm filling them in on what happened at the party.

Rylee sits next to me, concern etched in the lines of her face. "Megan and I left you alone for two minutes while you got drinks. It's not like we abandoned you, this is crazy. We always stick together. I feel like shit about it."

"There were way too many people in that house," Megan says.

"It's not your fault." I pause, taking a deep breath. "This is just my luck anyway. But now I know frat parties aren't for me."

"Yeah, you definitely weren't going to find your Prince Charming at that one, Cinderella," Megan quips.

Rylee places a hand on mine, drawing my attention back to her. "So after that guy came up on you and you took off, what happened?"

"I came back here. I don't know what happened to him."

"Well, I hope he gets what's coming to him," Megan says.

———

John

It's late, and I should've gone home hours ago, but grading papers is a welcome distraction. None of this year's students are as promising as a certain dirty blonde that I still can't seem to rid from my thoughts. As I scroll through essays on my computer, my frustration grows. It's getting harder to find anyone not using AI to write their work for them. Doesn't anyone think for themselves anymore?

A noise from the quad distracts me, and my head swings in that direction where I see a small group of female students congregating right outside my window. They look like they're dressed to attend a party, and I wonder which frat house they're headed to when I spot Emma. Blood rushes to every part of my body, my ears, my face, and my dick. My heart beats loudly as I try to process the flood of emotions hitting me. Anger, longing, and sorrow overwhelm me as I push away from my desk.

Where the fuck is my sub going dressed like that?

Except she's not mine. I was the one who ended things, pushed her away. I need to let her go. It was what was best for both of us. I have to be in control of this situation. I'm not in a place to get involved with anyone, even if I want her more than I've ever wanted anything in my entire life.

I should just stay focused on my work, but when I heard her laugh and saw her in that tight little dress from my office window, I knew I was fucked. There's no way I can concentrate when she looks like that. My siren is calling to me, and she doesn't even know it.

Minutes later, I'm out of my office and following them across campus. My earlier suspicions are confirmed when I watch them walk into the frat house.

It's killing me not knowing what's going on inside of that house. What is she doing here anyway? Since when are frat parties her scene?

Following along the tree line at the edge of the property, I cling to the shadows like a creep. Even though it's not nearly cold enough yet, I grabbed a hoodie on my way out of my office, and I tighten it around my face, praying no one sees or recognizes me. What the fuck am I doing? So I'm not only willing to break rules for her, but I'm also willing to break the law too?

Just when my common sense returns and I'm ready to leave, I hear voices on the patio and see her, watching as some asshole approaches her from behind. She elbows him, throwing her cups in the process.

When he chases her, I lose my shit and go after him, catching up near the side of the house. I drag him into the woods, grabbing him from behind so he can't see my face while he prattles on. My arms lock around his neck, cutting off his words.

"What did you do to her?" I growl close to his ear, my teeth grinding in anger.

"Nothing, man, we were just having a little fun. She was into it." He desperately claws at my arms.

"I can assure you she was not, you pathetic fuck."

I release his neck and punch him in the side. He doubles over in pain as he falls to the ground. I kick the spot I just punched, and he curls into himself. Stepping back so he doesn't see my face, I take off in the direction she went, keeping to the woods so I don't draw attention. When I see her enter her apartment, I breathe a sigh of relief.

I really am living up to her old nickname for me. Slinking through the darkness like a vigilante to slay her demons. What the fuck is wrong with me?

CHAPTER 21
EMMA

I try to focus on the positive, but lately my mind is consumed with the nightmares that have started up again —most likely because of that jerk at the frat party—and with Daddy Dom and wondering what he's up to now.

I'm still getting used to my new living situation. Since the dorms are for freshmen and sophomores, my options were limited, and I ended up in student apartments on the outskirts of campus. Because of the price of rent, living off campus wasn't feasible.

Most of my theatre friends are a year or two below me, like Megan and Rylee, so I went in blind with a roommate. The girl I live with is nice but keeps to herself and is barely around, so I'm mostly on my own again.

Our apartment is small, just a living room, with a small kitchen off to the side, a shared bathroom and two bedrooms. I've got the slightly larger of the two rooms on the back side of the apartment.

It wouldn't be so bad, but I was really hoping for some companionship, especially after my breakup.

Is it a breakup? We weren't really together, and I don't even know his name or what he looks like.

It's a Sunday night, and I'm studying in the living room when I think I hear a faint knock at the door. From my spot on the couch, I peer through the window, and when I don't see any movement, I drop my head, burying it back in my book.

The next morning, as I leave for class, something flutters when I open the door. I shove the paper into my bag as I rush across campus.

Dropping my bag beside me, I plop into the chair, grateful I made it before class starts. Jeremy takes the seat next to me.

"What's this?" he asks, leaning over and grabbing the flyer. "*I can listen no longer in silence. I must speak to you…*"

My head swivels in his direction as my brows furrow. When I notice the piece of paper in his hands, I grow more confused. "What are you reading? Is that Jane Austen?"

"I dunno, it was in your bag." He shrugs, handing it to me.

It's written in what appears to be the same handwriting as the first letter, but it's hard to tell without looking at them side by side. My eyes scan the page, reading quickly.

> *My love,*
>
> *I can listen no longer in silence. I must speak to you by such means as are within my reach. You pierce my soul. I am half agony, half hope. Tell me not that I am too late, that such precious feelings are gone for ever… I have loved none but you.*
>
> *Stay strong, my love.*
>
> *Yours*

"I didn't know you were dating anyone." I glance at his face, but there's no hint of emotion there. Am I disappointed he's not hurt at the thought of me dating?

"I'm not," I reply in a tone matching his.

My leg bounces in my seat for the rest of class. I can't seem to allay this feeling in my gut. Is Daddy Dom sending me these letters? Why would he do that? It doesn't make sense for him to end things only to keep me on the hook with sporadic love notes.

That, and he's never admitted he loves me, so why would he do it in an anonymous correspondence? But if it's not him, who could be sending them? I would suspect it's Alyx or Ella pulling a prank on me, but they're too far away and both would enjoy the *gotcha* moment too much to leave a letter and run without seeing my reaction. Plus, they both know how torn up I've been about Daddy Dom and wouldn't mess with me about this.

"I emailed you my notes." Jeremy's voice pulls me out of my spiral as I close my laptop.

"Huh?"

"You're normally a typing machine in class, and I didn't see you touch your computer or pick up your pen once. Figured you could use mine in case you want to review them."

"Thanks. My mind is kind of elsewhere."

"Because of the note?" He brushes his floppy blond hair out of his face.

"Yeah."

"So you're not dating anyone?" There's a hint of hope in his voice.

"No. I'm focusing on school right now." I cringe, hoping he won't see through my excuse, especially since he noticed my lack of focus today. "Well, normally I would be, but now I'm playing Sherlock Holmes in my brain."

"Well, I hope you and the mystery gang get to the bottom of it," he says with a boyish smile.

"I don't think Scooby Doo is going to help me." I laugh, thankful for the moment of levity.

A month goes by without another letter.

Rylee and I are walking into the theatre on our way to class. "Hey, Ems, I think that says your name." She points to the envelope on the call board.

I stare at it confused at first. People sometimes leave messages on the board for others, but it's usually about an audition, casting, or job. Rylee pulls out the pin holding the note and hands it to me.

"Watch this." She wiggles her eyebrows as she pinches the pin between two fingers and flicks her wrist, firing it straight into the cork in the most satisfying way.

"I'm starting to think you're part ninja," I tease.

"Brothers. But I came away with cool party tricks." She smirks and I laugh in response, thinking about the torture they must have put her through growing up.

I hold the letter in my hands, debating whether to open it in front of her. Only Alyx and Ella know about the letters, and I have no idea what excuse I'll give her if she asks who it's from.

"Uh, ya gonna open it?"

"Nah, I'm sure it's just about a summer internship I applied for," I lie, stuffing it into my backpack.

When I get back to my apartment, several hours later, the letter burning a hole in my metaphorical pocket the whole time, I pull out my phone and FaceTime Ella.

"Em!" she chirps. "Wait, you're not spelling the alphabet. Shit. What's wrong?"

It's a blessing and a curse, her ability to read me so well. I hold the letter so she can see.

"Shit, another one?"

I nod solemnly. "Can I add Alyx? I'd rather go through this once than repeating the story back for him too."

"Fine, call Mr. Fuck-around-and-find-out." I shoot her a warning look, and she holds her hands up in defense. "I'll be good, I swear. I know this is important."

Once I add Alyx to the call and fill him in, I pull out the letter and read it for them.

My love,

"He's more myself than I am. Whatever our souls are made of, his and mine are the same."

Whenever I read this quote, I am reminded of you and the soul that we share. Stay strong my love, we will be joined soon. I'm in awe of you and am happy to be your pillar of strength.

Yours

"I'll show you a pillar of strength," Alyx quips. I laugh. Alyx is always able to bring humor to the seriousness of the moment.

I catch Ella trying to hide her smirk as she rolls her eyes. "Ever the child. Can't you take anything seriously?"

"Who do you think it's from?" Alyx asks, ignoring her jab.

"I have no idea. They're not always addressed the same way, and only the first one was signed with a J. Though, I'm not convinced it was a J, it was kind of written all loopy and swirly."

Alyx sits back, and I can tell he's thinking through this like it's a riddle he wants to solve.

"Where even are you right now? You look like you're in a black hole. Is that a filter?" Ella's head tilts closer to the screen.

"Somewhere I will never see you grace the doors of." Alyx's jaw clenches as if the thought of my sister at Pulse makes him angry.

Ella rolls her eyes. "Well that's not cryptic as hell."

Since I recognize his background, I keep my mouth shut, looking off screen to distract myself.

"Em, you're doing that thing with your eyes when you know something, but you don't want to tell me. What do you know?"

"I don't know anything," I lie, then quickly change the topic. "And I have no idea who could be sending these, but it's starting to make me really flippin' uncomfortable."

Ella grunts, realizing we're not going to humor her.

"Do you know anyone with a J name?" Alyx asks.

"There's this guy Jeremy in the theatre department, but I really doubt it could be him."

"What's Professor A-hole's name?" Ella asks.

"Um, I dunno… Wait, I might still have a syllabus from his class." I shuffle through a notebook until I find it. "John."

"Oh my God! What if it's your asshole professor?"

I burst out in laughter. "That's a good one."

She blinks back at me on the screen.

"Wait, you were serious?"

"I mean, why couldn't it be?"

"Has he given you any indication that he's into you?" Alyx asks.

"Absolutely not. That man cannot stand me. And I haven't seen him since last spring. Besides, he has a stick so far up his hiney, even if he did like me like that, I could never see him revealing it like this. And before you ask, I don't think it's Daddy Dom either. He's still ghosting me since he ended things, and he lives in the city. There's no way he'd come out here to leave me letters if he won't even return my text."

Alyx cocks an eyebrow. "What if he had someone on campus doing it for him?"

"Or what if it's multiple people?" Ella adds.

"Okay, well, you're both no help."

"What about that guy from high school? Doesn't he go to Faith Union with you?" My sister's question causes a lead weight to sink in my gut. "Didn't you say he cornered you on campus last year?"

"The fuck?" Alyx snaps. "Why didn't I know about this?"

"Because sister bestie trumps fuckboy bestie."

"Can you not word it that way and make it sound like I'm her fuckboy?"

"Gross," I add.

"Agreed," Alyx says.

"Respectfully," Alyx and I say in unison and then laugh. We spend another hour coming up with theories and get no closer to solving the mystery, but I laugh more than I have in months.

CHAPTER 22
EMMA

It's the beginning of the spring semester, and that means auditions for *Twelfth Night*. If I'm going to do a play, it might as well be Shakespeare since I possess zero musical abilities. I think back to my time last year with Professor A-hole and shudder. At least I don't have to see his stupid perfectly chiseled jawline that's always covered with the lightest dusting of stubble.

I'm crossing the campus, bundled up in all my winter clothes. Even though it's only six in the evening, the sky is dark, and the air is bitter cold. After stomping my boots on the mat, I pull open the theatre door and take a place near the back row as I remove my hat and scarf, stuffing it in my bag.

I spot Rylee and Megan, waving as I watch them make their way toward me when a voice from behind startles me.

"Welcome to auditions for *Twelfth Night*. My name is Professor Ali, and I will be stepping in as the faculty advisor for Dr. Judy who is on sabbatical this semester." He points to the student at the front of the house. "And sitting down there in the front row is Mackenzie, your student director. We'll be getting started shortly."

"You've got to be kidding me," I grumble out of the corner

of my mouth as my friends sit next to me. I thought I was done dealing with this infuriating man.

"What was that, Miss Black?" he asks, zeroing in on me.

I silently curse the theatre and its stupid perfect acoustics. "Nothing, Professor."

He slowly crosses the aisle and plants a hand on either side of my chair, looming behind me, and I flinch at his nearness.

"I thought we were past that." He hovers close to my ear, but not close enough to draw suspicions. My entire body comes alive at his proximity, and the hair on my arms stands on end under my sweater.

"Past what?" I turn my head slightly and we lock eyes.

There's a small crease between his eyebrows, and he looks almost…hurt? He schools his expression quickly, reading the confusion on my face as he clears his throat. "Past this animosity. Aren't you tired of the endless bickering between us? We could give Benedick and Beatrice a run for their money."

It takes everything in me to not let my jaw drop to the floor. Benedick and Beatrice bicker because neither will admit their feelings for each other. Is this his way of saying he has feelings for me?

"'Tis a pity. I was looking forward to your witty comeback. Alas, you still prove disappointing."

My blood boils, and I open and shut my mouth like a fish when it hits me. "'A bird of my tongue is better than a beast of yours.'"

"'I would my horse had the speed of your tongue.'" He winks. "Alright, everyone, let's get started. Emma here has volunteered to go first," he announces as he sets a hand on my shoulder.

I don't flinch.

The nerve of this man. I want to take comfort in the fact that Daddy Dom's lessons were actually helping me. That someone other than he or a family member has touched me, and I didn't freak out. But I shrug off his hand before I can reflect too deeply on its meaning and make my way to the stage.

I should've known he'd be involved with this production, since he's the only Shakespeare professor on campus, but I was naively optimistic when I didn't see his name on any of the audition flyers.

With my back to the audience, I draw in a deep breath and release it slowly, willing my nerves to calm. I know most of the people in this theatre. The house is full of friends and familiar faces, the only unwelcome one is his.

I've performed in plays in high school, and while becoming an actor isn't my goal, I'm incapable of doing things halfway. It's all or nothing. When I turn, ready to start my monologue, I'm filled with determination. It doesn't matter if I get the role of Viola or not, but I will not let him be right about me.

———————

John

She's ravishing as she stands center stage, the light brown strands of her hair looking almost golden in the spotlight. Her chest rises and falls with each breath, and I can't help but stare at her perfect breasts hoping to catch a glimpse of a piercing, but her sweater makes it impossible.

I had every intention of walking away. I haven't seen her on campus or in the club in months, aside from that incident at the beginning of the school year. But seeing her right now has me questioning that decision. Her plump lips part, and as soon as she speaks, I know I'm fucked.

"I left no ring with her: what means this lady?"

The theatre is silent as everyone watches with rapt fascination. She commands the stage and my attention as she continues her monologue.

A smirk tugs at my lips as I watch her become Cesario and Viola. Her delivery is flawless, making it evident that she understands each nuance, the duality of a woman playing two parts. She encapsulates Viola's wit and intelligence.

"Disguise, I see, thou art a wickedness,
Wherein the pregnant enemy does much.
How easy is it for the proper-false
In women's waxen hearts to set their forms!"

Her direct eye contact on that last line has my heart rate picking up. Does she know who I really am? Does she know I'm Daddy Dom? She can't. She'd say something if she did.

I miss the rest of her monologue, too consumed in my thoughts. The audience claps when she finishes. I make an effort to appear interested in the next few auditions, but no one captures my attention like Emma. My body is keenly aware of her at all times, and I can feel her eyes on me.

Mackenzie slides a piece of paper with her casting notes on it, and I nod my approval, gesturing for her to proceed. I stand and close my notebook, clutching it against my chest as I turn to the students and lean back against the seat behind me.

I shouldn't revel in her gaze, but fuck do I want to. No, I want her to look at me the way she looks at Daddy Dom. With adoration and trust. With so much fucking longing.

As Mackenzie explains the next steps to everyone, I quickly glance at Emma and grin when I catch her looking at me with a scowl on her face. It shouldn't give me as much joy as it does.

Once the theatre is empty, I head backstage to turn off the stage lights, leaving a few work lamps on in the wings. My phone buzzes in my pocket when I push through the doors of the building, the bitter air assaulting my senses.

MARY

Can you spend the night over here tonight?

I wasn't planning on coming into the city. I have classes tomorrow.

Sam is gone and I'm lonely.

I let out a deep sigh, knowing it's going to be a long morning because I can't refuse a friend in need.

I'll be there.

Shoving my phone in my pocket, I make my way to the parking lot when I hear a familiar voice.

"Trent, stop."

"C'mon, just one date. I heard you're into all kinds of shit now."

I pick up my pace, and round the corner. Some pathetic fuck has Emma pinned against the side of a truck. It takes everything in me to restrain myself.

"Stop," she pleads as he moves in close to the side of her face.

What the fuck?

I'm on him in seconds, yanking him off her and pinning his back against the truck, my forearm holding his throat in place. "She said stop, and when a woman says no, it means no." Her eyes are on me as I work to calm my breathing. "Now get the fuck out of here and stay the fuck away from her," I growl as I release him. He scampers away, slipping on a patch of ice in the parking lot before he rights himself and retreats without looking back.

When I look over, her eyes are glassy like she's looking through me. It reminds me of that time after our first session when she cowered from me in the hallway. She slides down the truck, but I grab her biceps before she can hit the ground. I pull her up, shifting my hold to her elbows as she leans back against the truck.

"Are you okay?"

She nods slightly, and I know she's lying. "Do you have

someone I can call for you?" I ask, knowing I can't outright offer to call Alyx, or it'd blow my cover.

"The person I need hasn't spoken to me in months," she admits quietly, and a piece of my heart cracks. "I need him."

"How do I contact him for you?" I ask, even though it kills me. I wish I could be that person for her. I wish we could be out in the open, but it's not just my job keeping us apart. It's a rule I cannot break, not right now, and even if I did, I can't afford the scrutiny this religious school would unleash.

"I don't think he wants to hear from me." She looks down at her boots.

I crook a finger under her chin and tilt her face up to mine. "I doubt that's true."

What the fuck am I doing? This is reckless. It's not breaking a rule, but it's a gray area, murky at best.

She pulls out her phone, and I back away, dropping her chin as I look around to make sure we're alone. Using her teeth, she removes her glove, thumb flying over the screen.

"Are you texting him?"

My phone buzzes in my pocket, and I take another step back, clearing my throat, hoping she didn't hear it.

"He probably won't answer."

Well, fuck. I can't refuse her now even if I wanted to. The white knight in me won't allow it.

"Maybe he'll surprise you. Can I give you a ride? Are you in a dorm or off campus?" I know exactly where she lives, but she doesn't know that.

The look on her face is adorable: confusion mixed with a slight smirk. I've seen the way she checked me out all last year. I know she thinks I'm attractive, but what delights me most is that I don't see a hint of distrust, and given her history with men, that's huge.

"I'm in the student apartments behind the football field."

"That's a long walk. Why don't I drive you over there?" I turn to my car, knowing she'll follow.

"Okay." She sighs. I hear the snow crunch under her boots behind me.

I open the passenger door for her, and once she's in, I lean over her to buckle her in. "Sorry, it sticks, let me help." I'm way too close to the heat of her body as the blood in my veins starts to rush to my dick. Once I get her buckled, I move around to my side.

I pull up to student apartments, and she points out her building. Once she disappears into her apartment, I slip my phone out of my pocket. Her text nearly does me in.

Please, sir.

CHAPTER 23
EMMA

That night I have two nightmares. The first time I wake up screaming, I call Ella to calm me down. She soothes me back to sleep, telling me stories about her current flavor-of-the-month boyfriend. Since they change so often now, I have a hard time learning their names. I don't remember hanging up with her, so when I wake up screaming again, I end up waking her too.

She calms me down a second time, but I'm restless, so once we hang up I text Daddy Dom.

> Sorry it's late.

> Or early? Idk

> Had two nightmares tonight and I can't get back to sleep.

I'm here, pet.

His reply nearly knocks the breath out of me. It's been eight months since we've had any contact, and I honestly didn't expect him to respond. Before I can think how to reply, my screen lights up with an incoming call. I nearly drop the phone as I fumble to answer it with a breathy "Hello?"

"Emma," he rasps.

A tear slips down my cheek. "I'm broken. I don't know what's wrong with me. I'm sorry to bother you," I cry. I have no self-control when it comes to this man, but the organ in my chest doesn't seem to care.

"You're not bothering me, and you're not broken. You're the strongest fucking person I know. You went through a lot of trauma at a young age, and you've come out of it a tower of strength. I'm in awe of you."

I don't know how to respond to that because while I know he means every word, it doesn't feel true. Sure, some awful stuff happened to me and my mom when I was little, but until Professor A-hole pushed me to dig into my emotions, I couldn't even remember what had happened. And once I did, the nightmares slowly receded. So why have they started up again now? I know my therapist would remind me that healing isn't linear and that it's my brain protecting me from perceived threats. But it stinks when I feel like I've done everything right, followed my therapist's suggestions, only to fall back into the same trauma-fueled dreams.

"But you don't want to be with me."

The words hang between us. His breathing is soft as a tear slips down my cheek.

"I wish I could hold you while you slept so I could protect you," he says, surprising me.

"I wish you were here," I admit softly as my eyelids get heavy. "But at least I have your letter."

"Em?" There's a hint of concern in his voice.

Even though I should feel comforted that he called, that he showered me with praise, my heart hurts. His words are empty and he won't act on them. I hit the end call button before I can second-guess my decision.

———————

"What part do you think you got?" Rylee asks me at breakfast the next day.

Megan stomps over to us, plops into a chair, and drops her head on the table. "Coffee. Need coffee."

I hand her the to-go cup I grabbed for her. "Long night?"

"I wish I could regale you with an epic tale of debauchery, but I stayed up way too late writing a paper."

"Been there," Rylee and I say in unison.

"Emma, your audition was incredible, I'd be shocked if you don't get Viola."

"Agreed." Megan's head is still face down on the table as she gives us a thumbs-up.

"Are you sure you don't want to do more acting? You're really good at it."

I think about her words for a minute. I'm good at acting because I'm good at masking. No one would ever know what I'm going through by just looking at me.

I play a million different parts, but none of them feel like me. When I'm home, I assume the role of the dutiful eldest daughter, doing everything that's expected of me before I'm even asked. At school, I become the model student, turning into this people-pleasing teacher's pet trying to earn the respect of my professors and peers. Even though Ella is my best friend, school has been so hectic I don't get to see her anymore. And despite the fact that I'm doing all of this for Lizzy, to help others like her, I haven't spent much time with her outside of school breaks. Alyx has also been oddly silent since the holidays, and I'm afraid I've made things awkward for him at the club with Daddy Dom.

The last time I felt strong was when I was at Pulse at the mercy of Daddy Dom. But even he doesn't want to have anything to do with me. He's the only person that has seen the real me, the version I water down for others and dole out in small doses, making myself palatable. Not everyone understands me and my hang-ups, but he did. He embraced them, called them strength instead of the weakness they feel like.

I'm failing everyone, and the only men that show any interest in me are creeps. Maybe this is what I deserve. I'm too broken for anything good, so I just smile and take whatever crap life hands me. Of course I'm good at acting. I do it in every area of my life.

"Earth to Emma!" Rylee calls.

"No shouty-shouty," Megan groans.

I give them an awkward smile, letting them think I just can't take a compliment.

"Oh, there's Jeremy." Rylee nods to a spot across the caf. "He's really sweet, like you can tell he's one of the good ones."

Megan's head pops up as she nods her agreement. "He's not bad to look at either. He's got that skinny-hot-nerd-turned-surfer vibe."

I laugh. "That's oddly specific."

"And you know what they say about skinny guys. They have the biggest dic—"

"Diction!" I squeak as Jeremy approaches our table. "Diction is important, and I really should work on mine." My cheeks pinken in embarrassment as I try to cover for her loose lips.

"I think you have great *diction*." Jeremy has a boyish smile on his face.

It's obvious he's waiting for me to slide over in the booth so he can sit, but I don't budge.

"Wanna join us?" Megan asks, making room for him.

"We were just saying that Emma here should totally get the lead in *Twelfth Night*," Rylee adds. Her kindness should make me feel good, but I shift nervously under the praise.

"Couldn't agree more." Jeremy's focus is on me.

Megan turns toward him in the booth. "Maybe you'll get Orsino, and the two of you will be scene partners again."

"I'd like that." His eyes connect with mine, and I offer a polite smile. "This is kind of embarrassing, I was wondering if any of you had a meal credit left I could snag? Turns out this hungry boy went through all his for the month already."

"You can use one of mine." Megan holds her card between two fingers. "But will you be a doll and grab me another coffee while you're up? Today is a two-cupper."

"Absolutely. I really appreciate it." He gets up and heads to the food line.

I watch as he loads his tray. He seems genuine, and he was patient with me when we were scene partners last year. But his attention doesn't excite me like Daddy Dom's does. His touch doesn't make me feel like I'm simultaneously an inferno and a cold glass of water on a summer's day. I'm not sure if I'll ever find someone else who makes me feel like that again.

CHAPTER 24
EMMA

When the cast list goes out, I'm equally thrilled and apprehensive to find out I'm playing Viola. Professor A-hole was one of the lowest parts of my sophomore year. Despite his handsome features, his attention felt overwhelming, and I wanted nothing more than to shrink from his spotlight. And now I've found myself with a lead in a play where most of my free time will be spent in the spotlight. I'm sure he'll have lots of notes on how I could improve my performance. I just hope I don't have another breakdown like I did in his acting class.

But there's more than just Professor A-hole that's giving me anxiety about this show. As the female lead, I will inevitably have to touch the male lead at some point on stage. I just hope everyone is understanding about my unique issue. I feel fine sharing it with Mackenzie, but the thought of Professor A-hole finding out about it fills me with anxiety.

The first rehearsal is always exciting, and I pull out my script, lining up all of my highlighters and pencils, ready for the table read. It turns out Jeremy was indeed cast as Orsino. He takes a seat next to me, and I awkwardly smile when he nods. He was able to hold my hand in our scene last year, but it took time to build up to that, so the thought of kissing him on stage has my stomach in knots.

We make it through the first three acts without issue. Mackenzie stops us occasionally to share her ideas for the directorial vision and how she wants to make the production unique. Every so often I feel eyes on me, but when I look around the table, everyone's engrossed in their scripts, so I brush it off.

"This is the part where we kiss," Jeremy says near the end of act five. He's closer to my ear than I'm comfortable and I flinch, turning to look at him in confusion.

A throat clears across the table, and I lock eyes with Professor A-hole. For a second it almost looks like he's jealous, but I must be mistaken. I shake my head, clearing that thought as I look down at my script and read my line.

After rehearsal is over, I'm packing up my bag when Jeremy approaches.

"Hey, I'm headed over to the student apartments. You're over there too, right? Wanna walk together?"

"Um, sure." I look at him, noticing his warm smile. He's pushing his floppy blond hair out of his face, and he's actually cute in a boyish kind of way.

"I don't know about your place over there, but mine is a cinderblock shithole. But what can you do?" He shrugs as we pull on all our winter gear. "It was the cheapest option on campus."

Once we're bundled up and headed toward the door, a voice calls from behind me.

"Miss Black, can I speak with you?" I turn around and am met with the biggest scowl on an otherwise handsome face. What did I do now?

He has no power over me anymore since this isn't for a grade. The worst he could do is get me kicked out of the play, but I decide that wouldn't be the end of the world. I cross my arms over my chest and glare at him. "Yes, Professor?" I retort with a bit of a bite.

Jeremy hovers behind me, and I take a step closer to him. Professor A-hole just stares at me, looking between Jeremy and me. Again, it almost feels like jealousy, or concern, but I grow annoyed the longer he stares at us without speaking.

"Did you need something, Professor?"

He looks flustered, and I almost feel sorry for him as he opens his mouth to speak several times before saying, "Be careful out there, the snow is really coming down."

Now it's my turn to stare at him dumbfounded because it almost sounded like concern, and if I know anything, it's that this man doesn't give two thoughts about me.

"Don't worry, Professor Ali, I'll make sure she gets home safe." Jeremy wraps an arm around my waist. I flinch at the movement, dropping my bag, and break into a fit of laughter to cover up my blunder.

"Sorry, I'm just really ticklish." It looks like Professor Ali wants to say something else, and I quickly turn and head for the door. I do not need him to know what's really going on with me. And I certainly don't need his pity.

Jeremy and I walk over to student apartments, and I'm careful to keep enough room for the Holy Ghost between us. While I appreciate his kind gesture, I don't want him getting the wrong idea. There's only one man I'm interested in, and it's not him. He excitedly talks about the upcoming production, and I smile and nod along.

Once I'm inside my apartment, I toss my bag in my room and pull out my phone.

BATMAN DOM
Are you home?

Yes, just walked in from rehearsal. You?

I need to see you.

Now?

FaceTime?

Ok

MY HEART FLUTTERS IN MY CHEST. HE DOESN'T NORMALLY TEXT like this, and I'm usually the one begging to see him. The phone lights up with his call as I hold it out in front of me and lie on my bed.

When it connects, his screen is dark like he has his camera off.

"Are you alone?" he asks, but his voice sounds different. Like he's not wearing his mask.

"I am."

"Show me," he huffs. There's an uncharacteristic desperation in his voice.

"Is everything okay? You don't sound like yourself." I'm not even talking about his voice; his tone is off. He sounds like he's out of control and needs reassurance.

"I'm not in the mood for games. Be a good girl and show me you're alone."

Flipping the camera on my phone, I sit up and make a show of giving him a 360 of my room. It's not big, just a bed and a desk. Turning it back to my face, I smile, sensing this isn't the time for sass. "See? Alone."

He blows out a breath. "Okay. Thank you."

There's silence as neither of us speaks for several moments.

"I wish you were here. My roommate is gone for the weekend, and I have the apartment to myself."

There's a deep sigh on his end, and I know I'm not getting my way. "I've got to go. Just wanted to make sure you were safe. Something told me to check in with you."

Before I can unpack the meaning in his words, he's hung up and I'm left alone, again.

CHAPTER 25
JOHN

Rehearsal drags on as I sit in the back of the theatre and try not to stare at Emma. As the faculty advisor I have very few responsibilities. I mainly make sure the theatre is cleared and locked each night after rehearsal. I could sit in my office and just lock up after they finish since Mackenzie has everything under control, but I'm a glutton for punishment, so here I am staring at the woman I wish I could be with.

Being in her presence lately is starting to feel like too much of a good thing and not enough at the same time.

Commotion on the stage pulls me out of my spiraling thoughts. Emma drops to the floor hard, her knees pulled against her body as she rocks slightly. The fuck?

I'm out of my chair and on the stage in seconds.

"I'm sorry, Emma. I was acting on instinct. It felt natural to grab your shoulders. I didn't mean to freak you out," Jeremy says.

"What's going on?" I demand, giving Jeremy a death glare.

"It's nothing, I'm fine." Emma looks up at me.

I look at Jeremy and Mackenzie and am met with silence.

"Somebody better start talking," I grit through clenched teeth.

"I said I'm fine." Emma stands and brushes off her backside.

"We can just call it a day." Mackenzie claps her hands and backs away. "We'll pick up with this scene tomorrow."

"Miss Black, can I speak with you?"

Her eyes snap to mine, her brows are furrowed, and her shoulders are nearly at her ears. "Fine."

I wait until Mackenzie and Jeremy are nearly out of the theatre before I speak. "Tell me what's going on." It comes out like less of a demand and more of a plea.

She blows out a breath, and I'm fully prepared for her wrath, but her voice is low when she speaks. "Let's just say that physical touch isn't my love language."

My eyebrow lifts as I wait for her to continue.

"My father was abusive, and I think my body associates touch with him."

It's more than I expected her to admit, especially to me.

"I have to feel really safe and trust someone before I'm comfortable with them touching me."

"Thank you for sharing that with me."

"I didn't want to," she adds quickly. "But I figured it would make this rehearsal process easier if you knew."

Everything in me yearns to wrap her in my arms but I refrain. "I'm curious about something."

"What?"

"At the beginning of the school year last year, you let me help you up. Is it because I asked before touching you?"

She thinks for a second before shrugging.

"Have you figured out anything else that helps?"

Her cheeks pinken and my cock perks up knowing she's probably thinking about our time at the club.

"Actually, don't answer that. It's none of my business. Can I try something, though?"

There's a curious look on her face as I jog out into the

house to grab her parka. "Can you put this on?" I hand her the coat.

"Okay." She narrows her eyes.

"I thought that maybe if you were wearing more layers, someone could touch you without you flinching. With your permission, of course."

She pulls on the coat, lifting the fur lined hood over her face as I move behind her.

"Can I touch your shoulders, Miss Black?"

"Only my shoulders, though, right?"

"Only your shoulders," I assure her as I run one finger across her shoulder from right to left. "How was that?"

"I barely felt anything."

"Can I apply more pressure and use my whole hand this time?"

"Sure," she says on a big exhale.

Placing my palm on her left shoulder, I glide my hand as I walk around her body. Once I'm in front of her, I rest my palm on her right shoulder and grip the other one with my left, mimicking Jeremy's earlier movement. We stand there, me holding her, as she stands stock-still, her head dropped, hidden in her hood as her chest heaves with each labored breath she takes.

"Is this okay?" I ask gently.

When she looks up at me, her eyes are filled with tears as one tracks down her cheek. She wipes at it quickly.

"See how she leans her cheek upon her hand. O, that I were a glove upon that hand that I might touch that cheek!" My exaggerated voice is full of mirth as I crack a joke to ease her nerves.

The giggle that escapes her sets my heart back to its normal rhythm.

"You did it. I truly believe you're so much stronger than you give yourself credit for. A pillar of strength. That's why I pushed you so hard last year. Now look at you. You'll figure this out."

"And apparently all it takes is a heavy parka." Her voice is full of humor as she looks at me, her eyes stopping on my lips, before traveling up to my eyes.

I stand there, a blinking idiot, unsure where to look as I take in the delicate features of her face.

Her big brown eyes, surrounded by hundreds of long lashes that flutter rapidly under my scrutiny.

Her high cheekbones, makeup-free, yet covered in the lightest of blushes.

Her plump, round, kissable lips I've never pressed to mine, yet am dying to taste.

There's a voice in my head telling me to slide my hands down to her waist, pull her into me, and kiss her. Her eyes flick to my lips again, and that voice yells at me to take what I want, what we both want.

A door clicks closed in the back of the theatre, but when I turn in that direction, I don't see anyone. Taking a step back from her, the look of disappointment on her face nearly breaks me. It's like the universe is reminding me once again to keep my distance from her.

Emma

The next morning there's another letter taped to my door when I leave the apartment. I look around and don't see anyone outside. My roommate is hardly ever around. It could be for her, but it's unlikely. I open the envelope and unfold the paper.

My love—

I cannot fix on the hour or the spot, or the look or the words, which laid the foundation. It is too long ago. I was in the middle before I knew that I had begun.

We will be reunited soon, my love. Have patience and be safe.

Always Yours

I instantly recognize the first part from *Pride and Prejudice*. It has the same handwriting as the other letters and was taped to my door the same way, but this one was in an envelope, and not all of them have been. Since I'm cutting it close on time, I can't investigate further, so I head to the walking trail and make my way to campus. I read the letter a few more times when a voice pulls me from my thoughts.

"Hey, Emma!"

When I look up, Jeremy is walking toward me, and I offer him a polite smile. "Hey, I'm gonna be late for class." I shove the letter in my pocket and point to my watch.

He changes direction and falls into step beside me. "I'll walk you. I just finished a workout, and I'm kind of hungry. Any chance your class is on the way to the caf?"

"Kinda."

"I'm sorry about yesterday. I didn't mean to freak you out. I totally forgot about your touching thing. I should've remembered from last year."

"Oh yeah. It took some time, but we figured it out for that scene. We'll figure it out for the play." Maybe if I say it out loud, I'll manifest it. I don't mention the day he missed class and I had to run the scene with Professor A-hole. He grabbed my hand without all the rehearsal, and I still can't figure out why it didn't bother me.

"Was Professor Ali a dick about it when we left?"

I laugh, shaking my head. "Actually, he kind of helped me.

I told him about my issue, and he gave me some tips that might help."

We walk in silence for a bit, and my mind keeps replaying the moment on stage when Professor A-hole held my shoulders and told me I was strong.

"I truly believe you're so much stronger that you give yourself credit for. A pillar of strength."

There's something familiar about that phrase "a pillar of strength," but I can't recall where I might have heard it.

"See you at rehearsal!" Jeremy calls as we part ways.

I shove my hands in my pockets, determined not to think about that moment on stage. The moment when he looked at my lips like he wanted to devour them. Did I imagine that? I must have—there's no way my hot but uptight teacher would ever break the rules for someone he finds as infuriating as me.

Classes drag by slowly as I try to concentrate on my studies and fail, instead doodling in my notebook with ideas and thoughts about who could be sending me these letters and secretly hoping for the first time that they're from my professor.

CHAPTER 26
JOHN

I need to stop thinking about her. The way she looked at me at rehearsal. The way I wanted to pull her against me and consume her, feasting on every inch of her skin.

Mary let me know about several appointments coming up that I need to attend, and I should focus on that, not the sexy younger woman permeating my thoughts. I'm close to the end of the deal I made with Mary, but until then, I've committed to following through with her whenever she needs me.

MARY

I appreciate you helping me. Thank you.

I'm happy to and you have to stop thanking me.

But you've given up so much. I feel like all I do is take from you.

You're my friend, and it was literally a matter of life or death. Of course I was going to help you.

Thank you doesn't feel like enough, rafiq.

I smile at her text. "Rafiq" means friend in Yemeni Arabic—more specifically, it's someone you can count on. Over the past six years, I've learned a few phrases in her native tongue, but this one fills me with the most pride.

Just knowing you're alive and well is enough. You and Sam deserve the world, and I'll do everything in my power to make sure you're safe.

If there's anything I can ever do for you, name it.

I did want to tell you something.

Yes?

I've met someone.

That's amazing!

But it's complicated. She's a student at my college. Not currently my student, but she was last year. I met her before I knew she was a student though.

A younger woman? 😄

Don't worry, I'm still focused on the plan. It won't derail me.

I'm not worried about it. I'm happy for you.

I appreciate that. But I'm not sure how we could be together.

Seriously, John.

What?

You give so much to everyone around you, it's time you had a little happiness for you.

There are rules at play here.

Enough with your rules.

It's not that easy.

Will you get fired?

Actually, no. The university only has rules prohibiting me from having a relationship with a student in my class. Everything else is frowned upon but not actionable.

Your tenure would protect you?

Yes

Then do it. Go after what you want for once.

I set my phone down and blow out a deep breath. Could it be that easy? If Mary is okay with it and my job isn't at risk, could I pursue her? I'd still have to be discreet. We couldn't be out in the open with a relationship for at least another year. There are commitments I must honor and considering the amount of time I've put into this, it'd be foolish to fuck it up this close to the end.

Fuck it. I deserve this. We deserve this. Now I just have to make Emma fall for me the way she has for Daddy Dom.

I need to see you.

When?

Can you come to the city tonight?

I have rehearsal till seven, but I could come after. I only have afternoon classes tomorrow.

Come to my room. Text me when you get to the club.

Yes, sir.

———

I'm leaning against the counter when I hear a timid knock on my door. Emma is alone, and I crane my neck looking for Alyx.

"He's in his room. I came by myself." She walks hesitantly into the room as I close the door behind her.

Resting my forehead against the door, I blow out a deep breath into my mask. When I'm ready to face her, I turn and nearly lose it at the sight in front of me. Emma is stripped down to her panties and is kneeling, her palms on her thighs as if waiting for my instruction. A lone tear tracks down her face, and I reach out a thumb to swipe at it.

"Please, sir." She leans into my touch.

"I didn't say you could speak." My voice is weak. I'm running out of resolve, tired of fighting this need to claim her.

My thumb rubs along her cheekbone. Even though she's silent, her pleas are piercing.

I curse myself for putting her in this position, for pushing her away, because I can't fight this pull between us anymore than she can. "What do you need, pet?"

"I need to feel your lips. You can blindfold me again. I promise I'll be good. I just need to feel you against me."

Against my better judgment, I acquiesce, grabbing a blindfold and leading her to the lounger. She holds her hair back as I slip it over her eyes before sinking down into the deep curve of the seat. I pull her onto my lap and lean back, settling her against my chest as she straddles me. I know this is risky. I need her to crave this from John so when she finds out who I am she doesn't run, but I don't give a fuck when I feel her relax into me.

"I missed you." Her head jerks as though she's able to look at me, but the blindfold prevents it.

"Why?" she rasps, and I don't need her to clarify to know what she means.

Why did I push her away? Why won't I reveal who I am? Why can't we be together?

"Because this is complicated." We can't be together yet, and I need her to understand that.

"I've never felt like this before. And I've never tolerated someone's touch, let alone craved it. There has to be a reason for that. It feels like fate is pulling us together, but you keep fighting it. I can't stop thinking about you. What's wrong with me?" She drops her head, letting out a small sob against my chest.

"Absolutely nothing. You are exquisite." I wrap my arms around her, holding her tight.

"Then kiss me. Kiss me like you want me. Kiss me like we can be together. Let me pretend that while we're in this room, this means something. That it's as big and meaningful as it feels in my heart."

My rule about no feelings rings loudly in my head, but I push it away. As long as we haven't said those three words, haven't felt those big emotions, it'll stay a gray area.

Tilting my mask up, I pull her face to mine. Her lips are soft as I devour them, licking and sucking until she opens for me and our tongues meet. Euphoria crashes into me as her hand strokes my beard and she becomes pliant against me.

Nothing has ever felt more right than kissing this woman, and every reason for stopping this flies out of my head.

Her hips rock against me as we continue exploring each other's mouths. I've kissed every inch of her body but her mouth, so I take my time claiming her with my lips.

"I need you." Her moans are needy whimpers as I kiss down her neck.

"You deserve more than to have your first time in the

private room of a sex club," I growl into her ear, trying to mask my voice. "But I'll take care of you for now."

I slip my hand into her panties and groan at how wet she is for me. Circling her clit with my middle finger, she arches into me, pulling me close as she moans against my ear.

"Yes, right there. Please."

I want to slam into her, or at the very least, slide my fingers in and fuck her hard, but I keep my hand in place, repeating the same motion against her clit until she's bucking against me and crying out.

This is all I can give her right now. Stolen moments. Hiding her away when she deserves someone who is proud to be seen with her. A plan forms in my head, and I focus on that, determined to figure out a way around the few remaining obstacles keeping us apart.

CHAPTER 27
EMMA

It's been a week since I first felt his lips on mine and I can't stop thinking about them, feeling ghosts of them on my skin every night as I drift off to sleep.

Rehearsals have been going well. Using extra clothing as a barrier seems to help with the touching problem. I was nervous about sharing my issue with Professor A-hole, worried he would somehow use it against me, but he's been very patient and understanding with me this past week. I'm not sure how to feel about it. His shift in demeanor is throwing me. Where he once was cold and distant, throwing up walls and challenging every word out of my mouth, he's now becoming very encouraging, showering me with praise during rehearsal.

The teacher's pet in me is desperate to prove myself to him. I earned this role, and I want him to believe it.

Jeremy has been very understanding as well, and I'm thankful for that. It can't be easy to work with someone who recoils every time you touch them. I'd worry for his ego, but he seems to take it in stride. Nevertheless, I find myself complimenting him and his acting whenever I can. I don't want him to think my issue is any reflection on him.

Just as we're wrapping rehearsal, Jeremy pulls me aside. "I was thinking, maybe you and I should spend some time together outside of the theatre."

"Like a date?" I ask nervously.

"Kinda?" He gauges my reaction. When I don't jump at his words, he continues. "It doesn't have to be a date, but we can treat it like one if that helps."

"What do you mean?" I cross my arms over my chest as my heart rate picks up.

"I'm fucking this up, I'm sorry." He rubs his forehead. "I just meant that maybe if you got more comfortable being around me outside of the show, you wouldn't freak out when I try to hold your hand on stage. It was one thing when we did a scene in class, but a lot more people will see this. People are paying money to watch us fall in love on stage, and I want it to be believable."

"Oh." My nerves relax.

"If you wanted it to be a date, I'm cool with that too. You're hot, and I would definitely enjoy spending more time with you. But at the very least, if we hung out more, maybe you would be more comfortable with me on stage."

I want to tell him how this has never worked for me in the past. So many guys in high school tried exactly what he was suggesting, but the difference was they all wanted to get in my pants, and I think my body knew that. I'm not sure what Jeremy's true motive is, but as long as I'm suspicious, I'll never fully trust him and this issue will persist.

"Okay, I guess we could try."

He smiles at me, pushing his hair out of his face. "Great! It's a date."

"What's a date?" a deep voice asks from behind me. Professor Ali stands there, hands on his hips, a scowl on his face.

I glance between the two men, offering Jeremy a sweet smile before matching my professor's scowl. "Not a date," I assure Jeremy gently, then add more firmly to the professor, "We're just hanging out."

"Outside of here?" Professor Ali clarifies, waving a hand around to indicate the stage.

"Yes, outside of here. Otherwise it would just be considered rehearsing," I say, my tone biting. His emotional flip-flopping is messing with me, and I can't keep up with how he feels about me on any given day.

"I'm going to grab my stuff. Meet you outside?" Jeremy places a hand on my shoulder.

My eyes fixate on where he's touching me, and I wait for a reaction that never comes. Jeremy's eyes meet mine and he smiles. "Yeah, I'll be right there."

I watch him leave when a throat clearing pulls me back into the present.

"Is this what you want?" he asks tentatively. His forehead wrinkles in worry. Is he concerned about me?

"It's fine. You don't have to worry about me. I'm fine."

"You didn't answer my question." His face hardens, his eyes narrowing.

"I don't know what you want me to say," I admit. I'm not interested in Jeremy like that, but if there's another person who can help me with this problem, I'm open to exploring it. I can't wait around for my mystery man to admit he wants something more with me.

"I don't like that guy." He takes a small step closer to me.

His presence fills the space between us, and even though we're a few feet apart, it feels like he's inches from me. "I'm pretty sure he's harmless. He's just trying to help me, which is more than I can say for anyone else in my life right now." My eyes lock on his, and I cringe at my confession. Why do I feel the need to share every thought in my head when I'm around this man?

"I don't like it."

"You don't like what?" Now I'm starting to get annoyed. How dare he try to tell me what to do?

"I don't like you spending time with him."

"Well, you don't really have a say in that." I cross my arms, fully prepared to tell him off. If he wants to know how I really feel about him, I'll tell him.

"Just be careful." It feels like a plea, and I tilt my head in confusion. "There's more snow moving in tonight. Call me if you need anything." He hurries off.

I'm left standing there in total shock and confusion. Why would I call him? I don't even have his number. But why does he care?

———————

"I think he likes you." Jeremy leans over the table conspiratorially.

A laugh bursts out of me as I quickly swallow my drink. "Warn a girl before you launch into a comedy routine. I almost covered you in iced tea."

The cafeteria is mostly empty since it's a Friday night and everyone has better plans than being here. Except for me. And Jeremy, apparently.

"Seriously. It makes sense when you think about it."

"Are you delusional? How does it make sense? That man has been mean to me since the day I met him. He picks on me in class constantly, eviscerates my papers with his red pen, and trades insults with me, sometimes in Shakespeare."

"Are you hearing yourself?" He smiles, taking a sip of his soda.

"Yeah, he hates me. What am I missing?"

"Did you ever have a boy pull your pigtails in kindergarten?"

I laugh incredulously. "This is not that."

"It's exactly that, except now he's a grown-up. Same feelings, different behaviors. He can't pull your pigtail so he's doing everything else you listed."

"You're ridiculous," I scoff, but the seeds of doubt take root in my head. Is that what he's doing? It could explain his recent change in behavior. I'm not his student anymore, and suddenly he's nice to me.

"So about your little problem. Have you found anything that helps?"

I blow out a breath, unsure of how much to share with him. It's not like I'm giving him the cheat code to get into my pants, but it kind of feels that way. "It helps if you tell me before you touch me, so I know it's coming."

"Okay. I'm going to play footsie with you now." He grins as he taps his foot against mine under the table.

His teasing is unexpected, and I laugh. "Not exactly what I meant, but that works." I push my foot back against his in jest.

"This won't work in the show, though. I can't be like 'Prepare for thy touch, gentle lady.' That would totally kill the vibes."

"The Bard would roll over in his grave at an improv like that. We have time to practice those parts, though. I was able to hold your hand for our scene in class."

"But we never had to kiss in class. I have a feeling that one might be harder. And I would prefer not to be slapped every time I try to plant one on you."

"Who says I'm going to slap you?"

"Just a hunch." He grins.

His words sound innocent, but there's a look on his face that tells me he's not telling me something.

"I'll try my best to keep my hands to myself. Besides, we could always do a stage kiss," I suggest.

"That still requires touching, even if it's not on the lips."

"True."

"We could practice the kiss tonight if you want?" He sounds a little too eager.

"Actually, I need to study," I deflect.

"How about this? We finish eating and I walk you to the library, but you have to hold my hand or link arms the whole way. We can even recite our lines on the walk over if it helps."

Relieved that he's willing to let it go, I nod my agreement.

The trip to the library is brief but cold as the snow picks up, crunching under our boots. I loop my hand under his elbow, resting my palm on his forearm as we walk. It's not terrible and I don't have the urge to cause him bodily harm, so I'm calling it a win. When we arrive at the steps to the building, he releases me, dropping into an exaggerated bow.

"I must bid you adieu, m'lady."

His goofiness makes me laugh, and I breathe a sigh of relief. Maybe this could work. If I think of him like Ethan or Alyx, I could get through most of the touching. I'm just not sure how to navigate the kissing part.

Nearly two hours later, I'm standing on the library steps, the snow falling in heavy drifts. My apartment is a ten-minute walk from here, and I pull my scarf tighter to protect myself from the cold. As I walk, I replay Jeremy's words in my head. Is Professor Ali into me, or does he just find me attractive? Maybe it's all in my head?

There's one way to find out. I pull off my glove and swipe open my phone, pulling up the syllabus in the class portal.

This is crazy. I should just walk home and go to bed. But the thought gnaws at me. Could Jeremy be on to something?

Before I can change my mind, I dial his office number. It rings once before he answers it.

"Miss Black?"

"Um, how did you know it was me?"

"Lucky guess." I swear there's a hint of a smile in his voice.

"This is really embarrassing."

"What's wrong?" he asks, his mood shifting quickly.

"I was walking home from the library, and the path to student apartments hasn't been shoveled yet, and I think I twisted my ankle walking in the snow. I know there are some crutches in the prop closet, could you maybe—"

"Where are you?" he asks, cutting me off.

"At the beginning of the path behind the stadium, close to the theatre parking lot."

"I'll be right there." The call ends.

Minutes later and much faster than I expect, I hear footsteps approaching quickly, and I turn to see him running toward me, no crutches in sight.

"You couldn't find them?"

"What?" He pants, out of breath.

"The crutches."

"Didn't have time. I came straight here from my office. That would have taken too long."

"How am I going to get home?"

"Shit." He puts his hands on his hips. "It's really coming down. It's probably not safe to use them anyway."

He stares down at me as the snow falls around us. It's unusually silent, making my racing heart sound louder in my ears.

With all the snow and the few lights on campus, it's bright enough to make out all his features. His amber-brown eyes are intense as they search mine. Is this real? Is he interested? I've only had this rush of feelings for one other person. I momentarily wish I wasn't wearing a hat so he could tuck a strand of hair behind my ear. My cheeks heat at that thought, and my head drops in embarrassment.

He reaches out his hand, gently crooking a finger under my chin to tilt my head up to look at him. "Are you hurt?"

His words send a dull ache through my chest, and I rub at it without thinking.

"Wh–what?" I stutter, unable to look away.

"Your ankle." He breaks eye contact to look down at my boot.

"A little," I lie.

"I'll carry you, if that's okay?" he asks cautiously.

I nod, feeling like this must be a dream.

"I'd feel better if I could get your verbal agreement." He smirks.

"Yes, you can carry me."

Then he slides his big arms under my back and knees, carrying me bridal-style as I wrap my arms around his neck. He moves slowly along the path, and my body jostles with each step he takes.

"Are you okay?" he asks as he continues staring ahead.

I look at him. "Better now." My voice is a whisper.

He tilts his head toward mine as he slows his pace. Our faces are inches apart as he speaks. "I'm glad you called."

Not sure how to respond, I place my head against his neck and focus on my breathing. In and out. Each inhale smelling of woods, falling snow, and something else familiar that I can't place.

"I've got you," his voice soothes as he pulls me tighter against him. The path back to my apartment isn't long, and I don't want this to end.

There's something about the way he's carrying me. Something comforting about the way his arms feel holding me. And for once I don't think about my hang-ups, instead focusing on the way I feel cradled safely in his arms.

When I leave for class the next morning, I open my bedroom door and a piece of paper flaps from the motion. Was someone in the apartment?

"Hello?" I call out, but there's no answer. My roommate's door is open, which only happens when she's gone. Looking around my room for a weapon, I grab a dictionary and hold it in two hands like it's a bat, swinging it wildly each time I turn a corner in the apartment. When I'm satisfied that I'm alone, I walk back to my room, drop the book, and tear the paper off the door.

Emma,
I better not see you touch that fucker again. No one touches you but me. You belong to me.
Yours

I drop the letter like it's on fire. This one is nothing like the others. Even the handwriting looks off, the pen strokes hard and angry. Whoever is leaving these is getting bolder, breaking into my apartment to make sure I see them. I should call campus security, but I don't know what this person is capable of. Until now the letters had been sweet, but this one makes it clear I have no idea who I'm dealing with.

CHAPTER 28
JOHN

I'm desperate for a way to spend more time with her as John, hoping that I can build her trust, but I'm running out of ideas for how to do it without looking suspicious.

Mary may have given me her blessing, but I still have to be cautious about this.

Sitting in the back row of the house watching rehearsal, I can't stop thinking about our interaction a few weeks ago. I'd been surprised when Emma called, and I was fairly certain she was only pretending to be injured, especially after seeing her easily walk around the stage days later.

Does that mean she wanted to see me? I treasured the way her body curled into mine when I carried her home, but I left quickly after settling her on the couch, not wanting to draw suspicion from her roommate.

The actors onstage are nearing act five, and my stomach sinks when I think about what's coming. It's the end of March, and the show opens in four weeks. I've watched Emma try to get out of it. Hell, even though she doesn't know it, I've covered for her when it was clear she wasn't ready to block the final scene. But it's getting close to crunch time, and she will have to practice the kiss.

I watch as Jeremy whispers in Emma's ear, and she nods. Then the fucker places his hands on her cheeks to pull her into a kiss. Her body stiffens, and I fight the urge to march onto that stage and push him off her, wrap her in my arms, and carry her away from here.

Just as he gets close, she shoves against his chest, nearly knocking him to the ground.

"Emma, what the hell?" He stumbles over his feet trying to right himself.

"Do we have to do the kiss? It's not even in the script."

He takes a step toward her, his voice a little louder and more irritated. "I just asked you to marry me. The kiss is implied."

"But we don't have to do it, do we?" Emma asks, directing her attention toward the house.

"Stop!" Mackenzie yells from several rows up. "Emma, do you need a minute?"

She folds in half, bending at the waist and clutching her knees as she drops her head. I watch as Jeremy reaches out a hand like he's going to rub her back, and I'm out of my seat stomping toward the stage. "Stop!" I growl.

Jeremy lifts his arms in defense as the entire cast grows silent, looking between us, the tension palpable. "Whoa, man, chill! I was just going to rub her back."

"She clearly doesn't want to be touched, hence her reaction," I bark back angrily.

He stares me down, arms still in the air as he takes a step back at my approach. I drop into a squat in front of Emma, careful not to touch her. "Are you okay?"

She shakes her head and draws in a shaky breath, refusing to look at me.

"I did everything we talked about. I let her know I was about to touch her and she was okay with it. I didn't mean to upset her," Jeremy prattles on, but my focus is on Emma.

"What do you need?" I ask her.

"I need quiet," she softly replies.

"Follow me to the green room." I walk through the throng of students, clearing a path for her to follow me.

Once we're inside the room, she collapses onto a couch and starts crying. I want to pull her into my chest and soothe her, kiss away every tear that falls down her beautiful face, and tell her how proud I am of her. She's actively facing her fears, putting herself in a situation that she knows will be difficult for her because of her trauma.

But I refrain because I know that anyone could walk in on us here, which would not be discreet. Instead, I hand her a box of tissues and place my hands on my hips, standing in front of her.

"I can't do it. I have to quit the play. I tried, but I can't control the urge to punch him when he leans into me for a kiss. He wanted to practice the kiss, but I said no."

"He wanted to practice kissing?" I force down the bile rising in my throat at the thought of that little fucker's lips on her.

She wipes her cheek. "Yeah, he mentioned it that night you picked me up in the snow. I'm not sure it would help, though. This happened to me with every guy I dated in high school. As soon as they got close enough to make a move, I'd hit, kick, or laugh. I bruised more than just egos and developed quite the reputation, which has followed me here."

"How so?" I lean back against the arm of the couch opposite her, folding my arms over my chest.

"So there's this club, made up of my exes. It started in high school when a few of the guys I'd dated got together to swap stories about me. In order to save face, they all agreed that they'd tell everyone that they hooked up with me, even though none of them had."

No wonder she doesn't trust men. Between that and her abusive father, it explains why she has so many nightmares.

"And apparently, that reputation followed me here."

"What do you mean?" The hair on the back of my neck prickles at her words.

"Do you remember after auditions—"

"In the parking lot?" I cut her off, so she doesn't have to relive that encounter. It was the same fucker, Trent, that confronted her on campus last year during spring break.

"Yeah, that guy was one of the guys I dated in high school."

I nod, not letting on that she's already told me about this as Daddy Dom. "What does that have to do with what happened on stage just now?"

"So that night when it snowed, I was able to hold Jeremy's arm when we walked across campus. And then I saw you. But the next morning there was another letter taped to my door. This one had my name on it where the others didn't, and it freaked me out."

Others? She's been getting letters? I wait, letting her share more at her own pace. When she breaks into a sob, I walk over to her and sink onto the couch next to her, keeping space between us, but letting her know I'm here if she needs it. "What did the letter say?'

"It said, 'I better not see you touch that guy again. You belong to me.' Except it used more colorful language. I have no idea who sent it and... and..." She drops her head into her hands and sobs.

"You got this letter weeks ago?"

She nods and more tears spill over her long, thick lashes.

"And you're worried that whoever sent it will see you touch Jeremy in the play and come after you?" She nods. "Have you gotten any more letters since that last one?"

"No. But that's why I've kept to myself. I haven't been seen with anyone but Rylee and Megan on campus. I don't want to upset whoever's sending them. But I'm also kind of hoping he just moves on."

"Have you contacted the police or campus security?"

"I called campus security after the last one, but it was a week later, and they were no help. The other letters were sweet and romantic, and I… I thought they came from someone else. Sorry, I don't know why I'm telling you this."

"Do you think the guy from the parking lot sent the letters?"

"I don't know. Maybe? But if he started a new chapter of the Emma's exes club here, it could be anyone. Getting in my pants was almost like a game to them. Who could have me first?"

What in the actual fuck? How do I fix this? How do I keep her safe from this? For once the thought of chaining her to the cross in my private room at Pulse doesn't seem like a bad idea after all. And because I'm a sick fuck and a glutton for punishment, the thought of having her first makes my cock swell. I push down my lust, ashamed that I'm no better than the shitheads that taunted her in high school.

"I have a buddy in campus security. I'll follow up with him about this. Can you send me a picture of the letter? At the very least Nate can file a report, and I can see if they can have someone patrol student apartments regularly."

"Okay. Like text it to you?" she asks, sniffling.

Fuck, that would mean giving her my number, and she doesn't know she already has it saved under a different name. "Just email it to me."

—————————

Emma

When I get back to my room, I take a picture of the letter and email it to Professor Ali. I don't get a reply, but something in my gut tells me that he's already taking care of this. There's no logical reason for my feelings, but I haven't really followed logic when it comes to men these past two years—getting involved with a masked dom at Pulse, dealing with my crazy ex and his friends on campus, and flirting with my super-hot professor.

Ever since I started doing the play with him, he's like a different person. The cold, stern A-hole who tormented me in class has been replaced by this warm, caring individual, almost like he likes me more now that I'm not his student.

I still have feelings for Daddy Dom, though. He was the first guy who was able to touch me without making my skin crawl. While he comes across as unattached, his commanding presence should be intimidating. Heck, the man has tied me to a cross and spanked me. But he also treats me with so much warmth and care in the moments after a scene, in the way he listens to me talk about my sister and my dream job, and the way he shows up to comfort me when I need him most. He uses his hardness to grind away my pain and trauma, exposing the tenderness underneath.

But lately, seeing this softer side of Professor Ali has caused a rush of confusing feelings to flood my brain—and my panties. He's taken the time to console me when I've been emotional after a difficult rehearsal, listened to me without judgement when I shared about my past and the letters, and he's been so patient with me as I work through my aversion to touch. And then there's the fact that his touch, sparing as it has been, has not only *not* bothered me, but has become something I crave.

And I don't think I'm alone in the way I'm feeling. There have been times during rehearsal when I've felt his eyes on me. At least twice now, I've caught him looking at my lips while I'm speaking. I know he's a professor and I'm a student, and he's at least a decade older than me; by any other standards, or by school rules, this should be forbidden. But I want him. I doubt anything will come of it. He doesn't seem like the type to break the rules, and given our rocky history, I doubt he'd do it for me. But if I wasn't still so hung up on Daddy Dom, I might make a move on Professor Ali.

Part of me wishes I could have both of them. If I could combine the hardness of Daddy Dom with the gentleness of Professor Ali, it would be everything I was looking for in a man. Someone who can protect me yet also help me get out of my head. Someone to push me in the classroom, push me to be the best version of myself, but who would also push my limits in the bedroom. So focused on my pleasure alone that he finishes in his pants. I don't think there's a higher compliment a woman can receive.

And clearly, I have a type since both men are tall and well-built. They both have short beards, though I've only felt Daddy Dom's since he always wears a mask or blindfolds me. Their voices both hit that deep register that vibrates in your ears pinging around the dopamine center in your brain. And both have tattoos, though Professor Ali clearly keeps his hidden since I've only ever seen it peeking out from his sleeve one time.

What if they were the same person?

My mind races with the thought as I change into my pajamas. I mean, it would explain some things, like how he was able to get to campus so quickly last spring break when Trent confronted me outside my dorm. And why I didn't see much of him last year or go to the club, because neither of us were near the city. But there's no way that uptight Professor Ali, who works at a Christian college, would ever be seen at a schmex club. And there's no way he would be the kind of man Daddy Dom is in the bedroom, the kind of man I've come to crave.

As I get into bed, I fantasize about the best parts of each man, blending them into my perfect man, secretly wishing they were the same person.

CHAPTER 29
JOHN

"Professor Ali, can you come over here and help us settle a debate?" Mackenzie asks. I set down the paintbrush and walk out of the scene shop toward the stage.

"You have a little paint on your face." She gestures to my left cheek.

I lift the bottom of my already ruined shirt and wipe where she's pointing. There's a whistle from somewhere onstage, and I look down realizing I've grabbed the hem of my undershirt and not my top shirt, exposing my entire stomach and my very unique tattoos.

My eyes search the group for Emma as I lower my shirt. Did she see my tattoos? Would she recognize them at this point if she did? Do I want her to?

I'd be lying if I said that I had the strength to keep pushing her away. Maybe I want her to see them. To finally see me, right in front of her.

When I see the back of her dirty blonde head, my chest deflates a little.

"Well?" Mackenzie asks. Fuck, I wasn't listening to a word she was saying.

"Sorry, you're going to have to repeat that."

"We're trying to decide the order for curtain call, and Dominic and Monty think they shouldn't have to go first, since—"

"I'm going to stop you right there. You're in charge here. As director, it's your vision and what you say goes. I'm just the faculty advisor, and apparently the scenic painter since the student who signed up to do this never showed. So if you want scenery for this show in a couple weeks, I need to get back to painting."

I'm being a moody bastard, and I know it. Part of me feels bad for snapping. Mackenzie isn't responsible for my frustration. Nope, that responsibility is all me, and the intoxicating woman who lives rent-free in my head and in my spank bank.

"Sorry, you're right," Mackenzie stammers. "It's just hard dealing with all these big personalities sometimes. Actors can be… a lot."

"You've got this. Now unless anyone wants to help me, I'm headed back in there." I crook a thumb over my shoulder at the scene shop behind me.

My eyes scan the crowd looking for volunteers before connecting with Emma's. She arches an eyebrow and makes her way toward me.

"I don't have any lines for a bit. I'd be happy to help, Professor."

Nodding my head for her to follow, I stalk back to the flat I was painting. "Clean brushes are in the green cabinet, and there should be coveralls in there too if you need them." I don't look at her, I can't. Instead, I concentrate on the set piece in front of me.

"I see we're back to being Professor A-hole," she mutters quietly as she slips on a pair of coveralls.

"I'm sorry, what was that?" I turn my head to her, a smile creeping onto my face.

"Great Caesar's ghost. Did I say that out loud?"

I chuckle at her discomfiture. "Haven't heard that one before."

"Really?" Her surprise is evident. "I'm sorry, now I'm being an A-hole."

"You're right, though." I focus my attention back on my task and dip my brush into the paint.

"About what?" I can feel her warmth as she approaches, her soft floral scent tickling my nostrils.

I inhale deeply. "About me being an A-hole."

"Yeah?" There's a sense of pride in her voice, probably at getting me to admit she's right. When I don't respond, she continues meekly. "Why are you such a jerk?"

"Because you scare me." The words are out of my mouth before I can stop them. I keep my eyes trained on the flat in front of me, concentrating on the way I'm swirling the colors. Why the fuck am I admitting this?

"I… scare *you*?"

I make the mistake of looking at her, and holy fuck. She's inches from me, pulling her bottom lip into her mouth, tugging on it slowly with her teeth. I can't look away as I continue fixating on her perfect fucking mouth. The lips I worshipped not too long ago. I stifle a groan and will my cock to deflate as I take a step back, breaking the spell. I gesture for her to get some paint so I can show her how to stroke it.

Jesus Christ. How to apply brush strokes to the flat.

Her shoulders sag, and I can read the disappointment in her body. I've watched this woman for almost two years, from close up and afar, memorizing all of her movements and expressions. I can read her like a well-loved book.

Clearing my throat I point to the spot on the flat, and she raises her brush to it. "You're going to apply a highlight right there. You want to think about the direction of the light source, and keep your highlight close to it. Got it?"

She nods.

"Some of the magic will be added in the lighting design,

but adding shadow and highlights will make it pop even more, giving it depth." Fuck me now, why can't I shut up?

"So I should do one here?" She peers at me over her shoulder, fluttering her lashes. "I just want to make sure I'm doing it right. I don't want to disappoint you."

My cock swells at her words, and I swallow thickly, trying to tamp down the lust. I watch her track the movement of my throat and catch her rubbing her thighs together out of my periphery. "I don't think I could find you disappointing if I tried."

"That's funny, I distinctly remember you calling me disappointing at auditions."

"You never were one to let a man pick on you or push you down, if I recall." I search her eyes, willing her to remember the first rule I gave her in the club. She blinks several times, her brow furrowing slightly.

That's it, pet. It's me. Look under the mask and see me for who I really am.

She doesn't say anything, just continues to stare at me.

"I thought you came in here to help." I nod to the flat, and she moves her brush along the surface.

We work in silence for a while, side by side. Every inhale of her scent makes my slacks tighten. Every minute that passes makes me curse myself for all of my choices when it comes to her.

For pushing her away as Daddy Dom.

For pulling her back in as Professor Ali.

For being the biggest fucking coward as John.

Has she figured it out? If she has, would she say anything? *Fuck it.* I want her to piece it together. I want her to know it's me.

I clear my throat, getting her attention, and lift the hem of my shirt, pretending to swipe at sweat on my face as I watch her eyes rake up my torso, a look of lust clouding her beautiful features. When she notices the tattoos a little further up, I see her eyes widen slightly in shock as she takes in my ink, the wheels turning in her brain as she makes the connection.

Do not show weakness, instead show your abs. Jesus Christ. What am I doing right now? I've lost my mind.

"Get your fill?" I tease, dropping my voice into a low gravel.

"Yes, sir… I mean, what? No. I wasn't looking at anything. You look…"

"I look what?"

"Pretty." She shakes her head like she's trying to clear the fog of lust. "What? Who said that? Not me. Sorry."

Did I read her reaction wrong? I know it's been a while since she's seen me shirtless at the club, but I could have sworn she recognized my ink.

She turns to paint, and I pull my cell out of my pocket and fake a call. When she looks at me, I motion that I'm leaving and walk away like the fucking coward I am.

CHAPTER 30
EMMA

At this point I'm nearly convinced that Professor A-hole is Daddy Dom. But how can that be? Could he have been in front of me this whole time? Or am I just wishing it was true because of my dirty dream about both the other night?

The walk across campus is short, my legs move quickly carrying me away from the theatre as my mind races with thoughts.

It would explain why Daddy Dom pulled back right after we met; I showed up in his class. And he never revealed who he was that first year because he was my teacher. There had to be rules against that.

His rules.

Oh my God, it makes so much more sense now. He was such an A-hole because he had to be, to protect himself. But why would he end things with me once I was no longer his student?

He started being so nice to me this past year. Was that his way of showing me the real him without the mask?

It would make sense if my professor was Daddy Dom, but I need to know for sure. Once I'm inside my apartment, I pull up our text thread.

I think there's someone in my apartment.

Where are you right now?

Locked in my room.

I'm scared. Can you come over?

On my way.

Come to my window. I'll let you in.

It should feel wrong to lie to him. If it is Professor A-hole, he'll be here in minutes.

There's a knock on my window shortly after and I open it quickly, helping him as he climbs in. He's dressed in black, his hood pulled tight around his mask.

"You got here fast. I thought you were in the city."

"I came as quickly as I could. Have you checked out the rest of the apartment? Where did you hear the noise?" He walks to the door, ready to investigate.

"I lied."

He freezes. His shoulders and back expand with each breath. Then, slowly, he looks at me over his shoulder.

My heart is racing as I take a step toward him, pulling his arm and forcing him to turn toward me. "You're wearing a Faith Union hoodie." I point to the university logo. There's only one reason why my masked dom would be wearing a hoodie for my school.

He unzips it slowly, tossing it to the ground as he bears his naked torso to me. I take another step toward him and reach out to trace the design of one of the tattoos on his chest. It's a skull with a crown on it. I've seen it half a dozen times, but it looks oddly familiar now.

My eyes move lower, noticing the other ink on his

abdomen. The ink that Professor A-hole flashed in the scene shop earlier. My gaze slowly travels back up his chest as he grabs my wrist, guiding me as I trace the outline of the skull, and I watch as goosebumps pebble his flesh at my touch.

"It's inspired by *Hamlet*." My heart pounds, and a jolt of electricity and lust rushes through me.

The Faith Union hoodie.

The *Hamlet* tattoo.

I reach up and gently lift his mask, tossing it to the ground. It's him.

A rush of emotions hit me at once. Relief. Triumph. Hurt. Confusion. Elation. Lust. But I don't have time to process any of them when he reaches out and cups my cheek.

There's a boyish eagerness in his gentle brown eyes as he peers down at me. I've never seen my uptight professor look like this, like he's unsure how this could play out, worried I might reject him.

He swipes his thumb back and forth as if I'm the most precious thing in the world to him. I cover his skull tattoo with my hand, pressing my palm against his flesh as his rapidly beating heart vibrates under my touch. His eyes are full of hope and longing, like he's been waiting for this moment just as much as I was.

"I hoped it was you." I barely get the words out before he pulls my mouth to his, one hand threading through my hair while the other grips my neck, angling me exactly where he wants me. His tongue thrusts against mine, and I'm right back at the club, remembering exactly how he felt. Comfortable and familiar, yet new and unsure at the same time, and the dichotomy sends a bolt of lust straight to my panties.

"You have no idea how long I've been wanting to do that. To kiss you, claim you, without some stupid mask in the way."

His words are a balm to my soul. And I revel in them as he licks and nips at my neck.

"I don't want anything between us. No more mask, no clothes, nothing else."

He cocks a brow at me. "Nothing? What are you implying?"

I smile and nod. "I've never done this before, but I'm on birth control." He claims my mouth in a bruising kiss.

"Are you sure?" he asks between kisses.

"Yes," I moan as he licks a path down my neck.

"I get tested regularly for the club, and those have all been clear, but I haven't had sex in at least six years," he says against my shoulder.

I pull back, unsure if I heard him correctly. I'm not one to talk, I've never had sex, but the thought that this man who dominates women in a sex club has been celibate for years is unbelievable.

"I told you, I don't fuck subs. What I do at Pulse is about more than just sex. You're the only person I've been intimate with there. The only one I'd break the rules for."

He picks me up, carrying me to my bed as he gently sets me down, taking his time to undress me. When he pulls down my panties, I grin at the look of pure adoration on his face. I'm tempted to say something cheeky, but decide against it, not wanting to spoil the gravity of the moment. He kisses down my stomach and around my hips causing me to buck and squirm.

When his head pops up, he locks eyes with mine. "Stay still, pet. I want to take my time worshipping this body knowing I'm the only man who ever has and ever will. And then I'm going to devour this perfect virgin cunt so you're ready for me."

"I want that too," I murmur as he continues licking and kissing me. It's so hard to stay still, but I understand why he needs this, needs me to submit to him. I squeeze my eyes shut, forcing myself to focus on each stroke of his tongue and I gasp in surprise as he slowly moves lower, hovering just over my clit.

With just one lick up my slit, I'm a shuddering mess, grabbing fistfuls of sheets as I fight the urge to writhe under him. "Yes. Feels so good, sir," I moan.

He pulls back just an inch, and I look down at him for approval. "You're being so good for me, and it makes me so fucking hard. Now I need you to make a mess of my face, pet. Use my lips, my mouth. Ride them how you need. Make yourself come and fall apart on my tongue. Show me how badly you need it."

And then he descends on me, licking and sucking and it all feels so good. Just when I think it can't get any better, he pushes two fingers into me, crooking them against my inner walls as he rubs and pulses them against my G-spot.

"There!" I cry as my orgasm builds and I close my eyes. Tiny spots of light dance behind my eyelids as white-hot pleasure pulses up my spine. His tongue flicks rapidly against my clit as my orgasm barrels through me like a train at top speed. I'm powerless against it as I buck and cry against him.

"So fucking beautiful when you fall apart for me," he says against my skin, kissing my thighs, my hips, as he works his way up my body. He stops when he gets to my breasts. "You never cease to amaze me, pet. When I first saw these perfect tits, and realized they were pierced? Fuuuuck."

The coarse hair of his beard tickles my skin as he licks around the fleshy parts of my breast, taking his time to tease and nip at the skin, without touching me where I want him most.

"Tell me what you want, pet."

"I want you to play with my nipples. Tease them, lick them, suck on them until I can't take it anymore," I say in a rush, surprising myself with how forward I'm being.

A cocky grin lights up his handsome face. I've been staring at this man in class and in rehearsals for almost two years, wanting him more than anything, and not realizing who he really was.

He pulls a nipple into his mouth, using his tongue to slide my piercing back and forth. His hand teases the barbell on my other nipple. "Oh, sweet cheese and rice," I gasp as he sucks harder.

He chuckles against my skin. "I think I'd lose my mind if I heard you moan 'fuck.' But it would undo me if you moaned my name. Can you do that for me?" His face is earnest, full of longing as he slowly leans down to kiss me.

"Is that a command?" I bat my eyelashes, pausing to emphasize the next word, because I know what it does to him. "Sir."

"That bratty fucking mouth. Don't make me punish you, pet."

"Yes, sir," I purr, reaching down to grip him through his pants.

"Oh, fuck, I need a second," he groans, sitting back and dragging a hand through his hair as he exhales.

I push up on my elbows until I'm sitting in front of him, reaching to undo his belt.

"I don't know what it is about you that has me wanting to come in my pants like a goddamn teenage boy."

"I think it's kind of flattering. Plus, I've never done this before, so I'd kind of like to return the favor, but I'm going to need you to talk me through it."

"Jesus Christ, I'm never going to last if you keep talking like that."

"Please, sir." I give him my best pouty lips.

He exhales slowly, as if it pains him to speak. "We'll have time for that later. I'll show you exactly how much I'd love your lips wrapped around my cock. But right now, I want nothing more in the world than to fill you up. I need to be inside of you. Need to feel you pulsing around my cock as you come."

"I need that too," I beg as I help him unzip his pants and pull them off, throwing them haphazardly onto the floor.

His cock juts out proud, straining up his stomach as I reach for it. He hisses. "Please, I've never—"

"Fuck, are you telling me you've never even touched a cock before?"

I shake my head as I glide my fingers through the slit on the end, smearing the moisture there. He involuntarily bucks into my hand.

"Emma," he warns as I continue playing with the head.

"I'm ready, sir."

He has me on my back, pinned to the bed before I squeak out the last word. His warm head parts me as he glides it through my wetness, teasing me.

"Wait," I cry, suddenly nervous.

Pulling back, he cups my face. "We don't have to do anything you don't want to do."

"I know, it's not that."

He looks at me expectantly as I try to push down the embarrassment and form the words to continue.

"What's it going to feel like? I've heard some people say it hurts, but my sister didn't mention that. And if it does hurt, like how bad? Will I bleed? Will it feel good eventually? How long will it last? I'm sorry, I'm just nervous and I want to know what to expect. I feel like I've studied everything I can to prepare for how it should feel, but now I worry it wasn't enough and that I'll disappoint you."

His smile is reassuring as his hooded eyes stare back at me. There's so much lust and reverence in his gaze that it stuns me, momentarily knocking the breath from me.

"There's nothing you could ever do to disappoint me. And if you want to know what to expect, honestly, it's different for everyone. But I'm not going to lie, I'm bigger than average so it might hurt, but that's why I wanted to make sure you're nice and ready for me. I can't really tell you what it will feel like for you, but I can describe what it feels like for me as I'm going, and if you want me to stop, just tell me and I will." I nod, and he fists his cock, lining it up with my entrance. "Ready?"

"Yes," I breathe as he slowly pushes his head into me. "Oh God!" I cry as I stretch around him. It hurts, and when I look down at where we're joined, there's a lot more of him to go before he's fully inside me.

He immediately pauses his movements, a pained look on his face. "Emma, honey, talk to me. Do you want me to stop?"

"Don't stop," I moan as I pinch my eyes shut and he slides in a little further. "Oh shoot, wait. I can't..."

"Emma, look at me," he snaps, and my eyes fly open, locking on his. "It's taking everything in me not to rut into this perfect fucking cunt. You're squeezing me so tight, and I've never felt anything better than how you feel swallowing me, enveloping me. You feel so warm, so soft, so wet, and so much like home. This is how it feels for me. I want to live here, inside of you as you pulse and squeeze me. Nothing has ever felt like this."

His words wash over me like a tide, smoothing over every crack in the sand and filling me with his adoration. My body relaxes, and my nerves dissipate. "I can't imagine doing this with anyone else. I trust you. I trust you so much." I pull his face to mine, kissing him passionately, so I don't share more.

"So fucking much," he echoes, kissing me again. My heart skips, wondering if there's a deeper meaning there. Before I can fixate on it too much, he pulls back. "How do you feel?"

"So full. It hurt when you first pushed in, but that second thrust didn't hurt as much. I don't think any of my research truly encapsulated what this sensation would feel like. It's just overwhelming. I don't know how to describe it."

"I know." He places my hand on his rapidly beating heart as he rubs his forehead against mine. It's comforting knowing I'm not alone in this, that he might be feeling everything I'm feeling too. "Are you okay?"

"More than okay," I assure him. "Can I...can I try something?"

"Honey, you can do anything you want right now. I'm at your mercy," he whispers against my skin, kissing my forehead.

"Don't move," I beg as I glide my hands up his chest, tracing the lines of his tattoos to ground myself. My touch is feather-light and I marvel as goosebumps break out on his skin and his breathing picks up. Ever so slowly, I rock my hips against him.

"Mmmmm. Fuck," he rasps. I can tell he wants to move, but it feels too good having this kind of control over him, as brief as it may be.

"I like this." I move my hips a little faster. "It doesn't feel like anything I've ever felt before. Your tongue, your fingers, your..." I trail off, suddenly shy.

"Say it. Say 'cock' for me, pet."

I swallow the nerves and continue. "Your cock. It all feels different. I don't know which one I like best. But it doesn't hurt anymore." My hips move faster. "I think I want you to move."

"Are you sure?" His eyes are full of concern. "I'm only halfway in."

I grip his cheeks, forcing him to see my sincerity. "I need you to fuck me, John. I need you to move, fill me up, make me come, make me yours. Please, John."

"Fuck, I'm yours. I'll do anything you want." He grabs my face, kissing me hard as he takes over, pushing all the way in. The stretch feels so good, the burn nearly gone as he pumps in and out slowly building up speed. He sucks on my bottom lip, pulling on it hard before dragging it between his teeth. "I'm going to embarrass myself with how quick you're going to make me come. You fucking own me, pet. I need you to come on my cock. Choke me with that perfect cunt."

He slides a hand against my clit as he rubs it in quick circles. I'm not even sure his efforts are necessary since my orgasm hits seconds later, overwhelming me with its intensity. My walls flutter around his length as my clit throbs against his hand. "Fuck! John!"

"Yes, fuck, Emma. Oh fuuuuck," he growls against my lips, as his hips still and I feel his cock twitch in me, a warmth filling me up everywhere. His eyes are locked on mine and I'm stunned by the emotion I see there. He's looking at me with so much affection, so much adoration. Like this means everything to him. He almost looks like he loves me.

CHAPTER 31
EMMA

"I did it!" I squeal as soon as Ella's sleepy face appears on my phone.

"Did what? You're way too chipper this early in the morning." She yawns, propping her phone on a pillow as she pulls her covers up to her chin.

"Do you have your earbuds in?"

"Hold on." She disappears from the frame, and I hear rustling before she reappears, earbuds in place. "What's so important that you needed to wake me up this early, Em?"

"I had sex," I say softly.

Ella shoots straight up and grabs the phone, moving closer to the screen like she's examining me. "Are you fucking with me?"

"No, I actually did it."

"Did Dommy Batman take your V-card?"

I giggle at her nickname for him. "Daddy Dom, Professor A-hole..."

"*You* had a threesome? Oh my God, tell me everything!"

"It wasn't a *threesome*," I tease, hoping she'll figure it out.

"I'm not following."

"Daddy Dom *is* Professor A-hole. His name is John, remember?"

"Holy fucking shit, I knew it!"

"It was—wait, what?"

"Something about the way you described both of them. And it made sense why your professor was a grumpy asshole. He could only have you at the club since he was your teacher. I love when I'm right about these things."

"Why the heck didn't you tell me sooner?"

"Well, I did try to tell you, but you thought I was joking." She laughs. "So how was it?"

"It was everything I ever wanted, El."

"So nothing like my first time. Lucky bitch."

I can't help the smile that lights up my face as I think back to last night. The way he touched me, cared for me. "This might sound dramatic, but it feels like a breakthrough. Like when he first touched me, but so much more…momentous."

"Given your issues with touch, it makes sense that you'd feel that way. I'm so happy for you. Okay, mostly happy and a little jealous you got an orgasm your first time."

"How did you know?"

"You have that look. That 'I've had mind-blowing sex' look."

"It was mind-blowing. And not just the sex. It was *him*. The fact that it was him. I've had feelings for Daddy Dom for so long, but I've only recently started feeling something for John. And when I figured out they were one in the same, something just clicked. Like I should've been mad, but I wasn't. I just knew. I wanted him. I trusted him. And I didn't want to wait anymore."

"Are you going to see him again?"

"I hope so. I've got a bunch of papers and schoolwork to get caught up on. But I was thinking of surprising him in his office soon."

"You should suck him off under his desk. Guys eat that shit up. Or so I've heard."

John

I can't focus on grading papers, not when the memory of Emma's sweet pussy squeezing me permeates my thoughts. It's been three days since I had her. Three days since that perfect cunt gripped me as she screamed out her release. When I was her professor and adhering to my rules, I could go weeks without seeing her and not feel this crazed. Now I want to crawl out of my skin, and it's only been seventy-two hours. But between my class load and her upcoming exams, finding time to see her has been difficult.

Not to mention, she's still a student at my school. I can't just walk around campus with her without drawing attention. While it may not technically break any school rules, us dating openly would be frowned upon.

And then there's my obligation to Mary. We're not out of the woods yet—she still needs my help, and juggling her, my classes, my work at the club, and Emma is a lot to manage. But I've kept so much from Emma, more than she knows. And while I'm confident she'd be understanding if the truth came out, I can't risk it. Not yet.

There's a soft knock on my office door, and I look up right as Emma sneaks in, closing it behind her.

"This is a pleasant surprise." I push my chair back from my desk.

"Do you have any meetings right now?"

"No." I eye her suspiciously.

She locks the door and walks around the desk, swaying her hips seductively. My cock pushes against its fabric restraints, eager to play.

"Anyone that would just stop by for a visit during office hours?" She pulls her hair back.

"No. What are you doing, pet?"

She drops to her knees and crawls between my thighs under the desk. "Good, because I need that lesson now."

I love that she can't get enough, that she's seeking out her pleasure.

"There's something we still haven't done, and I'm eager for my professor's instruction. And attention." She flutters her lashes.

"What lesson?"

"You said you'd show me exactly how you'd like my lips wrapped around your…" She eyes the bulge growing between my legs.

"Jesus Christ."

"Can I, sir?"

"Only if you say it."

She swallows thickly, working up the courage to ask for what she wants. "I want to suck your cock, sir."

"Pull it out." I lean back in my chair, propping myself on the arm rests as she undoes my belt and zipper.

Once my cock springs free, she looks at me for direction, and I nearly come from the look of total surrender on her face. Never has someone's submission made me this hard, this feral.

"Such a good girl, on your knees for me, eager to swallow this cock. What did I do to deserve you?"

I'm testing her, daring her to speak, but she refrains. My eager fucking pet wants to please me, submit to me, giving me total control over our pleasure. She places her hands on my thighs, waiting for instruction.

"Spit on your hand, make it nice and wet. Then grip it firmly by the base and squeeze hard as you slide your hand up to the crown. Swirl your palm around the head and go down my shaft again. I like a lot of pressure."

She follows every step, working her hand up, around, and back down.

My jaw clenches as I try to stay quiet. "So fucking good," I grit out. "Now repeat the same motion with your tongue. Tease me. Make me beg to fill your mouth with my cock."

Her tongue follows the same trail and when she reaches the base again, I drop my head back, stifling a groan, whispering "again" on repeat. I'm so worked up, I'm pulsing against her each time her tongue swirls around my tip.

"That wicked fucking mouth," I groan, grabbing her jaw and halting her movements. "Relax your jaw, flatten your tongue, and slide down my cock."

She nods against my grip as she takes my cock in one hand and guides it into her mouth, sliding down as far as she can go until it hits the back of her throat.

"Don't move. Shit. Fuck," I rasp, willing my orgasm to hold off a little longer.

Saliva drips down my length as she takes shallow breaths through her nose, and I work to control the urge to rut into her hot little mouth. She's not ready for that just yet. "Stay just like that and slip your hand into your panties. I want you to circle your clit."

She obeys, dipping her fingers under the lace as she slowly works herself up, her mouth still stuffed full of my cock. Little moans spill out as her orgasm quickly approaches causing me to squirm each time the vibration from her mouth reverberates through my dick.

The minute I see her brow pinch and her shoulders tense, I grab her hand, yanking it away from her clit. "Not yet."

She lets out a low groan of frustration as I delicately stroke her cheek.

"Now close your lips around me and suck hard as you slowly move up, lightly grazing your teeth against me as you go." A low growl escapes me when she obeys. "Fuck, yes. Just like that."

Sitting back on her heels, she pops off my dick, looking at me for further instruction.

"The sight of you, on your knees, making a mess with your mouth all over my lap. Shit."

A small smile lights up her face as her tongue darts out, licking her lips in a circle like a goddamn tease.

"I need that perfect fucking mouth on me. I want to watch as my cock disappears between those lips, messing up that pretty lipstick while you come apart on your hand."

"Yes, sir." She sits up and pulls me back into her mouth, flattening her tongue on the downstroke, and sucking hard on the way up, using her hand to hold me in place.

"That's it. Just like that. Touch yourself. Come on your hand while I come down your throat."

I watch as she obeys, slipping her hand back into her panties as she tries to concentrate on both tasks. The sight alone has me coming sooner than I expected. "Don't swallow," I command right as I spill into her mouth, my orgasm crashing into me.

Her muffled sounds nearly do me in as she moans around my cock when her orgasm hits, careful not to spill a drop of my cum.

"Open your mouth and show me what an obedient little thing you are."

She opens, showing me her mouth full of my cum.

"Now swallow me down, pet."

And she does, delicately wiping the corners of her mouth before licking her fingers clean, showing me her empty mouth after.

I grab her other hand and suck her fingers into my mouth, cleaning the evidence of her orgasm from them. "Tastes like mine."

Then I lift her off the floor and into my lap, kissing her deeply. When I pull back, she looks worried, and my hackles rise. "How do you feel, pet?"

She shifts nervously in my lap. "I've never done that before. Was it okay?"

"What you just did was incredible. Anyone can get a dick wet and suck on it. What made it perfect was the way you followed every command I gave you. You just submitted to me perfectly. I've never been more turned on or satisfied in my life."

She preens at the praise and leans into me. "This is going to sound silly, but I've felt different these past few days. Like anyone looking at me knows I've had sex. Can people tell just by looking at me?"

I press my cheek against her forehead and chuckle. "No, pet, I don't think they can tell just by looking at you, but if you walk out of here with your lipstick like that, they'll know exactly what you were just doing."

Her head pops up. "Oh shoot, do you have a mirror?"

"I don't." I grab her face, gently holding it in my hand. My finger glides along the skin around her lips, wiping away the stain as my gaze focuses on her mouth. "There."

"Thank you, sir."

My cock stiffens at her words. This fucking woman. She knows what that does to me. I shift underneath her, trying to resist the urge to fuck her on my desk. This is risky. And even though I've broken almost all my rules when it comes to her, I'm desperate to keep some in place. "As much as I'm enjoying our time together, I think we should talk about the rules and boundaries here."

She wrinkles her nose. "I thought we were done with those. I get it now, why you had so many rules."

"Do you?"

"Well, yeah. You were my professor, and it was forbidden. That's why you wore a mask, right? You didn't want people to know you were involved with a student."

"Technically I wore a mask before you were my student.

And I was never involved with you as a professor. You only interacted with Daddy Dom when you were my student."

"But you *are* Daddy Dom. So technically you were involved with a student. It doesn't make it less true just because I wasn't aware who you were."

She's not wrong. These were the lies I told myself when I gave in and broke my rules. And her calling me out isn't helping quell my hunger for her. "I enjoyed sparring with you in class. Do you know how many times I had to hide how hard you made me with that goddamn lectern when you spoke?"

Her mouth drops open, the blush on her cheeks spreading, and I love that I can admit these things to her now.

"I wondered why you stopped walking through the lecture hall as the semester went on. And that time Daddy Dom asked me to flash my professor. Oh my gosh, it all makes more sense now. How did I not see it sooner?"

"It was incredibly hot watching you submit to me in my fucking classroom, and you didn't even know it."

"There's something I've been wondering. I get why you had so many rules since this is complicated. But the rules you gave me? Were those to control me?"

"No, pet. My rules exist to give me control over myself. The rules I gave you were meant to help you."

"Because you're a white knight dom. You like to help your subs," she says as if she's figuring out all the parts of me I've hidden behind the mask. "Your rules did help."

"I'm glad to hear it."

"You know, I never did negotiate rules when we were in the club. You shared your non-negotiables, but I never set mine."

"I'll happily negotiate any rules you want at any time. You hold the power in this dynamic, and I want you to feel safe and empowered." I slide a comforting hand along her thigh.

"Can we make our own rules together?"

"I'd like that. What shall we start with?"

She chews on her lip. "I'm still working on myself, my past trauma, and how it's still affecting me. I need you to be patient with me. It's not your job to fix me, I understand that. Even though I've come so far, I may have moments where I struggle with touch or have nightmares. I don't want you to think..." She drops her head.

I slide a finger under her chin, forcing her to look at me. "You are incredible. Strong when others would be weak. I'm so fucking proud of you. I would never think anything less than that," I assure her, leaning in to kiss her softly.

When I pull back, her eyes are misty and I look at her pleadingly, hoping she'll see the sincerity in my face. "Consent isn't negotiable. Saying 'yes' isn't a forever 'yes.' You can change your mind at any time without guilt or punishment. Your safety and emotional health are far too important to me."

"So I can use my safe word at any time, and you'll walk away?"

"If that's what you need, yes. I will do anything you ask of me."

She thinks for a second. "I know one of your rules was that I be honest with you, but I want that from you too. I get why you couldn't be for so long, but now that I know who you are, there's no reason to keep secrets anymore."

If she only knew what I was still keeping from her.

I swallow thickly, chewing on the inside of my cheek, trying to figure out what to share. I can't tell her everything, but I need to give her something. "I'll tell you what I can. I promise I'll tell you everything eventually, but if I keep something from you, I need you to understand that there's a reason for it. I may not be allowed to tell you for legal or safety reasons. And I understand that's cryptic as fuck, but there are aspects of my life that I cannot share right now."

"Like what you do at the club? Are you still seeing other subs?"

My shoulders relax when she doesn't press further, instead

letting her jealousy steer the conversation. "I'm not seeing anyone currently, and the last few clients I've taken on have been couples that I've only coached. I haven't had any other subs since I met you. You're it for me, Emma."

"What does that mean for us now? Can we be together? Out in the open?"

I pull her against me, wishing I could grant her that and give myself to her fully the way she deserves. "I'm still a professor, and you're still a student. It's not that simple. But I promise, that when I can, when it's safe, I will shout it from the rooftops and cherish you openly the way you deserve. But, for now, the rules still apply."

CHAPTER 32
EMMA

Now that I know that John is Daddy Dom, we've yet to visit the club, and that fact just feels plain wrong. I want to experience it all, without him holding back.

And sneaking around on campus is getting increasingly difficult when we both have roommates. Not to mention the creep that's leaving me letters. I haven't gotten any since the threatening one, and I'm hoping that means that whoever it was has lost interest.

When we walk into the club a week later, I'm elated to finally get my wish: to see John unleash his true, full inner dom.

He leads me down the darkened hallway toward his private room, his hand pressed to my lower back, guiding me. Once we enter his room, the noise of the club is muted and his crisp, masculine scent permeates my senses as he towers over me.

"Every word I utter is a command I expect you to follow. Every pause is deliberate. Intentional. I need your total obedience. Not just your body." He swipes a thumb across my forehead. His touch is feather-light. Delicate. "Don't think about anything else. Don't daydream. Don't let your mind wander. If

I sense you pulling away, I'll bring you back. I don't want part of your mind, half of your focus, or some of your attention. I want it *all*. It's mine. Nod if you understand."

I nod quickly.

He grabs my hand, guiding me across the room to a device that looks like a padded picnic table, but smaller. "This is called a horse bench. Remove your clothing and straddle the top. Put your weight on your hands and knees."

"Yes, sir." I undress and then he takes my hand, steadying me as I climb onto the contraption.

His fingertips graze my calves in measured strokes. "Clear your mind and concentrate on my touch. Focus only on the spots where you can feel me."

My nerve endings come alive everywhere his fingers roam. The bottoms of my feet, the sides of my calves, the backs of my legs. His fingers pause along the crease of my inner thigh, teasing me in a slow caress. A whimper escapes me.

"Do you know how sexy you look right now heeding my every command?" His hot breath tickles the hairs at my nape. "I'm going to restrain you now." His hands never leave my body as they trail down each of my limbs while he cuffs me to the bench.

He steps away, and I miss his touch instantly. He opens drawers and cabinets on the other side of the room, and I focus on my breathing and the arousal gathering in my belly.

There's nothing I want more than for him to touch me. I crave his hands on my skin, the press of his lips. Shivering as his tongue traces every curve of my body. I never thought I would get to this point with anyone.

"Focus on the sound of my voice. The weight of my fingers on you. The bite of the leather against your skin," he says as a new sensation lights up my senses.

I jerk my head in his direction, "Wh–what is that?"

He pops my backside lightly with the implement. "I gave you a command, pet, and it didn't involve you speaking."

My mouth closes involuntarily at his words, the response Pavlovian and automatic.

"This is a flogger." He holds it out for me to see. "Do you trust me, pet?"

"Yes, sir."

"Fuck, you know what that phrase and your obedience does to me."

My eyes travel to his crotch, the outline of his cock presses against his pants, aching to be free.

He drops the flogger and grabs his belt with one hand, removing it in one fluid motion as it cracks in the air, his tattooed bicep flexing with the movement. Immediately I clench my thighs against the bench, my arousal dripping from me.

"Look at me. Eyes on mine."

My gaze shifts up to his and I'm stunned by the affection I see. "Such an obedient pet. You're doing so well. Always the best student for me, giving your attention to what edifies you."

When he bends down to pick up the flogger, I watch enraptured, waiting for my next command.

"Place your cheek against the bench and close your eyes."

I comply easily.

The strands of the flogger rustle, and I imagine him stroking it in his hand. His movements halt and he tickles my arms and back with the leathery fringe. He takes his time, pulling the braids against my body, lighting up my flesh with each pass as goosebumps prickle my skin. I let out needy whimpers each time he circles my bottom.

Please. Please. Please. I need more.

More pressure.

More of him.

More bites of pain only for him to soothe it away with his tongue.

Suddenly my backside is assaulted with tiny sharp pricks of pain. It's oddly arousing, the discomfort lasting a second before my skin tingles in a delicious sensation. And then his warm hand caresses and cups each cheek. His touch feels reverent, and I fight to stay lucid as a surge of pleasure courses through me like a tidal wave threatening to pull me under.

"You like that," he muses, and I nod slightly against the bench.

He repeats his movements. Spending several minutes punishing my ass, gradually increasing the intensity and duration before lavishing me with soft touches, kneading and kissing my skin. I don't realize how much I'm bucking against the bench until his words pull me back.

"You only come when I tell you to, pet. And from what I can tell, you're three seconds away from humping that bench to completion. Can you feel the mess you're making rubbing that perfect pink cunt all over my bench?"

"Yes, sir," I whine. I'm needy and out of breath, stilling my movements. Barely holding on. I need this man inside of me. I need him to make me come.

The sound of his zipper opening is loud in my ears as I squeeze my eyes tight, bracing for the sensation of him filling me.

When the tip of his cock brushes my lips, slowly gliding back and forth through my wetness, I shudder. And when he pushes in seconds later, I gasp.

We've yet to try this position, and it's an entirely different sensation than the ones we've done before. It feels like he's everywhere, filling every inch of me, his cock impossibly huge as he gently pulses in and out so I can adjust to him.

"I will never, never get over this," His words are choppy, strained as he pushes in, punctuating each word with a thrust. "This." *Thrust.* "Perfect." *Thrust.* "Fucking." *Thrust.* "Cunt." *Thrust.* "The way it stretches for me." *Thrust.* "The way it flutters and pulses around me." *Thrust.* "The way I feel when you're stuffed so full of me, I can't tell where I end and you begin. Fuck."

His words are my undoing as I fall over the edge, my orgasm crashing into me in wave after wave, as bursts of light explode against the backs of my eyes. It's so intense, so unlike anything I've ever felt.

"That's it. Come on my cock, pet. Squeeze it, show me how good I make you feel. Make a mess all over me. I want to be covered in your cum, knowing I'm the only man to ever make you come undone."

His movements slow as I come down from the high of my orgasm. When he pulls out of me, I whimper loudly. The number of times this man has drawn that kind of sound out of me tonight should be embarrassing.

His warm hand caresses my cheek and my eyes flutter open. He moves slightly, blocking the overhead light from shining in my eyes as I squint up at him.

"Are you still with me?" He presses his mouth to my forehead, placing several soft kisses there. I nod my agreement.

There's gentle tugging at my wrists and ankles as he loosens my restraints and helps me sit up. Bending down to look me in the eyes, his stare is penetrating as though he's trying to peer into my soul.

"I think it's time for some aftercare while you come down."

I blink at him in confusion.

"It's common for submissives to enter a state of euphoria during an intense scene. Based on the way your pupils are dilated, I'm guessing you're feeling pretty good right now. Maybe like you're a little drunk or high?"

"Is this subspace?" I rasp, surprised by the sound of my voice. "I read about this."

He chuckles. "Of course you did. Ever the astute teacher's pet."

"I love when you use big words to say nice things to me. It's sexy." I giggle.

"Then allow me to elucidate how incredible you are. Meticulous. Fulgent. Ebullient."

"You know those aren't synonyms for incredible," I tease. When he swats my behind, I gasp.

"So clever. And Jocund. Jubilant. Docile. Lyrical. Demure. Jovial," He punctuates each word with a kiss as he slides his arms under my thighs and picks me up, pulling me to his chest so I can wrap my legs around his waist. The tip of his cock stretches up his abdomen, brushing against me with each step he takes. I tighten my grip around his neck as I rub myself against his rigid length.

"Fuck, baby, you're so wet. Is all this for me?"

"This is what you do to me. Only you."

He moves quickly over to the lounger, sinking into the deep curve in the middle of it, as he pulls me atop him. I melt against his chest, nuzzling my head into him as I trace the lines of his skull tattoo. His jaw flexes and he hisses in a breath as I get bold in my movements, grinding my center against him in slow quick thrusts.

"Did you finish?" The fingers stroking my back still.

"Tonight isn't about my needs." He cups my cheek. "It's about yours. You come first. You will always come first to me."

His tone is serious, making it obvious that he's not just talking about my pleasure. I tilt my head up to his as he slowly moves his lips closer to mine. "I love you, John," I whisper softly right before his lips touch mine.

He stiffens against me before pulling back abruptly, framing my face in his hands as his gazes searches mine.

"Don't tell me that right now."

Blood rushes to my face as I squirm in his hold, wanting to escape his scrutiny and his command. "What?"

"Do you trust me, pet?"

Reluctantly, I give him a single nod.

"Do you want to please your dom?"

Again, I give him a solitary nod of agreement.

"Then you have to obey every command I give you in here. And I'm telling you not to tell me that *right now*. Not when we're in the middle of a scene. Not when you're coming out of subspace and aren't fully in control of your mind and words. Not when I can't know for sure if it's the high of your orgasm making you confess what you think I want to hear."

He leans forward, pulling my cheek against his as he speaks against my ear.

"Don't confess the words I've been waiting to hear since the day you stood up to me about how I graded your paper. Don't get my hopes up when I can't be sure it's not the endorphins making you confess something you don't really feel. Don't make me fall more in love with you than I already am. Not when I can't fully be with you the way you deserve."

I'm not alone—he feels this too. This all-consuming feeling that keeps drawing us together like magnets. My heart beats wildly in my chest as our breathing slowly synchronizes. I turn over his words in my mind, trying to pull the unspoken meaning from them.

"I want to hear your words when you have a clear mind. I need them so goddamn much." His voice breaks on the last word, and I turn my head, capturing his lips.

And I kiss him. Hard. Slow. Deliberately. With all the love I have in me, pouring it all into the kiss. If he won't let me confess it with my words, I'm determined to show him with the press of my lips to his, the exploratory stroke of my tongue into his mouth, the way I dig my fingers into his skin to pull him closer as I thrust against his erection pinned between us.

We stay like that for what feels like ages, exploring each other's mouths with our lips, teeth, and tongues as our hands roam each other's bodies, groping, pinching, and caressing. It's one long confession of feelings passing between us, and I've never felt more at peace, never felt safer, like this is exactly where I was meant to be my whole life, wrapped in this man's arms.

My arousal is at a fever pitch, and my thoughts are consumed with pleasure, his specifically. This man has spent all night worshipping my body and I want to make sure he knows how much I appreciate him. How much I need him to fall apart at my touch.

Tilting forward, I press my chest against his as I lift up, snaking a hand down to line him up with my pussy. When I slowly sink down on his length he breaks the kiss, groaning in appreciation.

"Oh fuck, Em. The way your pussy feels gripping my cock is incomparable. I could live in this cunt every day." He slowly rocks up into me.

"I want that. So much. Every day, just like this. Oh God!" I can barely get the words out as I concentrate on the way he feels moving under me. The flex of his abs with each thrust. The press of his forehead against mine as he starts chanting my name.

"Oh shit, Emma. Need this. Emma, fuck. Need you so much. Em," he rasps against my lips. It's not a shout from the rooftops, but the intensity in his voice is palpable as my orgasm hits and my fervid cries spill from my lips.

Our heavy breaths fill the space as I drop my head against his shoulder. Strong hands glide up and down my back. I'm uncertain whether he expects me to get off his lap, but I've learned to obey his command, and he remains composed beneath me. When I shift nervously, he places his hands on my hips.

"Don't."

I blink rapidly against his skin, waiting for further instructions.

"Don't move," he pleads, digging his fingertips into my skin.

I exhale a shuddering breath, anticipation overwhelming me as I hang on his words.

"You feel incredible."

My chest expands and contracts as each rise and fall against him feels like a tether, tying our souls together.

"I don't want this to end." I whisper the words against his skin in a silent prayer.

Something shifts between us at my confession. He grips my jaw, forcing me to look at him as he presses a kiss to my forehead, his lips lingering as he speaks. "We can't..." He trails off, but I already know where this is going.

"There are rules. I know." I roll my eyes. I know being with him is complicated, but I long for the day we can be out in the open. Free to date with less restrictive rules. With just *our* rules.

CHAPTER 33
EMMA

The sneaking around is really starting to pick away at my insecurities. Our visits to the club have become more frequent in the past two weeks, and I know I'm being a petulant child with my whiny requests, but I can't shake the feeling that he's embarrassed to be seen with me.

"We need to be discreet. There are rules," he'll say. I know our relationship would be frowned upon at school since he's a professor, but I'm getting sick of his rules, especially when it feels like the only obstacle in our path preventing us from being together.

Since John had plans tonight and Becka needed a sitter, I happily agreed to help. Her family has doubled in size since I last saw her, adding a partner and another daughter and son to her clan. Maybe it'll be good that we have a night apart so we can come up for air.

"Thank you so much for babysitting, Emma." Becka pulls me into a hug and ushers me inside. "Bennett's parents had plans, Miles is out with friends, and I wasn't sure if you were free during the school year."

"Only sometimes. Finals are coming up and then there's the play, so it's good you caught me this weekend since I won't have a lot of time after this. I'll probably just study after the girls go to bed."

"Just make sure you cut them off at two bedtime stories, or you'll be reading *their* books all night instead of yours." Bennett chuckles as though speaking from experience.

"That's not an issue when I tuck them in," Robert adds. "You just have to make sure they know that two is the limit."

"I thought three was the limit?" Becka quips as she and Bennett laugh while Robert scowls.

"Why are you two laughing?" Robert grumps.

"It was a threesome joke." Bennett playfully slaps Robert's chest, and his scowl deepens. "Don't pout, B. You're just jealous that the girls like Fun Dad reading them more than two books." Bennett smirks at Robert, causing Robert's brow to furrow. "They know Grumpy Dad reads two and Fun Dad reads more."

"Okay, you two, not everything is a competition. Save it for the basketball court." Becka kisses each of her men on the cheek. "How did things go with that A-hole professor?"

I can't help the blush on my face at her question.

"I wanna hear about that later," Becka says.

I smile politely, looking for a reason to excuse myself from the conversation. "Are the girls upstairs?" I ask as the doorbell rings.

"Yup. Will you grab that on your way up? It should be my brother Jack and his wife. We're headed out on a double date with them." I back out of the room while he and Bennett debate what to call their group date since it's technically a double date with five people.

I open the door, standing behind it as I speak. "C'mon in, everyone's in the kitch—" I stop when the couple walks into the foyer and I get a clear view of who it is.

Holy shit.

"Emma?"

What do I call him? Daddy Dom? Professor Ali? A-hole

definitely feels most fitting right now. "John," I rasp, the shock in my voice evident.

We stand there staring, me gaping in disbelief, him blinking at me in confusion, his normally perfectly polished mask peeled back exposing a tempest of emotions underneath.

The woman beside him clears her throat. She's stunning with gorgeous skin and perfectly done makeup. Her dark brown hair is pinned up.

"Sorry, this is my wife, Maryam. Maryam, this is Emma. She's a former student."

I'm a former of all my titles now, A-hole.

He's *married?*

Oh my God, I'm his dirty little secret. It's why I've never seen his place. We always met at the club. He wasn't just hiding me because I was his student. It's why he said he couldn't be fully honest. My stomach rolls and I clutch it as I move past them and head up the stairs.

"Emma!" his voice calls after me as I close and lock the bathroom door behind me.

Somehow, I manage to get through the night. Hallie and Lexie are a welcome distraction, making it easy to shift my focus. Every time I had a minute to myself to spiral, one of them would run up or ask me a question and pull me out of my funk.

The waiting is the worst kind of torture. I didn't let him explain after he arrived, and I've been ignoring his texts all night. I can't turn off my phone in case Becka or her guys need to reach me. It feels like an agonizing countdown toward my heartbreak. Will he come back with them? Is this all going to implode in front of Becka, Robert, and Bennett?

Oh God, what if he's telling them about me? Will they ever want me to babysit again?

When I see headlights pull up thirty minutes later, I'm pacing and head to the kitchen to wipe down the counters and load the dishwasher. I hear someone climbing the stairs as footsteps move toward the kitchen.

"You can just throw those in the sink. I like to wash them by hand," Becka says.

My anxiety is spiraling out of control as I grip the counter, letting my intrusive thoughts spill out, convinced Becka knows all the sordid details.

"Becka, I can explain." I turn toward her, ready to face the music.

"Explain what?" She furrows her brow.

"Never mind. How was dinner?"

"It was good, but Jack seemed distracted and was on his phone all night."

"I have to tell you something," I say nervously.

"What's wrong? Were the girls okay for you? Oh God, were they awful and you're telling me you're quitting?"

"Gosh, no. Nothing like that. They were great." I twist my hands in front of me, unable to contain the nervous energy bubbling to the surface.

"Okay, good, because they adore you and there's no way I'll be able to find a sitter as wonderful as you."

Will she still think that when I tell her what I've done?

"Are you and Jack close?"

She stares at me in confusion for several seconds, blinking. "Not where I thought you were going, but okay. Robert recently reconnected with him. They were never really close, and when their brother Michael was killed, it really tore apart their whole family."

He's shared a little about his brother, but clearly I don't know the whole story. "That's awful. What happened?"

"Michael was beaten to death at school. It wasn't ruled a hate crime, but it was definitely because of his sexuality. It happened while Robert was in his freshman year of college.

His family was never the same after that. When we started family dinners, Robert decided that he wanted to reconnect with Jack. I think they each blamed themselves for Michael's death, and they both withdrew from the family because of it."

"Oh my God."

"Yeah. Luckily they were able to reconnect and talk through a lot of these issues. Why do you ask?"

My thoughts are moving a mile a minute thinking through everything he's said to me as Daddy Dom, Professor A-hole, and as John. This explains a lot about why he's so protective, why he feels the need to be a white knight and help others.

Becka clears her throat, and I look up, locking eyes with her. "Emma, sweetie, what's going on? Why are you suddenly interested in my brother-in-law?"

Tears flood my vision, and her silhouette blurs in front of me. She pulls me into a hug, and I sink into her warm embrace. "Jack is Professor A-hole, isn't he?" I nod against her shirt as a sob escapes me. "And he showed up here with his wife and you've just been sitting here in a panic. You're why he was on his phone all night."

"How did you figure all that out?"

"It's a gift. I've gotten really good at following bread-crumbs." She chuckles, stroking my hair and brushing it back from my face. "Do you want the good news?"

I look at her and nod.

"I don't think he loves her. We've hung out with him quite a bit the past few months, and tonight was the first night I met her. If one of my guys had his head buried in his phone at dinner all night, you better believe I would be annoyed. There's no way I wouldn't say something. But Mary was unbothered. And they definitely had friend vibes, not happily married, madly in love vibes."

"But he's still married, and he didn't t–tell me," I stutter out, trying to calm the emotions swirling inside me.

"True. But something tells me there's more to the story than how it appears. If I know anything about the Gardner men, they're a pretty easy bunch to figure out. There's not a thought in Robert's head that I can't read on his face. And Jack was easy to decipher at dinner. I knew something was up."

"Gardner? So his name is Jack Gardner?"

"His name is John, Jack is a family nickname. And Robert said he took his wife's name."

"Ali. I know him as Professor Ali, or John."

Becka laughs, easing my nerves slightly. "I think you've only ever referred to him as Professor A-hole to me, or I would have figured this out sooner."

My responding smile is weak as I run through all my lingering thoughts.

She places a hand on mine, squeezing it, and I imagine she's imbuing me with strength I don't have. "I think you should talk to him. Let him share his side of the story. I'm sure there's more to it than it seems. He doesn't strike me as the type to string you along."

Her words should comfort me, but I feel hollow. It hurts to know that she knows this whole other side of him that I've never seen. That clearly I don't know him at all. That his rules were there to keep things from me, little pieces of himself he was either unwilling to give or had already shared with someone else.

"I dunno. This week is going to be crazy with the play. I've got a lot going on, and I should probably just focus on that right now."

"Oh my gosh, we're so excited! We're all coming to watch —Bridget and Ethan, Robert, Bennett, Miles, and the girls. I think Alyx even said your parents are bringing your sisters to opening night."

"Yeah, the matinee is the only performance that isn't sold out. I think everyone I know is coming to opening night." I can tell my smile doesn't reach my eyes, but Becka doesn't call me out on it, instead she wraps me in a tight hug.

"I know it doesn't feel like it right now, but it's going to be okay. I promise." She releases me, holding my shoulders while looking directly in my eyes. "Take some time for yourself to gather your thoughts and then talk to him when you're ready."

I know I should let him explain, but I don't think I'm ready to hear his excuses. And what else could they be but excuses? He's married. I can't think of any possible explanation he could give that would make this okay, and I'm not sure my heart could take it if he tried. It feels like it's shattered into a million pieces during a windstorm and there's no way I could possibly find them all to make it whole again. There will always be fragments that are missing, lost to the wind, belonging only to him.

CHAPTER 34
JOHN

Fuck. Fuck! I've been so careful, or at least I thought I had. This is why I have rules. If I'd just stuck to them, it would've protected me from situations like this. What the fuck do I do? I can't lose her. But I've already committed to helping Maryam with her citizenship, and we're so close. I can't fuck this up for her now. Not when it could literally be life or death if she's deported back to her home country.

I've managed to keep this part of my marriage secret from everyone in my life. My colleagues, my family, the club. As far as anyone knows, I'm just a married professor. How did I screw this up so badly?

The waitstaff could have brought out a live fish that sprouted legs and did a jig on my plate, and I wouldn't have noticed. I keep checking my phone to see if Emma has replied to any of my messages. It gutted me seeing her face when we walked in. I had no idea she was my brother's babysitter. And this is definitely not how I wanted her to find out about Maryam.

Near the end of dinner, Maryam pulls me aside. "John, can I talk to you outside?"

My head shoots up, looking around the table, and my

brother Robert grimaces and nods to my phone. *Fuck, I need to focus.*

We walk outside, the humid May air causing me to tug at the collar of my shirt when Maryam unexpectedly pulls me into a hug. I'm not expecting it, and I stumble over my feet.

"You've been distracted all night. I'm worried about you." She examines my face.

"I'm fine."

"Does this have anything to do with all the tension I felt between you and the babysitter at your brother's house?"

The look on her face is understanding when I don't answer, just nod.

"Is that the girl you told me about?"

"It is."

"I see. And until tonight, it was going well?"

"It was. I love her," I admit, rubbing the back of my neck.

"John, you've done so much for me, now it's my turn to repay you. I want a divorce. Go be with her." Maryam places a hand on my arm.

"No, I made you a promise."

"But you love her. And I can still apply for a green card even if we divorce." She squeezes my arm.

"I know you can, but we're so close. And it's risky. What if they deny your green card? Or worse, deport you?"

"Since Samira fled to Canada, she's been a citizen for a couple of years now. Her path to citizenship there was faster than mine has been here."

"I thought she was a US citizen." *I'm an ass. As much as I know about this woman and her girlfriend, I should know this, but my mind has been preoccupied for a while now.* "Sorry, I'm a shit friend."

"You're not." She smiles instantly putting me at ease. "She has a work visa, but her company has offices in both countries. She'd probably be able to get me a job so I could move to

Canada, or she'd move back and sponsor me there till I could apply for citizenship."

"So you've thought about all that. Made a plan." I scratch the stubble on my chin.

"I've seen the way you've lived your life since we met. You always put others before yourself and it's admirable, but right now it's stupid. You're miserable, and you don't have to be. I'll never forget everything you did to get me here, but you don't have to be the martyr anymore."

"I still want to do this for you, Mary. It's important to me."

"I know it is. But you've served your time." She smiles, her dark brown eyes full of gratitude.

"You say that like this is a chore." I wave a hand between us. "You're a person, a person who deserves to love whomever you want and not be put to death because of it. You're not a chore. Nothing I did for you the past six years was a chore."

"Wasn't it? Look, I know it wasn't when this first started. And I understand your need to help others, to make a difference in the world around you. But what started as a sincere gesture has become an obligation for you over the past couple of years, and I have a feeling it has everything to do with your feelings for Emma."

She's not wrong. "I'm not going to divorce you when you're a few months from getting your green card."

"If there's a chance Emma isn't okay with this, then yes, you are. I'm not going to let you sacrifice anything more for me, certainly not love."

My mouth opens in rebuttal, but she narrows her eyes and I close it, thinking over her words.

"I was married to Ahmed for years when I fell in love with my best friend. When we couldn't be together, you gave us a chance. You brought me here and gave me space to be with her, all the while sacrificing yourself to keep up the ruse. If there's anything I can do for you, it's to end this marriage so you can be with Emma. I can talk to her, explain things."

Blowing out a breath, I put my hands on my hips and look up at the sky. Can it be that easy?

We head back inside the restaurant and finish our meal. Emma hasn't read any of my messages, and I decide the best thing I can do right now is to give her some space to process everything. Once she reads my texts, she'll understand, and we can talk. I just hope that she reads them and feels the sincerity in my words.

"Are you staying at the house tonight?" Maryam asks as we leave the restaurant and climb into the car.

Normally I'd stay in the city and meet up with Emma at the club since I couldn't take her back to my house with Maryam there. And I couldn't bring her to my room on campus since my professor roommate would not approve of me bringing a student back to his place.

"I'm going to take your silence as a no."

"I'm sorry. I should—" I cut myself off, suddenly unsure of what I should do.

"You want to be close to her in case she wants to talk."

"I'm sorry."

"Stop saying that. I totally understand."

"I don't deserve you," I say, hoping she sees my genuine gratitude.

"It's funny, I feel the same way about you. Why do you sell yourself short? How come you can't see the wonderful man that I do? You've given up the last six years of your life for me. You're a good friend, rafiq."

"I'm not a good man."

"And I'm telling you that you are. A little stubborn clearly, but a good man, nonetheless. I know you carry the weight of your grief over your brother's death on your shoulders, but I need you to hear this. You've helped me more than you know. You've paid your penance, not that you needed to, but clearly the guilt you've been holding onto about your brother is telling you otherwise. So stop beating yourself up and go after her. You deserve to be happy more than anyone I know."

———————

Once I make it back to campus and collapse onto my bed, I pull out my phone. Emma still hasn't read my texts so I decide to reach out to the only person I can think of who might know where she is.

Have you heard from Emma?

She's not at her place.

ALYX

She was babysitting for Becka tonight.

About that...

What the fuck did you do?

If you broke her heart, I will fucking end you, bro. Even if you do have a few inches and lbs of muscle on me.

Respectfully

Are you done?

Start talking.

I had plans with my brother tonight.

How does this involve Emma?

Becka is my sister-in-law.

Robert's your brother? 😬

Yeah, why?

...No reason.

Did you hook up with my brother?

…

Never mind, I don't want to know.

So, did you find Emma at your brother's
or not?

Oh, I did. And so did my wife.

THE FUCK?!?

BRO!

YOU'RE MARRIED!?!?

I can't really get into it through text, but I need
to talk to her.

Please, it's important.

If you hurt her, I'm not the only one you'll
have to answer to. You know that, right?

I'm not trying to hurt her. I love her.

Oh shit, I thought you were just spanking her.

Jesus.

Do you know where she is? Is she safe?

CHAPTER 35
EMMA

"I don't like lying to him. Can I at least tell him you're safe?" Alyx asks, sitting next to me on the couch.

"I don't want him to know I'm here."

"I'm still pissed about the married part and the lying too, but he's really torn up about it. Look." He tilts the phone screen so I can read their last few messages.

My eyes get stuck on three words.

I love her.

Three words he's yet to speak out loud to me.

Three words he's hinted at and yet danced around.

Three words he's probably telling his wife right now.

And suddenly his rules make sense. His cryptic words whispered in moments of passion that felt like they held a deeper meaning, come crashing into me.

It isn't that he's a professor, and I'm a student.

"Don't make me fall more in love with you than I already am. Not when I can't be with you the way you deserve."

It isn't the school rules keeping us apart, or the rules at Pulse. It isn't even his list of dom rules that's the issue. We can't be together because he already has a life with someone else, already promised her forever and made vows to love her.

"Hey, it's gonna be okay." Alyx throws an arm over my shoulder, tugging me into his side. It's an awkward hug with the way we're sitting on the couch, yet I still find comfort in his touch. I'm not able to contain my emotions any longer and tears spill over my lashes, making what I'm sure are black streaks down my face.

"I don't see how," I cry as his hand squeezes my shoulder.

"For what it's worth, I've never seen him with anyone at the club. And he definitely doesn't treat his other subs the way he treats you. Also, he's never asked me to reach out to anyone before."

"Is that supposed to make me feel better? He was doing all that while still cheating on his wife. She probably doesn't even know about his whole secret life as a dom. It's probably all a lie." I'm aware that I'm coming across like a whiny child, but I couldn't care less.

"Something tells me that's not true. I think there's more to this than you realize."

"Do you know something?" I ask suspiciously.

"Nothing I can confirm, but I can tell from his texts that you mean something to him."

"If I meant something to him, he should've told me the truth. Instead, he spent a whole year lying to me, pretending he was only my teacher while talking to me as Daddy Dom, and a whole 'nother year not telling me he was married."

"I'd bet anything there's a reason he didn't tell you."

My eyes narrow on him. "You're so good at keeping everyone's secrets, but you seriously need to tell me what's going on."

"Even if I knew something, it wouldn't be my story to tell. I've met a lot of people in my time as a sex worker, and you know the main takeaway I've learned?" He pauses, waiting for me to answer. I cross my arms over my chest and tilt my head, signaling for him to continue. "More than anything, people are desperate for a connection. They want to feel like they matter to someone else. Most of the people I interact with at the club aren't there because they want to fuck."

I shoot him a disbelieving look.

He holds his hands up in surrender, letting out a hearty laugh. "Okay, okay, they want to fuck, but that's just on the surface. Deep down, most people are searching for something more, craving a connection at a deeper level. They want to be seen, want to know they matter. If it was just sex, they could take care of that with a hand or toy. People come to me because they want more than the orgasm they can provide themselves."

"Why are you telling me this?" I say, fully aware of how exasperated I sound.

"That man doesn't say or do anything he doesn't want to. And if he spent two years patiently pursuing you, it tells me that he's desperate for that connection too. Maybe he's not getting it at home. I'm not condoning cheating or lying, and I'm not justifying his actions, but I think you should keep an open mind."

Letting out a deep breath, I think over his words. Maybe he's right. "Even if I did give him a chance to explain, I can still walk away from him if I don't like what I hear."

"But are you really going to walk away from the only man who's ever solved your touching problem?"

"Ugh." I drop my head into my hands, then pop my head up suddenly as something hits me. "What if my nightmares come back? Between Daddy Dom's sessions and Professor A-hole pushing me to unlock the memory that caused my nightmares, they had pretty much stopped. But they came back when he broke up with me."

"Do you wanna sleep in my bed?" Alyx offers.

"I don't need your woody poking me all night."

"Oh my God, no one calls it a woody anymore." His groan turns into a laugh. "Besides, I'm not popping boners *every* night and I'm definitely not popping one for you, sis. Respectfully."

"I know you're not, but it's biology, and I'd prefer to remain ignorant to all things involving your crotchal region."

He barks out a laugh. "I'll build a pillow barrier."

"Ethan's old room is fine."

"Then I'm sleeping on the couch so I'll be close by if you have a nightmare."

"Your room is like ten feet from my door."

"I promised your brother that I'd look out for you. Please? It would ease my mind."

"Fine," I relent with a sigh.

We sit in silence for several minutes as I think over Alyx's insight. While I appreciate his optimism, I'm having a hard time believing it. And what's so disappointing is that so many other men in my life have let me down. John was the first person who broke through my sexual barrier, and it's unfathomable that he could already be committed to someone else.

"Okay, you need to get out of this funk. Need a laugh?"

"Yes." I lean back against him on the couch.

"I may have given John's brother a BJ."

"Cheese and rice! You're joking!" I say through a fit of laughter as I push up to see if he's serious.

"To be fair, I didn't know it was John's brother at the time."

"Wait… You and Robert? Does Becka know?"

"Not my—"

"Story to tell, yeah, yeah." I roll my eyes.

"Exactly. But I can confirm she was present for it. I won't say any more out of respect for their privacy."

"I'll have to ask her about it after the next book club meeting."

"Actually, lemme just text her now so she knows you know." He pulls out his phone as his fingers rapid-fire across the screen.

"So you're like secret friends with everyone, aren't you?"

He mimes locking his lips with a key when there's a knock at the door.

"Please tell me that's not—"

He shakes his head, cutting me off as he gets off the couch. "It's not him, it's just"—he opens the door—"your annoying little sister."

"Fuck you, Alyx. There is nothing little about me." Ella rushes over to me, her big personality filling the space as she plops down into my lap, wrapping her arms around me.

"Lovely, as always." Alyx rolls his eyes. "And I was referring to your age."

"Then you should've said younger, not little. And I'm almost nineteen now, so you can stop treating me like a baby."

"Stop acting like one, and maybe I'll stop treating you like one," Alyx volleys back.

"What are you doing here?"

"I texted her. I figured I'd let you two catch up. I knew you'd need your support system right now."

"Thanks." I smile.

"I'm gonna get outta your hair, let you two talk," he says, heading to his room.

"Use a condom!" Ella calls out after him.

Without turning around, Alyx pauses in the doorway, holding up his middle finger.

"You're gonna need more fingers than that if you ever want to make anyone come," Ella barks back.

Alyx grips the doorframe, his biceps popping as a small smirk lights up his face. I swat at Ella's thigh as Alyx disappears, closing the door behind him.

"Still not able to finish what you started, I see," Ella yells at his closed door.

There's a thud against the door in response and then silence before I turn to her as she scoots off my lap sitting next to me. "He's a really good friend. I know you two get on each other's nerves, but besides you, he's the only person that's been there for me."

"And I love that for you, but any day that I don't have to see his face is a good one as far as I'm concerned." Ella's arms are crossed as she continues to glare at his closed door. I'm not sure if she's waiting for him to reenter the room or if she's placing a silent curse on him. I clear my throat, drawing her focus back to me.

"Sorry, I just don't know if I'll ever get over how he treated me when we were kids, and every time I see him, I want to throat-punch him. But he did text me to come saying you and John were having issues. How can I help? Are we making voodoo dolls tonight?" She crosses her legs, facing me on the couch as she rubs her hands together. "I know who I'd like to make one for." Her eyes snap to Alyx's room.

"Seriously, what happened when you were kids that you're not telling me? I remember you following him and Ethan around all the time and then suddenly you stopped." I point over my shoulder in Alyx's direction, lowering my voice. "And he's never said an unkind word about you, so I'm kinda confused why you hate him so much."

"Are you fucking kidding me?" she yells, and seconds later Alyx's head pops out of his door.

"You just tell her the part where he's married?" Alyx asks, looking at me.

"What the actual fuck is happening right now?" Ella shouts.

I shake my head. "I have not told her that yet." I shoot him a withering look, and he holds his hands up in defeat.

"Sorry."

"Okay, one of you better start talking." Ella's delicate features scrunch into a scowl.

An hour later, I've filled her in on everything that's tran-spired with Professor A-hole. We're sitting on the couch, Alyx in the middle, my feet propped in his lap while he massages my foot through my sock. Ella is on the opposite end of the couch, practically sitting on the armrest to avoid being near Alyx, her legs tucked tightly against her body.

She wiggles a finger between us. "You two have the weirdest co-dependent relationship I've ever seen."

Alyx gives me an annoyed look before turning his face to hers. "Says the girl who hops from guy to guy because she hasn't dealt with her daddy issues."

"You're one to talk, fuckboy. How many flavors have you been through this week?"

"Jealous?" He grins.

Ella squeaks out an awkward laugh. "Oh, you've got jokes now?"

"You're the one attacking me for being friends with your sister. There's nothing wrong with our friendship. And labeling us co-dependent just because you don't understand it is ignorant. Physical touch is hard for her, but she can handle mine. So what if I rub her feet or shoulders? I'm not trying to get in her pants."

"If there's nothing wrong with it, why doesn't Ethan know about it?"

Alyx pauses his massage at her words, thinking carefully about how to respond.

"On more than one occasion, he's been suspicious that something was going on with me and Emma because she kept showing up here. It wasn't my place to tell him about her aversion to touch and how I'd helped her. I'm not sure there's a way to explain it to him that he would understand. He told me not to fuck with his sisters, but he also told me to watch out for her."

"He did?" I ask, touched as Ella speaks at the same time.

"What about me? He didn't tell you to watch out for me?"

"Jesus, Ella, not everything is about you." Alyx drops his head back onto the couch in exasperation. "Just like how I knew that Emma was capable of taking care of herself, I knew

Ethan was worried about her, but he was also pretty distracted at the time."

"Maybe I need someone to take care of me," she pouts.

"Something tells me you can take care of yourself just fine." He swivels his head to her.

I can see all the emotions she's holding back as she glares at him.

"So what's the plan, are you going to talk to him? Hear him out?" Ella shifts her focus to me.

I groan. "I just want to keep my head down and get through this week."

"Are things any better with that actor guy? Jeremiah?"

"Jeremy," I correct her. "Kinda? We've been able to get through the show with minimal issues. He's been really understanding and respectful of everything I've asked of him. He even blocked a stage kiss where he tilts me upstage and covers my mouth with his thumbs so he can kiss them instead of me."

Alyx shifts his attention back to me. "So he hasn't tried to make any moves on you? Ethan would want me to ask."

"No, he's harmless. If I were attracted to him more, I'd probably give him a chance, but I don't like him like that. He's just a friend."

"What about when the play's over and you don't have to see John at rehearsal anymore? Are you going to talk to him then?" Ella asks.

"Ugh, I dunno. I probably should, but I can't even think about that. I just feel numb. I can't believe any of this is real."

"It'll hit you. Breakups are kind of like grief that way. You're still in denial. You'll go through all the phases: bargaining, anger, depression, before you get to acceptance. Trust me."

"Is that what happened with you and Chad?" Alyx asks, his tone teasing.

Ella doesn't break eye contact with me, a look of sadness washing over her when she speaks. "Sure, Chad." Something tells me she's not thinking about her breakup with Chad, but I wrack my brain for what breakup could be affecting her like this.

"Okay, I love you guys, but I have to go to bed," Alyx says through a yawn.

"Then go to bed," Ella snaps.

"You're kinda sitting on it." He leans back into the couch, stretching his arms up, exposing a sliver of his abs. I watch Ella's eyes fixate on it.

"You have a bed, dumbass," she says, looking annoyed.

"I'm sleeping out here in case this one has any nightmares." He hooks his thumb, pointing at me.

"Well, if she does, I'll be there to help since I'm sleeping with her."

"Nuh-uh. You're not staying here. Ethan would kill me if he knew two of his sisters were spending the night at my place. I love the guy, he's my best friend, but sometimes I think he looks at me like I'm only after one thing, so he gets really hung up on the idea of me hanging around you two too much. Just because I fucked around a lot when we lived together doesn't mean I'm going to fuck anyone I see. He tends to over-react when it comes to his sisters."

"He's just really protective," I agree.

Ella nods. "He practically raised us since Dad was always working. Sometimes I worry more about his approval than Dad's."

"So we agree, you're leaving," he says to Ella.

"Uh, no, I'm not."

They stare at each other for several minutes, neither backing down until Alyx walks to his room, speaking over his shoulder. "I'm going to grab some pillows. This room better be empty when I return."

CHAPTER 36
EMMA

It's been a stressful week full of tech and dress rehearsals. The first several shows went well, and I'm relieved that this matinee is our final performance. Avoiding John during those has been surprisingly easy. It's in the quiet moments of the evening, when I'm lying in bed, that my mind drifts to him. I still haven't looked at his texts. If I don't look, then his excuses won't let me down. I've officially moved on to bargaining, with a side of ice cream-fueled depression.

We're nearing the end of Act Four as I stand in the wings, taking deep breaths, pushing these thoughts down as I will the nerves away.

"Stage fright?" a voice whisper asks behind me. I turn to see Jeremy and offer him a small smile.

"Something like that," I say, tight-lipped. We've come a long way in rehearsals, and I've been able to handle his touches with little incident. With some creative blocking, we were able to stage our kiss so it looks real. I've built it up in my head, but our actual kiss is just a quick peck. And that quick peck is all that's standing between me and the end of the show. Once I get through this, I can go back to my apartment and sink into my bed as I wallow in my married professor-induced grief.

I shake out my hands, hoping to dispel my nervous energy.

"Want some water? I haven't had any yet." He unscrews the cap and hands it to me.

"Thanks." I gulp down nearly half the bottle.

"Easy there, tiger." He laughs as I hand it back to him.

There's a blackout on stage, and we stand there, waiting for our cue.

Once we make our entrance, the scene moves along smoothly, the audience laughs at the appropriate parts and gasps when the hidden identities are revealed. But something feels off. I look out into the audience and make eye contact with a man in the front row. It's hard to focus, and I suddenly feel dizzy, like I've been drinking. The man peers up at me, clenching his jaw. He looks peeved. Wait, is that John? It looks like John, but it's hard to tell since my vision feels foggy and he's blurring in and out of focus. I squint my eyes, trying to make him out better.

"And since you called me "master" for so long,
Here is my hand. You shall from this time be
Your master's mistress."

Jeremy speaks next to me, but my gaze is stuck on the man in the crowd.

Is it him?

Suddenly, I'm yanked against a body, and I stumble over my feet. This isn't what we rehearsed. My mouth goes dry as I struggle to hold my head up. I look down at my arms that are trapped between us. Rough hands cup my face, as thumbs stroke my cheekbones. For a second it feels like a dream, and I shut my eyes, picturing John's face peering back at me. But when I open them, I see Jeremy's face coming toward mine as he leans in and kisses me directly on the lips. I feel light-headed and I try to push him away, but everything around me feels like it's in slow motion yet quickly spinning at the same time. The kiss feels like it lasts forever, but I'm too weak to stop it.

What's happening?

When he breaks the kiss, he scoops me into his arms and my head lolls against his shoulder.

"M'lady is overcome with the news, I must bid you adieu," I hear him say. Is he ad-libbing now? The scene isn't over. Why are we going backstage?

The sound of applause is distant as I lose the battle to keep my eyes open as everything fades to black.

John

The minute she comes back onstage for Act Five, I know something's wrong. She hits all her cues, but her speech is slightly slower. And when she looks at me with those glassy eyes, alarm bells go off. She almost seems... drunk? Emma doesn't drink, but maybe she did a shot to ease her nerves?

And then that fucker throws everything we'd worked on in rehearsal out the window and actually kisses her. She struggles against him—it's subtle, but I know every movement Emma makes. I have watched her submit to me at the club, know every twitch, every shudder, every microexpression, and her body is screaming to me for help.

Turning my head, I scan the crowd for Alyx, but I don't see him. I'm not sure if she has anyone at today's matinee. Maybe they all came to an earlier show.

I watch as Jeremy carries her off stage and I'm out of my seat, not waiting for the curtain call.

When I get to the door that leads backstage, it's locked.

Fuck.

I pat my pockets, feeling for my keys, but come up empty, realizing they're across campus in my office. There's a distant roar of applause, and I run back to the theatre, making my way down the aisle during the standing ovation and discreetly slip backstage.

It's chaotic and crowded in the wings as the cast and crew run around excitedly. I see Mackenzie near a dressing room, and I call out getting her attention.

"Where's Emma? Is she okay?" I force myself to ask calmly, even though I'm screaming on the inside.

"Yeah, Jeremy said she was acting weird backstage earlier. Told him she didn't feel good. It's probably the nerves mixed with the heat from the stage lights that made her pass out. He said he was going to take her to the hospital to get her checked out just in case." Her tone is distracted as she speaks, waving at people and hugging others that approach.

Am I making things up? Why isn't she more concerned? Maybe I'm overreacting.

"Did he say which one? The nearest one is a forty-five-minute drive." Panic rises in my throat. Something isn't sitting right with me about all this.

"He didn't actually, but I can text him and send you an update."

"Okay, I'm going to head in the direction of the nearest hospital he might have taken her to. Text me as soon as you find out where she is." I don't give her the chance to respond; I take off for my office to grab my keys and start the drive to Columbus to find her.

CHAPTER 37
EMMA

My head hurts, and my mouth feels like sandpaper.

"There she is," a muffled voice says nearby.

Is that Jeremy? Am I at the hospital?

I squeeze my eyes tight to shield from the harsh lighting, then try to blink them open. Jeez, this pillow is hard. I attempt to rub my eyes, but I can't move my hand.

Slowly, my senses start coming back to me, and I feel something hard beneath me. Definitely not a hospital bed.

I'm lying on my stomach on a wooden bench and my hands are bound behind my back. And Jeremy is standing over me. I look around, trying to focus my eyes. We're in one of the practice rooms in the basement of the music building.

"You can scream if you want to, but these rooms are sound-proofed."

My heart pounds as fear courses through me. I discreetly wiggle my wrists to test how much give my bindings have. That's when I realize that there's something tied to my ankles, preventing me from closing my legs. Oh God, what is he going to do to me?

"Don't think about trying to get out of that. I got a merit

badge in Scouts for my knots. Those aren't coming loose anytime soon."

"Jeremy, what's going on?" I ask sweetly, hoping I can win him over and get him to release me.

He paces in front of me, my eyes fixate on his boots as he speaks. "You know, I watched you for months. I saw the way you fawned all over him. It was desperate and needy, and you're better than that."

My head hurts as I try to make sense of his words. "Who?" I croak out.

"Your professor boyfriend," he spits. He grabs a chair and spins it backwards before he straddles it so his knee is inches from my face. "I think it's time for a little story. You wanna hear a little story?"

I pinch my eyes closed, willing myself to wake up. This has to be one of my nightmares.

"Oh, that's right, I don't give a fuck what you want!" he yells, and I flinch as his laughter follows. "It's not like you're going anywhere right now."

A tear pools in the corner of my eye, and I tilt my head slightly allowing it to escape, suddenly terrified of what he's going to do to me. This isn't the nice guy I've gotten to know over the past year.

"Once upon a time, I met a guy named Trent. Ever heard of him?" I'm unsure if he's waiting for me to answer, but when I refuse, he continues. "A buddy of mine invited me over to his place. We played *Call of Duty* and shot the shit. I thought it was just guys hanging out, but once a few people left and it was just a handful of us, he told us about this chick he'd been with in high school. Told me all about *you*." He pokes me on the last word.

"He said you came off like a good girl, but you were a freak in bed. Told us that he'd pay someone a hundred thousand if we could prove that we'd been with you."

So there actually *was* a club? I joked about it, but it was real?

"It was kinda weird and I thought he was bluffing, but when I looked into his family's finances, he had the bank account to back it up. I don't think anyone else took him seriously, but I needed the money, so I devised a plan."

I shift against the bench as the edge of it digs uncomfortably into my thighs. He leans down; his lips close to my ear as he speaks. "Stop squirming, or I'll give you something to squirm about."

My body goes stiff, and I take shallow breaths.

He leans back. "I played the long game, signed up for that acting class with that dick of a professor, and purposely sat next to you, became your scene partner. When I learned about your little issue, I was pissed. I thought Trent had set me up. There was no way he ever slept with you. But I decided, fuck it. I needed the money, and I didn't care." He places his hand against my cheek, smashing my face further into the piano bench.

"You're a psychopath," I grit out, barely able to understand myself.

"Undiagnosed, so you can't prove it, but probably. Anyway, halfway through our acting class sophomore year, Trent mentioned that he'd pay me more if I fucked you and filmed it. I don't know what you did to piss him off, but I couldn't pass up that kind of money."

Flashbacks to my encounter with Trent over spring break that year fill my head. This is my fault.

"I watched you that first year, learned your habits, saw who you hung out with. Oh, by the way, you probably need new friends. It wasn't hard to convince Megan and Rylee to talk you into going to that party earlier this year. All I had to do was flirt a little with those vapid bitches and they took the bait. I was planning to make a move, but that frat bro at the party fucked that up. What was curious was when I saw a certain professor beat the shit out of him right after. Why would he do that?"

"I don't know what you're talking about." I really don't. I don't remember seeing John on campus that night, and he never mentioned it to me.

He leans closer, getting right in my face as he pulls a knife out of his pocket and glides the dull side along my cheek. "Yes, you do, don't play dumb with me. I know there's something going on with you two. I just can't figure out when it started."

I bite my tongue, not willing to share John's hidden identity. Things may be strained between us, but I'm not going to betray him like that.

"So I followed your little professor friend. Learned everything I could about him. Did you know he's married? No wonder he was sneaking around with you. He didn't want anyone to know you were his dirty little secret. I knew I had to do something."

"What did you do?" I ask. Anything to keep him talking, hoping it will buy me time for someone to find us down here.

There's a gleam in his eye, probably a reflection from the light hitting the knife in his hand. "I sent you letters, of course. I'd hacked my way past his alarm and snooped around his house when I came across those letters he sent his wife. It was actually genius on my part. I took them and started leaving them for you."

"But I got the first one at the end of my sophomore year." I cringe, worrying I've just admitted our tryst, but he continues unbothered.

"I saw the way he looked at you during our acting class that semester, but you were clueless about his interest in you. I figured I'd speed the process along."

"I don't understand. You wanted us to be together?" I ask, keeping him talking to stall as long as possible.

"I wanted him to slip up and kiss you on campus or something so I could expose him as a cheater preying on one of his students. I thought it'd be obvious to you that the letter was from him. Then I would swoop in and comfort you, and that money would be mine."

"And when that didn't happen?"

"Then I waited for my opportunity. I played the friend for months, gaining your trust, hoping you'd fall into my lap on your own. Then when we were cast in the play, everything started coming together. The theatre department always needs more guys for their shows, and I was able to bluff my way into the leading role opposite you. I was going to just offer to help you with whoever you had to end up kissing, but it worked out better that it was me. But then that fuckface professor started getting more involved, wanting to talk to you after. I watched as you let him put his hands on you after rehearsal, as he carried you home after I left you at the library, when you snuck into his office."

His admission causes a wave of nausea to hit me, knowing that this man spied on intimate moments between John and me.

He moves closer, waving the knife wildly as he gets more and more upset. "So I kept sending letters, trying to find ones that were obviously meant for someone else, hoping you'd think he was cheating on you."

"And the threats?"

"All me, baby. Nobody touches what's mine. And make no mistake, you belong to *me*. And today I'm finally going to claim my reward. Not everyone has a rich mommy and daddy. Some of us have to bust our ass just to make ends meet."

He stands, kicking the chair away, and it hits the wall before toppling onto the carpeted floor. His tall figure looms over me as he cracks his knuckles.

"Please don't do this, please!" I beg as my muscles tense and my trembling hands grip the bench tightly. He runs his palm up the back of my leg, lifting my skirt as he goes. I recoil against my bindings.

"I promise I'll make this good for you."

CHAPTER 38
JOHN

"She's not at the hospital. I went to the one you mentioned, and she wasn't there. I called all the other major ones in the city, including the ones that would've been closest to campus, and no one has a record of her." Actually, I had Mary call most of them while I stopped at the ones that were on the way back to campus. I wanted to stay in the city, in case one of Mary's calls located her. But when it became clear that Jeremy lied, I gunned it back toward Faith Union's campus.

What the fuck is going on and how did it go this far?

"I'm sure she'll turn up." There's a little too much pep in Mackenzie's voice. It's a stark contrast to the panic that has a chokehold on my heart.

"Have you gotten ahold of Jeremy?"

"He's not answering his cell."

"That's bullshit!" I yell into the phone.

"Professor Ali, are you okay?"

"No, Mackenzie. I'm not okay. I have two missing students, one who may still be unconscious and in need of medical attention."

"Wait, is this, like, serious? I just thought Emma was dehydrated or something, and Jeremy took her back to her room or the doctor or something."

I pinch the bridge of my nose. "You're the one who told me that he took her to the hospital."

"Yeah, when I called Jeremy after the show to check on Emma, he said she still wasn't feeling well, and he was gonna have her checked out at the hospital. I figured she woke up and was throwing up, or she had the flu or something."

"Mackenzie, listen to me carefully. Something is seriously wrong. Why would he tell you he was taking her to the hospital, and they have no record of her? And why wouldn't he take her to the closest one?"

"Maybe she woke up and told him she was fine, and he just took her home?"

"She's not in her apartment, nor is she at the campus nurse. I had my buddy Nate from campus security check. Can you call him again? Text him?"

"Do I need to call the police?" she asks in a panic. "I'm sorry, I kinda thought you were just overreacting. You can be kinda intense sometimes."

"Let's see if we can get in touch with Jeremy first. Nate is patrolling student apartments and her usual hangouts on campus. He'll notify me if he sees anything."

We hang up, and I try Emma's cell again, but it goes to voicemail, the mailbox full. When I pull into campus, I head toward the theatre. The building is dark. It's been several hours since the show ended.

I pull out my phone to send a quick text.

> Hey Nate, I'm over at the theatre. No sign of her. Find anything?

> Nothing at the library. Heading back from student apartments. I'll check out the buildings near the theatre. Check in with me in fifteen. If we come up empty, I'll call it in.

An eerie silence permeates the space, and I walk through the building looking everywhere I can think of: the green room, dressing room, costume closet, scene shop, rehearsal spaces, classrooms, even the light booth and all the catwalks above the house. The administrative offices are locked, and I look over at the doors that connect the theatre building to the music building. There's a light on. No one should be in here; the theatre has long been emptied, but there are music students that occasionally use this building on the weekends.

As I'm turning off the light, I notice the door to the basement practice rooms is slightly cracked open. It's not an unusual sight, but something in my gut tells me to check down there just in case.

I'm walking through the corridor when I see a light on in a room at the end of the hall and I quietly hustle over to it. Most of the rooms are fully soundproofed, but a few at the end of the hall are older and still need updating.

A muffled cry comes from inside, and I rush to the door, sickened by what I see inside.

Emma is face down on a piano bench, her wrists bound behind her, her ankles tied to a broom that's attached to the legs of the bench. The broom is holding her legs open like a spreader bar.

"I'll make this good for you," Jeremy's muffled voice says as he kneels between her legs and moves his face close to her cunt. *My* cunt. I'm about to open the door when I notice the knife in his hand.

Fuck.

I pull out my phone and silently curse when there's no signal. I can't leave her here to call the police. There's no telling what that sick fuck will do, and she's already lived through enough nightmares.

A plan forms in my mind, and I swallow down my nerves at what I have to do. I pull up the camera app and hit record, sliding my phone in the front pocket of my shirt with the camera facing out.

Jeremy's face is inches from her body when I violently throw the door open, startling him. He falls back onto his ass, nicking his leg with his knife in the process.

"Back the fuck away from her."

He recovers quickly, adjusting his grip on the knife and scooting closer to her exposed skin. Her skirt is flipped up, and there's a scrap of lace on the floor from where he must've cut her panties off.

He drags the tip of the knife up the back of her thigh as she whimpers, chanting "Please don't do this, please don't do this" on repeat.

I want to kill the sick fuck. But first I need to get him away from her. I inch closer, letting go of the door as it snicks closed behind me.

"Don't come any closer!" he shouts, a manic edge to his voice. He doesn't sound like his normal self.

"I said, back. The. Fuck. Up." I take a step toward him, and he points the knife at me.

"You really don't want to come any closer." There's a crazed look in his eye and his voice is eerily calm, which is really fucking unnerving.

When I take another step, he drags the knife along her skin, holding the blade against the upper part of her thigh. "Do you know how quickly she'll bleed out if I nick her femoral artery?"

I freeze at his words, my heart beating rapidly as the room starts to feel like it's closing in on me.

"Minutes. She'll be gone in minutes, and it will be *all your fault*." He pulls at his hair with his free hand, tugging on the blond strands.

"Okay, let's be calm and talk about this. We can figure something out." I hold my hands up in surrender, taking a step back.

Emma is in the same catatonic state, still chanting, her face pressed into the bench.

I drop to a knee, and Jeremy's head pops up. "What are you doing? Don't do something stupid."

"I'm just going to take her pulse," I explain. Leaning closer to her ear, I repeat it for her. "I'm going to touch your neck and take your pulse. Okay?"

She grows silent, nodding her head slightly.

Gently pressing my fingers against her neck, I count silently as I stare at my watch. As expected, her pulse is racing, but it slows slightly at the end of my count. "You're doing so good for me. Deep breaths, okay?"

"Einstein," she rasps, turning her head toward me, and I nod at her as my heart breaks. When a tear streaks down her cheek, I swipe it with my thumb, spreading the moisture around her face as I try to comfort her with my touch.

I hear the faint squeak of a sneaker on the polished floor of the hallway and remember that I hadn't checked in with Nate. Hoping I'm not imagining things, I stand, backing away slowly to make Jeremy think I'm retreating. I see what looks like a flashlight out of my periphery.

"You can have her," I say loudly.

Emma shudders as several tears fall down her face.

"What the fuck are you talking about?"

I swallow down the bile in my throat, sick about what I have to do next. "I know when I'm outmatched. Clearly you two have something going on. And she just gave me her safe word. She told me she'd only say that when she wanted out," I lie. "She's not mine anymore, and I know when to walk away." My voice is loud and clear, and I hope that whoever is in the hall can hear us.

"Just like that?" he asks, confused.

I grab the doorknob as I crack open the door. "Yup. I suggest you ditch the knife, though, unless you're into that sort of thing. No judgment if you are. I'm not shaming anyone's kinks."

Nate pushes the door open, his gun propped over the hand holding his flashlight, and he nearly knocks me over as I throw my body over hers.

"Drop the knife," Nate booms as I snake my hand between her legs in an attempt to shield her and push the knife away.

The knife falls to the floor, and Jeremy lifts his hands.

"Called it in. There's an ambulance en route. It'll probably be out there if you want to get her out of here," Nate says, restraining Jeremy.

I pull Emma's skirt down and untie the ropes. Once her legs are free from the bench and broom, she sits up, and I quickly work at the knots around her wrists. When I get her free, I scoop her into my arms and move quickly down the hall.

There are EMTs and a stretcher rolling up to the building when we walk outside and I watch in slow motion as they take her from me and start strapping her in.

I follow after them as several police officers hustle up the path. "Can she not be restrained? Some psycho had her tied up in the building just now. Campus security has him detained."

Two of the officers walk past us into the building while another stays by Emma's side as she's loaded into the back of the vehicle.

"Sir, you're bleeding." An EMT points at my hand.

I wave her off. "I'm fine. Where are you taking her?"

The officer motions me over, takes my info down, and I agree to follow them to the hospital so I can give my statement.

CHAPTER 39
JOHN

When I finally make it into her room in the ER, I pause in the doorway, staring at her small form curled on the bed. I knock lightly on the doorframe, and she shifts, her gaze meeting mine.

"You're here," she rasps, her voice still hoarse.

"The nurse said you were back here. I got here as fast as I could."

"Took you long enough." Even though her tone is playful, her words land their mark, bruising my ego. "My parents were here earlier, but I sent them home an hour ago, hoping I'd be discharged by now."

I lift my bandaged hand. "Turns out my cut needed a few stitches."

"I'm so sorry."

Offering her a small smile, I pull a chair next to her bed. The triage rooms are small, so I feel like I'm bumping into everything as I try to get comfortable.

"I know I'm probably the last person you want to see right now, but I needed to know you were okay."

She nods slightly, moisture pooling in the corner of her eye.

I reach out to swipe at it. When she doesn't flinch, but instead leans into my touch, I breathe out a sigh of relief.

"I looked for you after the play. I'm sorry I didn't get there sooner. Mackenzie told me Jeremy took you to the hospital, so I just started driving—heading to the closest one I could think of. I checked almost every hospital in Columbus, and Mary called the rest. If I knew you never left campus, I would've found you sooner."

"Something told me you'd find me. Since I met you, when something bad has happened to me, you've been nearby, ready to swoop in and help. I should be creeped out that I have a stalker, but it was always oddly comforting knowing you were looking out for me."

"A dom takes care of his sub." A tear slips down her cheek. "I should've found you sooner." I hope she can hear the desperation in my voice.

"You were worried about me."

"I was terrified. I didn't know what he was capable of and how much he'd been doing right under my nose."

"I had no idea until he laid it all out for me before you showed up."

"What did he say?"

"I already relayed everything to the police, I don't have the strength to go through it again." She leans back into the bed. "Did the nurse say when I'll get to go home?"

"No one will tell me anything, since I'm not your husband or family. I got lucky getting back here. I think the nurse let me in because the cop vouched for me, and I complimented her stitches." I lift my hand again.

"Are the police still out there?"

"No, they left after I gave my statement. I'm pretty sure they had enough proof to lock that fucker up for good."

Her brow furrows, and she lets out a deep exhale as she sits up, pulling her legs against her chest and my eyes land on the bandage on her inner thigh. It takes everything in me not to grab her and hold her to me. When I stand, her eyes flick to mine in concern. "May I?" I ask, reaching for her leg.

"I'm not wearing anything under this. He cut my—"

"I know he did. And I've seen all of you before. This isn't about that. I need to know you're okay. Can I do that?"

She nods. I gently glide my fingertips up her thigh, gauging her reaction. When I get to the bandage, I trace the edges, applying a little more pressure. When she shivers, I look over and notice her eyes closed, head dropped. "Pet?"

"You can't call me that. You can't just come in here and act like the last week or so never happened. Like you didn't rip my heart out of my chest twice now."

I withdraw my hand, but she grabs my wrist, keeping it in place, still refusing to meet my eyes. "I didn't say I wanted you to stop."

My fingers continue stroking along her thighs until I see her visibly relax under my touch.

When she finally looks at me, her pupils are blown wide, and a few tears spill over her lashes as I lean over to swipe them.

"I need answers. I need to understand what's really happening. It feels like I'm living out some ridiculous Shakespearean play and everyone knows their part but me. What am I missing?"

"What do you want to know? I'll tell you everything. I'm done hiding from you."

"Does Mary know you're here?"

"She does."

"So she knows about me?"

"She's the one that encouraged me to pursue you."

Her brows pinch in confusion. "I don't understand. Do you have an open marriage? I did meet you at a sex club so you could be into all kinds of kinks I don't know about."

"I don't have an open marriage. What I do have is a *legally binding* marriage in the eyes of *the law* with a woman who is a dear *friend* of mine." I try to emphasize certain words so she'll pick up on my meaning.

"That's not answering my question," she says, growing agitated.

I blow out a breath, moving her legs so I can sit on the edge of the bed as I lower my voice.

"I used to do a lot of missionary work for the university. A little over six years ago, I went on a trip to Yemen. And one day this woman walked into my line at the soup kitchen. I could see the desperation on her face, hear the sadness in her voice. There wasn't a romantic attraction, but *something* was pulling me to her. Once I finished serving, I sat at her table. It didn't take much to get her to talk, and I was surprised at how eager she was to share with me."

"What did she say?"

My shoulders relax, relieved that she's willing to hear me out.

"Her husband was threatening to report her to the authorities, and she needed a way to get out of the country."

"Maryam was already married?"

"She was divorced by the time we met. Where she's from, people like her can be put to death, and that's why she wanted to leave her homeland."

Her brow furrows in confusion as she shifts on the bed. "People like her? Women?"

"Women who love other women."

She looks at me unblinking, her brows raised. "She's gay?"

I nod. "When we met that day, she told me all about how she fell in love with her best friend Samira. Mary felt pressured by her parents to marry a man and she obeyed, but she was never truly happy, and the man she married was not a kind one. He suspected something was going on and divorced her, threatening to go to the authorities if she didn't leave quietly. But she's lived in fear of him ever since. The day we met, he'd just threatened her again. She was confident that nothing would come of it since he didn't have any proof, but I could tell she was terrified."

"What would've happened if the authorities found out?"

"She could've been thrown in prison or stoned to death."

Silence stretches between us for several minutes. The clock's ticking growing louder with each passing second as she processes my words.

I hesitate to say more, knowing I haven't shared these details with anyone but Mary. It's important that she hears my truth, so I take a deep breath and pull her legs onto my lap as I muster the courage to continue. "There's a reason why I felt called to help her."

"Why?"

"Because I couldn't save him."

"Couldn't save who?"

"My brother Michael. I knew how much he was struggling. My brother Robert may not have known what was going on with him, but I did. Michael told me he was gay. He was going to come out to our parents. I told him it was a bad idea. That there was no way our mom and dad would handle it well. I was too much of a coward, and I hid in my room while he did it. And I knew he was being bullied at school, and I didn't do anything. He was a year behind me, and he was weird and different, and I was a stupid middle school boy that just wanted to blend in, and being around him at school forced us to stand out. So I ignored him. I didn't stand up for him when I knew he was being picked on."

"Oh, John." She rests a hand on my shoulder and squeezes gently, and I feel instantly grounded.

"I have seen firsthand the power of hateful words in the mouths of bigoted people. I know what that hate is capable of, and I'd be damned if I ever stood by and watched that happen again, not when I could do something about it. Not with Maryam, and not when I felt like I had a second chance to help."

Exhaling, I continue. "I was the one who found him." The admission feels like a lead weight in my chest. "When I didn't see him at the parent pick-up line, I went looking for him, knowing how mad our mom would get when we were late. He wasn't at his locker, and I ran through the school, searching every place I could think of when I saw a group of kids huddled in the back of the gym in this alcove behind the bleachers next to a door that led to the football field. The way I burst through the door must have scared them, and they took off."

It's a struggle to speak as emotion clogs my throat at the memory still as vivid in my mind as the day it happened. "I almost didn't see him. He was lying so still. Too still. At first, I thought the guys that ran off had left behind a pile of clothes. Something told me I needed to go over there. And when I got closer, I recogni— I rec— it was his shirt. His stupid One Direction shirt that he wore practically every day. I'd know that shirt anywhere. But it was covered in his blood. They'd—"

Swallowing, I summon the courage to continue as her hand strokes along my arm. "They'd beaten him to death. I didn't even recognize his face," I say through tears, willing the rising emotions to abate. "But I knew it was him."

"Because of the shirt?"

I nod. "Because of that stupid shirt that I used to tease him about relentlessly. And because of his shoes. He had this pair of Vans that he'd drawn rainbows on. I couldn't stand those shoes. It used to bug the crap out of me. Not because he drew rainbows on them, but because they didn't match. His left shoe had a thin rainbow while the right had a thicker one that disappeared into a cloud. It made my eye twitch. I remember wanting to grab some sharpies and make both rainbows even. He used to give me shit about that." I smile briefly at the memory. "But I knew it was him because of those stupid fucking shoes and that shirt. I shouldn't have ignored him even if he did bug the shit out of me. I should've stood up for him even if it put the spotlight on me. And now I'd give anything to get my annoying baby brother back."

She leans over and pulls me into a hug. It's stiff and awkward with the way we're sitting. I'm turned at an odd angle, but I lean into her as much as I can, finally relieved to have someone else to share this burden with as I cry on her shoulder.

"I can't imagine what that must've been like for you. And I'll say this, because you need to hear it and I'm not sure anyone has ever said this to you, but none of that was your fault. You're not to blame. Not for his death. Not for the way he came out, or the fact that he did, and certainly not for your parents' reaction to it."

My eyes blur with tears at her words and I blow out a breath as I wipe my face.

"It explains a lot, though, if I'm honest."

I blink at her in confusion. "What does?"

"Your need to help others. To save people. You have a soft spot for LGBTQIA+ causes. The friendship you've struck up with Alyx at the club. It makes sense why you would offer to help Maryam."

"Holy fuck," I say as I process her assessment.

"You said you were a white knight dom. You like protecting others and solving their problems," she says like she's piecing together the puzzle of who I am.

"You're totally right. I couldn't ignore the woman in front of me that needed actual help and just go back to serving soup in foreign countries. Here was an opportunity to do actual good, so I took it. We established a long-distance relationship through letters, emails, and texts. I even made a couple of trips over there so we had more evidence. There was enough proof that she could refute her ex's claims that she was gay, and enough to establish credibility so we could apply for a K1 visa. It took two years to get it, and we got married a few days after she made it to the States. Then she had to apply for a green card."

"You didn't push me away because you didn't want me."

"Fuck no. I've never wanted anything more in my life than how badly I want you."

"And I was your student."

"There was a reason we couldn't be together until now. I had to make sure that my marriage looked legitimate so Mary could get her green card. She could still get it if we divorced at a certain point, but I didn't want to chance it."

"What did that require?"

"It had to look like we lived together. We have a mortgage in our names, have joint banking accounts and tax returns, and I even changed my last name to hers."

"That explains why I didn't figure out your relation to Robert sooner."

"Yeah, we only recently reconnected, and I couldn't put off him meeting Mary any longer without either hurting his feelings or him getting suspicious."

"But you don't have a ring." She glances at my left hand.

I lift my right hand and wiggle the finger with my ring. "Rings are worn on the right hand in Mary's culture."

"What happened to Samira? Did she make it to the states?"

"She did. She and her son were able to escape to Canada as refugees and are now citizens, but she's here on a work visa."

"Do you all live together?"

"I rent a space near campus during the school year. Since Sam travels a lot for work, Mary gets scared of being in the house by herself, and I stay there when that happens. She lived in a war zone for most of her life, and it's the least I can do to provide her some comfort."

"What about the letters?"

"What about them?"

"Jeremy said he stole some letters from you. Those were the ones that kept showing up on my door. I was having a hard time following what he was saying because I was groggy from whatever he drugged me with. One of them was addressed to M and signed J. At first, I thought you sent it to me because you've called me Em before. And the letter talked about you not wanting to be separated from me, and it arrived right after you broke things off."

"Jesus, if he got my letters to Maryam, that means he was in my fucking house in Columbus. No wonder she's been scared to be alone in there. I wrote those to Maryam while she was still in Yemen. We wrote to each other regularly, and we saved all that mail as proof of our relationship so we could apply for the K1."

"So you didn't mean anything in those letters to her?"

"No. We just needed it to look like we were in love. After a few months of penning my own, I just started using letters and love declaration passages from literature. You're lucky I didn't use any James Joyce for those letters, or you would have been really embarrassed."

"Oh my God, my sister and I found a letter he wrote his wife in a book at the library once. He went on for ages about doing it in the butt while his wife farted. Ella and I almost got kicked out of the library from laughing so hard."

"Yeah, I didn't think the government needed a letter like that as proof of a relationship." I laugh.

She looks up at me, her brown eyes shining under the fluorescent lighting. I'm suddenly overwhelmed with love as I stare at her.

"I'm sorry I've been avoiding you. I kept telling myself that I needed to get through this week with the show before we talked about all this."

"Are you sure you want to talk about this now? We can wait until you've gotten some rest," I ask, rubbing her leg.

"It's okay. I'm okay. I'd rather talk about this right now. Honestly, I told myself that there was nothing you could say to justify keeping all that from me. That any excuse you gave me for not telling me you were married was going to be total crap. And then you had to go and tell me the only thing that could justify everything you did. All the lying, all the secrets, all the rules."

"I wanted to tell you. So many times. And it's not that I wouldn't trust you with that secret, but I haven't told anyone. Besides Mary and Sam, no one knows. Not even my family. Hell, I didn't even invite any of them to the wedding. And it's been eating me alive for six years. Other than Mary, I've had no one to talk to about this, and while Mary and I are close friends now, I couldn't really tell her how isolating it was, how lonely I felt. How I felt like I had no control over my life. But I was happy to do it for her, and I refused to make her feel guilty for my decision."

She looks at me, her brow furrowing as she works out her thoughts in her head, careful with her words when she speaks. "Is that why you became Daddy Dom?"

"Partly. I've always been into BDSM, and never shied away from exploring my dominant side, but once I became a married man publicly, I essentially agreed to become celibate. I had it in my head that I couldn't risk it ever looking like I was cheating on my wife if I wanted our union to look believable. If anyone ever saw me at the club, I could explain that I just worked there, but it was the only outlet I had to control these urges I could never act on. And I didn't want to get involved with anyone because I knew I couldn't pursue it as long as I was married. I didn't want to jeopardize her citizenship, and I couldn't imagine any partner I had being okay with waiting all those years for me to get a divorce. So I created rules that allowed me to indulge in a scene at the club in private while also protecting myself from getting attached. And I pushed you away when I felt myself falling for you."

"That's why you wore the mask and disguised your voice. Does Alyx know all of this?"

"He knows some. He didn't know I was married, though.

He knew I was a college professor and knew my first name. And he figured out that I was Professor A-hole pretty quickly."

"And I just thought you were uptight."

"Far from it. I'll never forgive myself for the way I treated you in all of this, pushing you away and then pulling you back in. You trusted me as your dom to provide for you, and I broke that trust. I'm so fucking sorry, pet. You deserve to be worshipped and adored, not hidden away like my dirty little secret.

"I need you to know that I didn't mean what I said in that practice room when he had you—" I take a shuddering breath and squeeze her leg still in my lap, grounding myself to her as a reminder that she's okay. "Fuck, Em, I was so scared, seeing you restrained like that, not knowing what he was capable of. And when you said your safe word, I knew I had to do something to distract him."

"I remember saying it, and some of what you said after, but parts are fuzzy. My heart felt like it was going to beat out of my chest, but when you touched me, I knew you would keep me safe."

"He was so close to you, it took everything in me not to beat his ass right there, and I would have if he didn't have a knife. There's nothing I wouldn't do to keep you safe, Em. No length I wouldn't travel to find you. I'd walk away from it all right now if you asked me to. My job. My marriage. The club. If you asked me to leave, I would. There's nothing you could demand of me that I wouldn't do for you."

Reaching out, I stroke her cheek with the back of my hand and revel in the way she leans into it. She grips my wrist holding my hand in place.

"As much as I should be mad at you, I'm not. Don't get me wrong, I was furious when I found out. Devastated. And if you had come to me then I don't know that I would've given you the time of day. But you gave me space because you knew

I needed it. You supported me quietly in the background even when I wasn't aware. And if you hadn't been at the show, I don't know what Jeremy would have done because no one even noticed I was gone. All my family came to earlier performances. You were the only one there for me today."

"I'll always be there for you, if you allow me."

"But you lied to me. You hid things from me. And while I understand your reasoning, it's going to take time to earn back that trust."

My gut twists at her words, but I deserve it. "I won't lie and pretend like I didn't have my own selfish reasons for keeping you in the dark. If you knew who I was earlier, you may have walked away. If you found out I was married sooner, you may not have been willing to wait for me. And I wanted you so fucking badly. I wanted you to want me. I wanted to be the only one that could truly provide you with what you needed, even if I couldn't give you all of me at the time."

"I want that. All of you. No more hiding behind a mask. At least metaphorically. It's kinda hot in a scene sometimes."

"No more hiding," I agree.

"So what happens now?" she asks, hope lighting up her face.

I rub the back of my neck as my jaw flexes. "Maryam asked for a divorce. She wants me to be happy."

"Would that make you happy?"

"Divorcing her? No. Not if it means she could be deported."

"Would she?"

"There's no telling. She's confident that it'll be fine. And it's possible to get a green card if you're divorced, but we're so close to the finish line, for her safety, I don't want to risk it."

She nods solemnly, blinking rapidly.

"But if you ask me to, I will. If it would earn back even one iota of your trust, I'd do it," I admit.

We sit in awkward silence as she processes everything I've said, her eyes occasionally drifting to me, then back to the door as nurses walk past. I want to confess how I truly feel, wrap her in my arms and finally say those three words. I know she feels it; I think she knows that I'm feeling it, but I've already shared a lot with her, and I don't want my confession to be in an ER triage room after she's just been brutally attacked. The drugs Jeremy gave her probably aren't fully out of her system. And I want her fully cognizant when I declare my love for her. I want her to remember every word.

"Once they discharge you, I'm going to take you to Alyx's."

Her swollen eyes lock with mine, exhaustion evident in them.

"Will you wait for me?" It's a shitty thing to ask her, and I'd totally understand if she said no.

When she nods her head, I breathe a sigh of relief. "This is bigger than me. Bigger than us. I couldn't ask you to risk her safety for my own selfish desires."

I cup her cheek, pulling her forehead to mine, my words a whisper. "Let me say it again so it's clear: I would if you asked me. If you needed me to, I wouldn't hesitate. Mary made some very convincing arguments that have eased my guilt. So if you change your mind, I'll do it for you." I kiss her forehead, mouthing the words against her skin that I want to say out loud. "Now get some rest."

CHAPTER 40
JOHN

A sense of calm washes over me as we walk into my private room at Pulse. This is the first time I've had her alone since everything went down after the show. It's the first time we'll be intimate since that fucker violated her in front of me. Anger wells in me as I clench my fist, hearing her close the door behind me.

Her soft hands wrap around my wrist, gently tugging me back and pulling me from my thoughts.

"John, what's wrong?"

I keep my back to her as I take deep breaths to calm the anger inside of me as my brain relives the scene with Jeremy.

"Do you not want me?" There's a break in her voice, and I spin to face her, taking her hands in mine as I lean down and kiss her forehead. She releases me, wrapping her arms around my waist and I breathe a sigh of relief.

"Baby, there's not a minute of the day that passes when I'm not overcome with thoughts of you. There's no one else on this earth and nothing in this life that I want more than you."

A tear falls down her cheek, and I tilt her chin up to kiss it before covering her face in kisses, finally landing on her lips.

"I'm really starting to rethink this no-bed-in-my-room deci-sion," I say between kisses.

"I don't need a bed. I just need you to touch me."

"It makes me so fucking hard to hear you say that. To see how far you've come since the first time we were in this room."

Her body melts into mine as we hold each other, our kisses growing more and more frenzied before I pull back.

She looks at me, her brows raised. "What's wrong?"

"I'm sorry I lied to you. I'm sorry I hid from you. It felt wrong keeping this from you, who I really was, why we couldn't be together. I know I sound like a broken record, but I'm just so fucking sorry."

"I'm not. I got to fall in love with you twice. I didn't under-stand it at the time, but I was never bothered when you touched me as Professor Ali. You'd grab my hand or arm, and I never balked. And part of me felt so torn reveling in the touch of two different men."

"I'm not going to lie and say that I didn't feel bad about that. But it was also really fucking hot watching you use all my rules against me as your professor."

A blush stains her cheeks and my cock hardens at her reac-tion as she trails her fingers slowly up my chest. "I just wished I figured it out sooner. What if we made new rules? Rules that we promise not to break."

"Such as?"

"Well, if this is going to work and we're going to rebuild trust, how about we always tell the truth? Be honest, yet kind. And we tell each other everything—no more hiding parts of ourselves from each other. Inside this room, I trust you implic-itly, even if I shouldn't. But outside this room... that will take some time."

"Done. What else?"

"You were the one with all the rules, Professor, you tell me."

"When we're in here, you're mine to control, mine to command. You will submit to me fully."

She lets out a shaky breath, and I watch the way her chest rises and falls as her breathing picks up. "I like that one."

"Tell me, if I were to touch you right now, would I find you dripping for me?"

"Yes, sir. What about your old rule about being with subs?"

Pressing my erection into her, I crowd her against the door. "You're not just my sub. You're my everything. The air I breathe. The sunlight that brightens my day. The sustenance that nourishes me. The balance I need to ground me. And most importantly, *mine*. You are mine, pet. I don't fuck subs, but you're more than that. You're my fucking world. And I will do what I want with you when and where I please."

"Is that a rule?"

"Yes." I press my forehead to hers, breathing her in.

"I think those are good rules to start with, but there's still something that's bothering me." Her voice is soft as she leans back to look up at me. Long lashes blink rapidly, and I steel myself for her admission.

"Should I change your name to Bruce Wayne in my phone or keep it as Batman Dom?"

I bark out a laugh, cradling her cheeks as I force her to look at me. "You're incredible, Emma, and I'm so deeply in love with you. I love you. Your joy, your curiosity, your zest for life. The way you make me laugh. The way you trusted me with your trauma, your body, your fears. I've spent most of my life helping others as a way to atone for my sins. Thinking that if I did enough good in my life, I'd finally be worthy. That I had to earn the love of others. I didn't think I deserved to be happy. But you make me feel seen. Wanted. Needed. And if you allow me, I'll spend the rest of my life making it up to you. Proving that I'm worthy of you, loving you the way you deserve."

"You don't have to prove anything to me. I see who you are under the mask, and I love every version of you."

I barely let her get the words out before I capture her lips with mine. My hands roam up and down her body, desperate to claim her and touch every inch of her. She whimpers against me, hiking a leg up my hip before I lift her off the ground, wrapping her legs around my waist.

She's soft and warm in my arms as she grinds her pussy against me.

I love you. I love you. I love you.

The sentiment a chant on repeat in my head as I whisper the words against her skin, kissing every inch of her exposed flesh.

"Okay, now I'm kind of wishing there was a bed."

I nibble at the skin where her neck meets her shoulder. "If I'm going to make love to you, I want to have somewhere I can spread you out and worship your body."

"I don't care where we have to go, I want that," she whines.

An idea pops into my head, images of me leading her around the club on a collar, claiming her in front of everyone, but I shove it down, not sure if she's ready for that.

I gently set her back on her feet, and she whimpers in protest. Moving over to the lounger, I drag it to the center of the room, motioning for her to join me.

She pushes off the door and walks toward me slowly, her hips swaying with every step. My cock hardens in my pants from her obedience.

"Permission to speak."

"Emma, we're not in a scene right now. You can speak freely." I cup her face, stroking my thumb along her cheekbone.

"What if I want to be in a scene? What if I want to be your sub right now?" She sounds nervous as she looks at me for approval. "I want you to treat me the way you would anyone else you bring here. I want you to… I need you to reclaim me."

I search her eyes, wanting to be sure I'm understanding what she's asking.

"When I was having nightmares, you helped me. Every time I closed my eyes, the monster in my dreams came after me, and you healed that. The way you touched me before, when I had my nightmares, that's what I want right now. I want you to put your hands on my body, reclaim me, make me think of your touch there and not his."

Not Jeremy's, she means.

I want to give her exactly what she's asking for, but part of me worries about triggering her trauma. Fuck, what is wrong with me? I wouldn't have given her request a second thought before, so why am I hesitating now?

Because I love her. Because she's not some random sub. Her reaction, her mental health actually matters to me now.

I grab her wrist and guide her over to the tall end of the lounger, running a hand up her spine to push her down onto the curve. I waste no time pulling down her skirt and panties as I kneel behind her. Running my hands up the backs of her legs, I start at her ankle and pause when I get to her knees as images of Jeremy kneeling behind her flood my brain. Without even realizing it, I've put her in nearly the same position he had her in and I hesitate, worried about her reaction.

I want to erase every memory of him here from her brain and replace it with me. How good I can make her feel. How good we are together. Slowly, I continue running a single finger up the back of her thigh, the one he held a knife to. When I get to the exact spot, I press a kiss to it, swiping my tongue over the area as delicately as I can.

A soft moan escapes her lips as I continue worshipping her upper thigh, but after a few minutes, her frustration becomes evident.

"I'm not fragile, John."

My head pops up. "I know you're not."

"Then why are you treating me like I'm going to break? Daddy Dom would have tied me to that cross and claimed every inch of my skin. He wouldn't treat me like a breakable doll. I need that beast to come out to play. Touch me. Touch me like you did the first time you saw me in here. Spank me. Be rough with me. I need your bite to replace the memory of him. When your hand smacks my thigh, I want that pain to remind me of you, and only you."

Fuck, that does something to me, and I sink my teeth into her. "Do you want to please me, pet? Are you going to be good for your professor? Be my good little teacher's pet?"

"Yes. Yes, sir."

"Don't move an inch or you'll be punished." I walk over to the cabinets on the other side of the room and pull out several toys: a riding crop, a flogger, and a whip, along with a slender vibrator. When I walk toward her, I crack the whip, and she flinches slightly.

"You know your safe word still applies. Do you need to use it?"

"No, sir."

"It's important to me that you're completely comfortable. Are you sure?"

"I'm sure. The loud crack just surprised me." She closes her eyes and lets out a breath.

I set the toys down on a small table next to me, keeping the riding crop in my hand. "Do you remember the first toy I used on you?"

"The crop." I slowly guide the stiff part of the handle up her inner thigh.

"That's correct, Miss Black." Her breath stutters at the use of her name, and I smile at the reaction. I've only called her that in class, but I like the way it feels on my tongue now. "Let's see how you do under the rest of my instruction."

I push the stiff rod of the crop up, guiding it between her pussy lips as I move it back and forth, coating it in her wetness. The muscles tighten in her back and thighs as she does her best to remain still. My eyes track the rapid inhale and exhale of her chest. The way she pulls her bottom lip into her mouth as she drags it ever so slowly against her teeth. When she releases it, taking a sharp inhale, I know she's close. I slowly pull the crop toward me as the tip emerges from between her legs, dripping in her arousal.

Her eyes fly open and her brows pinch.

"I told you not to move. That includes flinching at loud noises. So now I'm going to edge you with each of these toys, bring you to the brink of orgasm without letting you have the release you crave."

Moving to the side of the lounger, I drag the crop up her back, to her shoulder, and then down her arm, flicking the leather tip against her. "You should see the mess I'm making on your back. You were dripping on my crop, and now I'm covering you in it like a filthy girl."

Each little smack against her skin has it prickling into goosebumps. I walk around her, spanking the other side of her body, then swap out the crop for the flogger.

The leather fringe fans out on her skin as I softly stroke it down her body. Starting on one shoulder, I drag the flogger down to her ass before giving it a pop. I repeat the movement on the other side of her body, and she cries out with each spank. After a few more repetitions, I drag the silicone handle down the crack of her ass, and she lets out a long moan.

Once I position the tip between her thighs, I hold down the button turning on the vibrations and push it into her tight cunt.

She lets out a surprised gasp followed by a long low moan as I move the toy in and out, teasing her.

"This toy is my favorite. Capable of so much pain and pleasure in one little device. Do you want me to make you come with it?"

"Please, sir."

I continue moving it in and out, pressing it against her G-spot watching as her spine elongates and she drops her head. When I remove it, she lets out a needy whine. Setting it on the table, I grab the whip, holding it by both ends as I slide it around her neck and pull her up, until her back is pressed against my front.

Tightening the thong of the whip against her throat, I lean down pressing my lips against the shell of her ear. "Use your safe word if you need to stop."

Her breath hitches, and I watch the rise and fall of her chest as she nods. The barbells of her nipple piercings catch my eye as she relaxes against me.

"I know this is new to you, hell when you walked in here two years ago you couldn't handle a man's touch. But it's been incredible watching this transformation in you. Seeing you eager for me. Not shying away from how I touch you or what I touch you with. I promise we will work up to the pain and pleasure this whip can bring you. But for now, I want you to grab the vibrator on that table and hold it against your clit. See if you can make yourself come."

I adjust my grip on the whip so I can restrain her, leaving my other hand free to explore her body as she grabs the toy and slides it between her legs. "Keep it on the lowest setting." I growl into her ear.

She gives a small nod and rubs it around her clit. Her legs squeeze together, her frustration tangible.

"It's not enough. Is it?"

She shakes her head.

I release my hold on her and she places a hand against the lounger, steadying herself now that she can't lean against me.

"Do you want to see what I can do with this whip? How it'll feel against your skin?"

"I do, but I'm…"

"Scared?"

She shakes her head. "Apprehensive. Can you describe how it'll feel?"

"It will sting initially. You might feel uncomfortable. But the pleasure that blooms after the pain will light your skin on fire."

"Okay. I trust you with my pleasure."

"Fuck, that makes me want to bend you over this furniture and slam into you hard," I say, distracting her as I pull the whip back and crack it on the meat of her ass. Two quick pops.

"Oh, damn it." She drops the vibrator and uses both heads to steady herself.

I wait for her to use her safe word, knowing I pushed her harder than I have before. When she doesn't, I drop to my knees, releasing the whip, as I cup her ass cheeks in my hand and lick the red welts already blooming on the surface. My touch is gentle, reverent as I worship her skin. She pushes her ass into me and I smile at her eagerness.

"Such a good fucking girl for me. So desperate to please your professor."

She rubs her thighs together and I can tell she's eager to come, so I pull back and stand.

Grabbing her wrist, I lead her to the cross, and she assumes her position in front of it with her back to me. "Turn around. Let me see that beautiful fucking body."

She spins on her heel and locks eyes with me. "I like this. Seeing you without the mask." I fasten her hands to the end of the cross.

A wicked smile takes over my face. "Did I say you could speak, pet?"

She closes her mouth quickly, and I lower my head to her breast pulling her nipple into my mouth as I tug on her piercing with my teeth.

"I— oh, sugar!"

I release her nipple with a wet pop and smile. "Such a naughty girl today, not following your teacher's rules. Tell me,

Miss Black, where do you come up with these alternative curses?" I slowly glide a hand down her taut stomach, until I reach the apex of her thighs and make slow circles against her clit.

"I dunno. They just…" I pinch her clit between my fingers. "Oh fuuuudge, they just come out."

"Shall we make this a rule? Or can you behave?"

"I'll be good."

"Good, because I'd like to keep your legs unbound, but only if you compose yourself."

I drop to my knees and position myself between her open thighs, gripping her hips, I press the blunt ends of my nails against her skin as she squirms against me.

An idea forms in my head, and I grin wickedly, looking up at her. "I think it's time for a little role reversal, pet. I want you to teach me."

"What am I teaching you?" she asks breathlessly as I blow against her pussy.

"You're going to teach me exactly how you like to be eaten."

"I don't know if that's something I can teach you. You're already so good at everything. Anything you do feels good. I don't know what you want me to teach you."

She's rambling, and I tut several times, shaking my head. "Don't make me punish this gorgeous cunt." I smack my palm against her warm wet heat and she moans in response. "You like that, Miss Black?"

"You know I do."

"I'm going to need more instruction than that if you want me to continue." I remove my hand and look up at her.

"Slap me again."

I follow her command and slap her pussy a little harder this time.

"Ughnhn. Can you put your head between my—oh, frick. Between my thighs. Yes, like that. Your tongue feels so good. It's touching my…flicking my—"

I pull back, blowing cool air over her heated and sensitive skin. "I need to hear those words leave your lips. Knowing that you say them only for me, that I can bring that out of you, corrupt your perfect, prim little mouth. Fuuuuck."

"Only in here. Only in this room. And only for you."

"Is that a rule?" I chuckle against her skin.

"Rats, I think it is."

I smack her ass, hard. "Try it again."

"Fuck. Fuck, it is."

"Listen to that sweet little mouth saying those dirty words. Feel what it does to me." I stand up and crowd her, thrusting my cock against her slit, desperate to remove the clothing preventing me from feeling her skin against mine.

"So corrupting me, that's your kink?" She pushes her hips against me.

"Absofuckinglutely. I'm the only one that's taken your mouth and your cunt, and one day I'll fuck this hole as well," I say, trailing a finger between her cheeks, pushing at her tight ring.

"Can you take your clothes off?"

I quickly disrobe then sink to my knees again and position my mouth inches from her dripping cunt. I stick out my tongue to catch the wetness gushing from her. "You taste so fucking delicious, pet. Is all this for me? Are you dripping at the sight of me on my knees for you?"

"Maybe it's the way you've been edging me."

"Then you better teach me exactly what you need to make you come, because I'm only going to do what you tell me."

"Lick the seam of my lips from my opening until you find my clit."

I do exactly that, at a painstakingly slow pace, savoring the taste of her on my tongue.

"Put your mouth on my clit and lick around it in a circle. Oh frick, that's nice."

My tongue continues making circles waiting for her to tell me more.

"I think I need it harder. Oh yes, harder is good. Just like that. Keep doing that."

She's bucking against my face now with each swirl of my tongue, and I reach down to fist my cock, hoping to relieve some pressure.

"Now flick your tongue back and forth on my clit. Oh fuck, just like that. Keep going. Oh! I'm so close, I need more. Add your fingers," she moans.

Knowing what she needs, even if she can't vocalize it, I pinch her clit between my lips, applying pressure as I continue flicking my tongue against the tip. I snake a hand up to hold her in place with my forearm.

"Oh God, keep doing exactly that. Oh yes! That's it. I'm going to come. I'm going to come. I'm going to come. Oh God, I'm coming."

Seconds later she squirts, covering me in her arousal. I'm like a dehydrated man in a desert, lapping up every drop I can as she twitches against me.

"Holy crap. That didn't feel like it normally does. Oh my God, what did you just do?"

"You just taught me how to make you squirt."

"I did?"

Pushing up, I stand in front of her, one hand still fisting my cock as I release one of her bindings one-handed. I grip her free wrist and guide it to my cock as she takes over stroking me while I free her other hand.

When she attempts to drop to her knees, I catch her by the bicep and haul her up, throwing her over my shoulder.

"Oh my gosh, John. Put me down."

I swat her ass, giving it one quick, sharp pop as she squeals. I sink into the curve of the lounger, lowering her onto my lap.

"You don't know what you just did. What you just unleashed."

She looks at me flustered, a mixture of confusion and arousal on her face.

I grip her chin in one hand as I line the tip of my cock up with her entrance. "I'm going to make you come until you're begging me to stop." I thrust into her. "Until you can't handle one more orgasm." I move my thumb to her clit and push against it. "Until your body is shaking so hard, your legs are so weak, you can't stand up." I dig my fingers into her hip holding her in place as I rut into her. "Until you say your safe word and force me to stop."

As soon as the words are out of my mouth and I build up the perfect rhythm, I know I'm all talk. There's no way I'm going to be able to do all the things I promised. Her greedy cunt is going to make me blow faster than a pubescent teen.

"Oh shit. Oh fuck, John!" She shudders against me as her pussy pulses around me, squeezing my cock as I will my orgasm away. Once she comes down, I flip us over, putting her on her knees against the taller curve of the lounger, and pull her ass toward me.

My cock has a mind of its own as I push inside, gripping her by the hips as I rut into her, the sounds of our skin slapping filling the space around us. "Fuck, baby, you feel so good like this. So tight. So fucking perfect around my cock. So fucking mine."

Each thrust in makes her perfect ass jiggle in the sexiest way as the force of my movements causes ripples through each cheek. Like a feral animal, I claw at her, gripping and marking her as she moans beneath me. No one has ever made me this wild, this crazed, like I only feel at peace when I'm inside her. Only feel whole when she's clenching around my length.

I watch as her cunt swallows my cock each time I thrust in and out. That familiar flutter starts, and I know she's close.

With one hand, I gather her hair into a ponytail, wrapping it around my fist as I pull her body flush with mine.

"I'm going to— I'm gonna—"

"That's fucking right. I'm going to make this perfect fucking cunt come again. Make you feel so fucking good as you milk this cock for my cum. You want me to fill you up, pet? Fill you so full of my seed you can't move without feeling me drip down your legs?"

Her hands flail around, scrambling for purchase as she struggles to grip my arm, a guttural cry escaping her. I let go of her hair and wrap my arms around her as I push deep inside her and still, my orgasm hitting me quick and hard as my cock pulses, spilling my cum deep in her pussy. We stay there, holding each other, our breaths in sync as we both come down. Her heart thumps rapidly against my arm as I press a kiss against the place her shoulder and neck meet.

"That was…"

"It was," I agree, not needing her to finish the thought, knowing exactly what she's thinking.

Once I've claimed every inch of her skin, I pull her against me, sinking into the lounger, smiling at how it's become my favorite spot to lay with her. The curve of it allowing me to lean back and pull her against me at the perfect angle.

"How are you feeling, pet? Are you comfortable?" My hands glide up and down her back as her warm skin heats mine.

"I think this is my favorite part."

"What is?" My words come out deep and rumbling as she smiles against my chest.

"The part where you hold me after. When your voice is husky and low as you come down from the scene. And you take care of me."

"That's the best part. Everyone thinks being dominant is about bossing around your sub and controlling them, and sure, that can be part of it. But I like these moments when you're fully sated and submit to me naturally."

"And here I just thought you liked spanking me." She wiggles her ass.

I swat at it lightly. "Watch it, pet."

"Did you mean everything you said? In the scene?" Her eyes are still glassy, and I cup her cheeks, pulling her face to mine.

"Every." *Kiss.* "Fucking." *Kiss.* "Word." *Kiss.*

EPILOGUE

EMMA

It's been a few months since the incident with Jeremy, and so much has happened. My parents were initially shocked to learn that I'd had a stalker for over a year and had never told them. When they came to the hospital after the kidnapping, I'd told them that I was dehydrated and exhausted from the show and the end of the semester. I was scared to tell them everything initially, and I didn't want my mom to worry after everything I'd been through with my biological dad.

My mom is a huge believer in love and was thankful that John was in my life and was there to save me from Jeremy. Since I'd previously told her his name was Don, I had to explain that it was a nickname I'd given him. It took a little longer for my stepdad to come around. While he was initially grateful for what John did for me, he had a lot of concerns about my relationship with him since he's thirteen years older than me and my professor.

The way my sister Ella lost her mind about that was comical. She argued that it was sexist that Ethan could date someone sixteen years older than him, so I should be able to too.

Telling Ethan was nerve-wracking as well. He's always

been like another father to me. I didn't want to disappoint him. There might have been a few angels whispering in his ears, because he didn't seem shocked when I told him. He just nodded his head and pulled me into a hug asking me if I was happy. I'm pretty sure I have Bridget and Alyx to thank for that.

John and I spent the summer together at his house in Columbus, sharing the space with his wife and her family. There was plenty of room for all of us, and we all agreed that we wanted to give Maryam the best path toward citizenship. John and I had already been pretty discreet on campus, so a few more months wasn't going to break me. And when we wanted time to ourselves, the private room at the club was our safe haven.

The fall semester started a few weeks ago, and since I've spent the last few summers taking classes, I'm on track to graduate in December. I'm applying to a few programs for graduate school, but I'm hoping to get into a state school in Columbus. It's a two-year program, and it's close enough to Faith Union that the commute wouldn't be too terrible for either of us.

Tonight, though, we are at Alyx's moms' restaurant, Mangia Bene. Since my brother Ethan and Alyx are both chefs here and Alyx's family owns the restaurant, they've closed it down for our private event.

When I look around the table, I can't help but smile at the chaotic scene.

It might be weird that we've all gathered to celebrate John and Maryam's divorce, but I think it's rather fitting. Maryam's green card was approved two months ago, and we kept planning a group dinner to celebrate, but between all of our schedules, none of us have been able to find time until now, the day after the divorce was final.

My mom is talking to Ethan, and my stepdad is out on a work call, like usual. It's probably for the best, though, because if he caught the way Ella keeps checking out Alyx, he definitely wouldn't be happy. I know she's had a crush on him since we were all kids, but she's never admitted it to me. I'm convinced it's why she bickers with him so much. Throughout dinner, she vacillates between scowling and openly checking him out, her gaze lingering every time he pushes up a sleeve and reveals his forearm tattoos.

Maryam, Sam, and her son are tucked in the corner completely absorbed in conversation. Ella is sitting next to Alyx, currently giving him a death glare, but Alyx is completely oblivious as he talks animatedly to Bennett. The two of them laugh when Robert leans into Bennett, kissing the side of his head three times before he excuses himself from the table.

"I'm going to call Miles and check on the girls, I'll be right back." Robert pulls out his phone and steps outside.

"Is it normal to be this attracted to your husband's butt after years and years of marriage?" Becka leans into me as she watches Robert walk outside.

I giggle, taking a sip of my water as she bounces her attention between me and Bridget. "This is nice. I wish us girls could all hang out together more often. Ooh, I know! We should all go to book club together." Becka claps excitedly. "I've always wanted a girl gang."

"Can I get in on that?" Ella asks, snapping her attention away from Alyx.

"Absolutely!" Becka says.

"How did I get roped into this?" Bridget complains.

"Because we'll tell our brother you were being mean to his little sisters if you don't." Ella smirks.

"And that's why you're my favorite sister. I always forget how crafty you are." Bridget laughs.

"Hey!" I object.

Bridget holds her hands up in the air. "I'm kidding. Kinda."

"If you're all serious, there's a book club meeting this Sunday. It's at The Spicy Shelf." Becka says the last part to Ella since Bridget and I have attended book club with her in the past.

Ella turns to me. "Could we hang out after? I need some advice." She's quiet, unlike her normal boisterous self.

"Everything okay?"

"It is, I promise."

There's laughter down the table as Alyx and Bennett pull our focus. Ella's eyes are fixed on Alyx, a look of frustration and longing on her face.

"Does it have something to do with you still harboring a secret crush on Alyx?" I ask.

Her head whips to mine as anger flashes in her eyes. "It absolutely does not," she grits through clenched teeth as she fakes a smile. "I can promise you that."

I lift my eyebrows in concern, and she offers me a small smile, her way of telling me that we'll talk later.

A hand grips my thigh under the table, and I look over at John. His gaze swivels to meet mine, and he puts his hand on the back of my neck, pulling me into him as he kisses my cheek. With his face still close to mine, he whispers into my ear.

"I forgot to tell you the best part of the divorce. Maryam got the house."

I pull back in confusion, searching his face for what he's not telling me.

"The movers are coming next week to pack my stuff."

"Are you going back to the place you were renting near campus?"

"Nope." There's a cocky grin on his face.

"Then where are you going? Because I'm not sure all your stuff will fit in your room at Pulse."

"There's a place I want to show you. It's halfway between Faith Union and the city. The drive wouldn't be bad for either of us once you get into grad school. If you like it, I'll put in an offer. If you don't like it, my realtor has a list of other properties we can check out."

My mouth drops open in shock as heat creeps into my cheeks.

"What do you say, pet? Will you move in with me?"

I nod quickly as he grins. When this man smiles, my panties instantly dampen every freaking time. And he knows it.

"You want to buy me a house?"

"I do." He presses a kiss to my lips.

"Did you tell her?" Maryam leans over, pulling us out of our bubble.

"Just did." John beams.

Maryam reaches across the table and grabs my hand, squeezing it in hers. "Sam and I cannot thank you enough for what you did for us." She shifts her eyes to mine. "Both of you."

I squeeze her hand in reply, looking at John, whose eyes are still on me. When I think about the things he's accomplished, what he's sacrificed, the good he's done, I smile back at him, so thankful for him and all his broken rules.

Want to find out what happens when John finally gets to collar Emma?
Download the bonus scene at
https://dl.bookfunnel.com/4tn91d2ixz

ACKNOWLEDGMENTS

Immigration into the US is a complex and ever-changing landscape, and when I first began plotting this story, the reality looked very different from what it is today. Throughout the writing process, I was constantly reminded of how deeply personal and emotional these journeys can be. To everyone who has navigated these systems—your courage touched my heart as much as it shaped this story.

KT, thank you for sharing your knowledge about the K1 and Green Card process. It's one thing to research a topic, it's another to pick the brain of someone who's lived through it. Thank you for sharing your experience and helping me as I navigated through the narrative. This book exists because of you. Love ya, bestie!

Sarah, my amazing editor, thank you for loving my characters. And thank you for not making them laughing idiots like I keep trying to do. Especially this one. Those rom com moms can laugh like idiots all day! Thank you for pushing me to be the best storyteller I can be! I appreciate you so much!

Emma goes through a lot in this book and I wanted to make sure her journey with her therapist felt real and authentic. Thank you to Hannah G for the therapist sensitivity read. Your insights and suggestions were incredibly helpful.

My beta and sensitivity readers are the best! Every reaction, emoji, comment gives me such joy. Thank you for reading my stories in their rawest form. Your feedback on this one was crucial, appreciated, and helped shape it in so many ways. Stacey, Ashley, Arni, and Hannah H. Stephanie your sensitivity read was so helpful. Thank you for taking the time to read this story.

Amanda, the best alpha reader in the world. I live for your reactions and voice memos. Making you fall harder for each MMC is my favorite thing in the world. And seeing your reactions to chapter one was one of my favorite parts of writing this story.

To my Romance Era girlies, Layla, Bianca, and Amanda. You are the best friends in the world. Our DMs are my favorite part of the internet. I never know what's gonna poke me in the eye when I open them. Thank you for shouting about my books. I can't wait for everything 2026 has in store for us!

To my author support group. You all give me life. Talking about thirst traps, creamy Lucky Peens, sharing covers and art, and talking all things books and author struggles. Erin, LJ, Berlin, Kay, Sky, Mauve, Loren, Ruby, Taccara, and Jen.

Shelly beans. I love you. I love our journey. Even if you never read these because romance isn't your thing. You have been with me since I was 1 year, 11 months, and 9 days. And I know our best years are ahead.

I want to thank my amazing street team. Every post you make, graphic you share, comment and review you leave—it matters. I appreciate all you do to shout to the world about my books and characters. Thank you for your support, it is everything to me.

Sandy, there are tattooed men in my next couple books. I'm sorry. (Not sorry.)

To the love of my life, my ultimate book boyfriend and my favorite grumpy A-hole. Writing this story took me back to college and sneaking around that campus with you. Every scene in a dorm or student apartment has a piece of our story in it. Thank you for listening to me talk for hours on end about books. I love you!

ALSO BY MYA MORE

The Broken Series

All Her Broken Pieces

Bridget and Ethan's story. An age gap (she's older), forced proximity, black cat/golden retriever spicy romance.

All Our Broken Vows

Becka, Robert, and Bennett's story. An MMF, bi-awakening romance with found family, a single dad, and friends that become so much more.

All His Broken Rules

Emma and (John) Professor A-hole's story. An age gap, forbidden romance with a professor/student who break all the rules.

All Their Broken Promises

Coming 2026

The Chestnut Mountain Series

The Santa Rules

A holiday rom com with a single mom, a single dad, two kids, and a whole lot of fun.

The Lucky List

A rom com with a tired single mom, 2 active little boys, an Irish firefighter, and a whole lot of luck.

The Summer Plans

A rom com about a single mom with 3 kids, a single dad firefighter, an unforgettable vacation, and a second chance to get it right.

Coming May 21st, 2026

ABOUT THE AUTHOR

Mya has always had a passion for storytelling and has a background in theatre, film, and education. She lives in the Midwest with her husband and children, working a nonromantic job by day while writing romance at night. Her books are contemporary romance with more love, more spice, and more HEAs. When she's not writing, she enjoys reading, singing karaoke, playing mermaids in the pool, and doing puzzles.

I love hearing from readers! Check out my socials below or email me at myamorewrites@gmail.com

www.authormyamore.com

instagram.com/author.mya.more
tiktok.com/@myamorewrites
amazon.com/author/myamore